Around
VARANASI
in **ASSI** Days

Raja started his journey in chemical engineering at an IIT, only to discover it's more about mind-melting calculus than alcohol or pipelines. His 'skills' led him to roles at Wall Street, tech firms and global financial services, where he morphed from an engineer and tech strategist into a consultant armed with a deadly arsenal of business frameworks. Over two decades, he advised and led firms in insurance, banking and high-tech industries, all while becoming a slave to MS Office (and later, Mac Office).

After countless detours in life, including surviving education at four global institutions and a few snake and piranha encounters, Raja now calls himself an author.

This is his first work of fiction, and if readers make it through, he threatens them with two more next year.

You can connect with Raja on:

LinkedIn: https://www.linkedin.com/in/nrajav/
Facebook: https://www.facebook.com/raja.venkateswar/
Instragram: https://www.instagram.com/nrajav/
Twitter: https://www.x.com/nrajav/

Around
VARANASI
in ASSI Days

RAJA VENKATESWARA

RUPA

Published by
Rupa Publications India Pvt. Ltd 2025
7/16, Ansari Road, Daryaganj
New Delhi 110002

Sales centres:
Bengaluru Chennai
Hyderabad Jaipur Kathmandu
Kolkata Mumbai Prayagraj

P-ISBN: 978-93-6156-962-3
E-ISBN: 978-93-6156-365-2

First impression 2025

10 9 8 7 6 5 4 3 2 1

The moral right of the author has been asserted.

Printed in India

Around
VARANASI
in ASSI Days

RAJA VENKATESWARA

RUPA

Published by
Rupa Publications India Pvt. Ltd 2025
7/16, Ansari Road, Daryaganj
New Delhi 110002

Sales centres:
Bengaluru Chennai
Hyderabad Jaipur Kathmandu
Kolkata Mumbai Prayagraj

Copyright © Raja Venkateswara 2025

P-ISBN: 978-93-6156-962-3
E-ISBN: 978-93-6156-365-2

First impression 2025

10 9 8 7 6 5 4 3 2 1

The moral right of the author has been asserted.

Printed in India

*For
my parents;
and
Nalinee and Pavitra*

Contents

Author's Note

This book is primarily in English, but with an Indian setting, base and structure. Several idiomatic expressions, phrases and exclamations in Hindi, Bengali and Tamil have been faithfully recorded in their original languages, accompanied where possible by an appropriate English translation. An effective way would be to also peruse the 'Handy Guide to IT Lingo', which offers explanations for some of the more esoteric descriptions and metaphors used.

The story is set in the early 1990s, a time before India emerged as the economic powerhouse it is today. It was a nation still grappling with its so-called 'Hindu rate of growth'—a term that, despite its racist and derogatory connotations towards the peace-loving Hindus, was largely ignored by a pliant Hindu populace and a leftist media. It was also a time when the competitive instinct that can only arise when a billion people jostle for honest work capable of ensuring a reasonably comfortable lifestyle was accessible to only about a quarter of the burgeoning population.

This is a work of fiction, though, as is often said, all fiction is based on factual imagination—a phrase that might seem oxymoronic but is probably the truth. As Sir Arthur Conan Doyle wrote in *A Case of Identity*:

'Life is infinitely stranger than anything which the mind

of man could invent. We would not dare to conceive the things which are mere commonplaces of existence. If we could fly out of that window hand in hand, hover over this great city, gently remove the roofs, and peep in at the queer things which are going on, the strange coincidences, the plannings, the cross-purposes, the wonderful chains of events, working through generations, and leading to the most outré results, it would make all fiction with its conventionalities and foreseen conclusions most stale and unprofitable.'

This little work is like that. A significant portion of the events described here happened in real life, and many readers may marvel at the eccentricities captured in these pages. Some may even shake their heads in complete disbelief. The cities and places mentioned in the book exist much as they are described, within reasonable artistic license. The institute of technology within the Banaras Hindu University campus (now the Indian Institute of Technology [IIT], after the politicians made the change that added 'Indian' to it, something pending since 1971— welcome to Indian bureaucracy) remains a prestigious engineering institution, churning out some of the world's finest engineers. The campus itself is breathtaking in its beauty and the buildings inspiring in their countenance, steeped in history and accomplishments in education and scientific advancement.

Varanasi and Calcutta, the two cities where this story unfolds, are places of rare character—one of unknown antiquity and the other more modern but both throbbing centres of vitality, art and culture; chaotic and maze-like, yet brimming with humanity, humility and honesty.

If this book appears to be a far cry from the present and no longer offers a reasonably realistic portrayal of life in an engineering school, then I can only quote Gabriel García Márquez—'Life is not what one lived but how one remembers it.'

I look back two decades to what I believe was among the very best periods of my life, if not the best.

But again, despite everything said, the initial disclaimer remains—this is indeed a work of fiction!

Introduction

Strange ideas, but I always thought I was a good writer. There was some limited proof to support my notion, but then, as I would point out to myself, there was none against it either.

My teachers at school, of course, did not share this belief, and my friends were convinced—perhaps rightly—that someone who only read fiction could never be a writer.

'Raja? Write? Ah, well…yes, he did write three articles for the school magazine.'

Throughout my school years, I remained an intensely shy, reticent and awkward adolescent. I often stammered in my restless eagerness to say something intelligent, to dispel the perceived cobweb of idiocy that seemed to hover over me like a brooding cloud. Incredible then, this insane desire to see my name in print.

I often contributed to the school magazine and to those published every year during the Durga Puja. However, their circulation was so limited that they rarely reached a discerning audience. After all, what class 10 student anywhere in the world actually reads the school magazine?

Strangely enough, I did get to see my name in print on a much larger scale—not once, but twice within the span of four weeks. The first time was on 31 May, when the IT (India's premier engineering institutions) results were announced; the second was on 30 June of the same year, when the results of the West Bengal Joint Entrance Examination (JEE) for admission to the Regional Engineering Colleges (now National Institutes of Technology) were published.

The sheer ordinariness of my existence was evident from the fact that my name had never once appeared on the school noticeboard, neither for exceptional academic performances nor admonishments—I led such an unremarkable existence.

To be accurate, I did not actually see my name in print on the IT noticeboard. I learnt about it only four days later when someone informed me that my name had appeared in bold letters, securing position 1680 in the IT JEE results. This delay was entirely due to my absolute confidence in myself—that I could achieve nothing in life. I believed I was destined to remain a stammering straggler, condemned to a nameless existence like so many others in India. Convinced of my mediocrity, I had accompanied my parents on a pilgrimage to a few temples in South India.

The IT results were announced on 31 May with the same monotonous efficiency that India's finest engineering colleges prided themselves on, an efficiency that mere mortals like us could only aspire to. At 10 a.m., the gates to the offices opened, and young hopefuls, accompanied by their even more hopeful parents, walked on hushed feet into the hallowed halls to check the noticeboard. I missed all this excitement for the simple reason that I was on the Madras Mail, heading from Calcutta (now Kolkata) to Madras (now Chennai), blissfully unaware of the inflexion point occurring in my otherwise mundane existence.

My cousin, Srikant, held a vastly different opinion. With reasoning that was entirely his own and difficult to explain, he was certain that I would secure a rank in India's toughest entrance examination. To this day, two decades later, he has yet to articulate why he believed in me. Perhaps his steadfast refusal to consume alcohol has something to do with his inability to express such an ephemeral rationale coherently. With certainty in his heart, hope in his soul, and a rupee for the bus fare, Srikant made his way to Camac Street in south-central Calcutta, where the offices of IT Kharagpur were once located. There, he confirmed what he already knew in his heart—I had earned a place in India's so-called intelligentsia!

Now came the difficult part—how to convey this news to me. Remember, this was before telephones were common, and mobile phones were something only seen in James Bond movies. At that time, rapid communication channels were limited to the telegraph—and no, I do not mean the newspaper we all grew up reading in Calcutta.

Rather conveniently, my grandfather, uncle and aunt were leaving for Madras on the Coromandel Express the very next day, with the intention of meeting us in a temple town called Palani on 5 June. They were obviously thrilled that their ward had accomplished something no one else in the extended family had managed—quite remarkable considering I come from a family of erudite, intelligent, educated and God-fearing Brahmins. So, it was in that beautiful temple town that I received the news, and the scene is imprinted in my mind without the sepia-tinted haze that often colours memories from over two decades ago.

My parents, younger brother and I were walking back after visiting the temple when I spotted a lady in a blue saree running along the second-floor balcony of our lodge, approximately half a kilometre ahead of us. In the sleepy atmosphere typical of a small temple town in South India, a lady running certainly stood out, so my attention was immediately drawn to her.

As we crossed a footbridge and the lodge disappeared from immediate view, my focus shifted. But a few seconds later, I could again see her again, now running down the stairs. Just when I was considering commenting on her speed to my mother—who was strolling behind us men—that I realized, upon closer inspection, that it was my aunt.

Wondering what could possibly have made her move like a steam engine in overdrive, I quickened my pace. Before I knew it, she was hugging me and screaming in delirious joy right outside the lodge lobby—'You have been selected for IT.'

Soon, I was surrounded by a crowd of well-wishers; everyone encouraged me to return to the temple—to walk up the steep incline and the hundreds of stairs leading to the sanctum sanctorum. That was the most exhilarating walk of my life—I knew then that I had truly arrived.

This book is all about what happened next.

1

Himgiri Express

The Himgiri Express stood proudly, as always, on Platform 8 of Howrah Station, ready to depart on its daily journey from the mouth of the Ganges to somewhere near its source. Back then, there was only one station under the Eastern Railway; this was before the authorities had the rather misguided idea of adding yet another complex for the South Eastern Railway on the southern side, further contributing to the already overwhelming congestion and pollution at India's largest railway station.

I was filled with a nameless fear, tinged with anticipation for what lay ahead. After all, I was leaving behind the city I loved like a sweetheart, the innumerable friends and relatives, and, most importantly, the sense of comfort and familiarity that only comes from spending a lifetime in one place. I was headed to a city I had never seen, with a university campus as unfamiliar to me as fresh, clean water is to a particularly lazy pig. Above all, there was the acute realization that I was about to face what almost every engineering student in India must endure in the first few weeks of hostel life—ragging. I had already had a small dress rehearsal for this at IT Kharagpur, where I had gone to fill out, in descending order of preference, the engineering disciplines I was most interested in and my college of choice.

For the uninitiated, the Joint Entrance Examination for admission to ITs and the Banaras Institute of Technology (BIT) at Varanasi is conducted annually. The 2,000-odd students selected are deemed extremely lucky and intelligent. As one could appreciate, in my case, the general sentiment among friends and immediate family was that my selection was purely due to luck, with almost no involvement of intelligence—and for the more envious souls, it was attributed to a computer glitch.

I had the fortune of attending the selection process— called counselling—at IT Kharagpur with my father, who insisted I take up Chemical Engineering. A voracious reader, he had pored over various magazines and literature and concluded that this was the engineering discipline of the future.

My father's presence did nothing to intimidate the older college students, who pounced on the opportunity to interact with the freshers, some of whom would soon be their juniors at the institute.

Fresher–Handy Guide to IT Lingo

I was called aside by a group of seniors at the end of the preliminary counselling session conducted by the Dean of IT Kharagpur. A bespectacled moron, who was at the forefront of the group and had difficulty speaking without pronounced pauses—probably searching for appropriate words—asked me to name the last blue film I had seen. As an Iyer Brahmin, wide-eyed and innocent, having led an extremely sheltered life in a joint family set-up, I had absolutely no idea what he was talking about. Lacking comprehension but fearing I might sound naïve, I was about to blurt out 'none' when I remembered I had seen *Twenty Thousand Leagues Under the Sea* a few days earlier. Figuring nothing could be bluer than a movie almost entirely set underwater, I gave an honest, down-to-earth reply.

'I...I...I can think of one, actually,' I stammered.

'One, eh... Which one?' asked one of the stragglers.

'Twenty Thousand Leagues Under the Sea,' I replied.

The next thing I knew, I felt like a caged animal surrounded by laughing lunatics, much like a chimpanzee in a zoo enclosure that spectators paid good money to watch lead a normal day-to-day existence—carrying about its mundane affairs like eating a banana handed by a good Samaritan or jumping through a hoop which the zoo-keeper had so thoughtfully provided.

'A fresh one,' somebody declared from the holy congregation gathered around me.

'The bugger is actually serious,' another exclaimed, looking at me with the same astonishment a batter felt when Anil Kumble sharply turned the ball from leg to off on a benign first-day pitch.

'*Abe, naya dhakkan aya re,*' one of the chaps in the crowd yelled to another group that was enjoying a nice tête-à-tête with another bedraggled fresher. Roughly translated, that meant 'We have a new joker in town.'

Abe, Naya and Dhakkan—Handy Guide to IT Lingo

At this, the other group, seemingly looking for fresher (pun intended) pastures, trotted over to where I stood, eyeing me with no little curiosity. I was still trying to figure out the reason for their extreme reaction to what I thought was a perfectly routine answer to a routine question, when the same question and answer were repeated to the new group, who also seemed to enjoy it thoroughly.

'*Abe, pondy nahin padha kya?*' one of them asked. Loosely translated, it means, 'Haven't you ever read a pondy?'

Pondy—Handy Guide to IT Lingo

Before I could muster enough courage to ask him to kindly elucidate (though I was not about to inquire about any special precautions for visiting a Union Territory like Pondicherry, where, incidentally, my cousin used to go for some rather eclectic eye treatments), my father appeared, looking for me and exclaiming that I needed to fill out more forms.

With a feeling of mystification at the peculiar ways of the senior world in the ITs, I followed my father out, sensing the seniors' eyes following my movements with sheer amazement.

'*Abe, yeh to BIT mein mar jayega,*' I overheard someone telling his neighbour, pointing in my direction. This literally meant that I would die in BIT (the engineering institution I was getting admitted to). The remark left an indelible imprint on my mind and considerably increased my already heightened sense of unease. I had heard horror stories of midnight raids on freshers' quarters by packs of seniors and the indescribable acts of terror inflicted upon them, and this last comment struck me where it hurt most.

I had just finished reading *Alice in Wonderland* on the train journey from Kharagpur to Calcutta when, probably as a result of the extreme reactions stirred by this enduring classic and my close encounters with the seniors throughout the afternoon, I felt an urgent desire to write a poem. It was like the first impulse of Bollywood heroes to break into a sad song during moments of distress. This is how it turned out:

> *You have no notion how horrible it will be,*
> *And it will be no great fun, you will see,*
> *When they take us in and throw us to the deep ITian*
> *sea,*
> *Where the seniors shall be waiting with unconcealed glee,*
> *And despite our entreaty and our heartfelt plea,*
> *Shall dip us headfirst into the deep ragging sea.*

Such were the thoughts that July night as I stood at Howrah Station, waiting to board the Himgiri Express once the compartment inspection was over. I watched with unseeing eyes as hundreds of people wandered in all directions, the air punctuated by assorted sounds in Bengali, Hindi, and the occasional cry in English.

My youngest uncle, chosen by consensus in my family to perform the Good Samaritan act of depositing me at my new address, broke my reverie.

'Raja, don't start drinking out there.'

I looked at him and nodded in the typical South Indian way, where a horizontal motion of the head means 'Yes' and a vertical shake 'No'.

'And don't mix with bad company. Look for boys from good backgrounds, with studious nature and pleasant habits.'

Another affirmative nod from me.

'Come, let us get in. The doors are open; the authorities must have completed their inspection,' my uncle said as I clambered into our compartment, holding on to the large suitcase containing enough clothes to last a month. He followed closely behind, carrying a large overnight bag that included, among other things, a bottle of homemade pickle and a set of bed sheets and pillows.

I made my way through the throng of people standing in the passageway and squatting on the seats, finishing last-minute monologues and taking advice from their friends and relatives about to leave on their respective journeys. As is customary in India, any departure by loved ones is almost always accompanied by crying and emotional displays. This exercise in demonstrating sorrow implies that the more one cries at the time of departure, the more affectionate they are deemed to be. As usual, the whole family presents themselves in all their finery to visit the station and give a ritual send-off for their loved ones.

Somehow, I managed to push and weave my way to our berths—one middle and one upper berth—my uncle trailing behind, looking much worse for wear, his notoriously long hair dishevelled after the battle to reach our seats. My uncle pointed to the upper berth, indicating that I should climb up without delay.

Panting in sheer exhaustion, he placed the overnight bag down, sat on the lower berth, and mopped his forehead with a large towel, observing, 'This place gets more crowded with every passing day. You would think the whole city has made its way to the station to see somebody they love off. Good thing Sundari, (my mother's nickname) did not come to see you off; she would be crying too. This city is going crazy, and it's a good thing you decided to seek education elsewhere.'

I pointed out that there could be no greater fan of the city than yours truly and, grinning in a way that my uncle found most irritating, said, 'Why, missing Usha already?' referring to my uncle's secret sweetheart.

I received a baleful glare in return and an admonishment to try and get some sleep, as I had a tough day ahead. Shaking my head, I lay down, my thoughts again turning to the perceived ordeal ahead, wondering how a man in his early youth could doze off with the prospect of facing the hangman's knot the next day.

Sunlight streamed through the open window, making my eyes blink in sleepy fury. Suddenly, I realized I had fallen asleep sometime during the night and had woken up due to my uncle's incessant desire to share a cup of coffee. I roused myself from the arms of Morpheus and blinked away the last vestiges of what had been, in the context of my anxious state, a remarkably good night's sleep. I noticed that my ability to sleep amid the commotion typical of Indian trains in the late morning—close to 10 o'clock—had drawn the attention of my co-passengers, who were looking at me with a mixture of amusement and amazement.

'Good morning,' my uncle declared.

I wondered what was so great about the morning, given that I was being sent off to the place where all newcomers got a solid welcome party from the seniors. I was preparing to face the day the same way a philosophical goat would, when confronted with the prospect of being introduced to the friendly neighbourhood butcher. I slid down to the lower bunk, next to my uncle, and reached for the cup of coffee he had so thoughtfully purchased from a passing vendor, and wished him a good morning. I sipped the coffee with some trepidation and muttered, 'Horrible! Wonder what will happen in the next four years. Can't brew a proper cup. Imbeciles!'

'Better get used to this. It is all you will get for the next four years. It's extremely important for home-grown dicks like you to get a taste of the real world.'

Coming from a man whose only claim to fame was not leaving Calcutta despite all the best job opportunities in the world, it sounded extremely funny.

I, however, preferred to quietly finish my cup of strong medicine and went off to the toilet, which, as I had feared, looked as though an entire herd of buffaloes had just defecated in it and failed to clean up after. Ultimately, the stomach rules the bowels—and for my digestive system, the coffee was the catalyst for the early morning activity. Muttering under my breath and bracing myself for what the hostel facilities might look like, I returned to meet my uncle's triumphant gaze. I knew the early bird had indeed cleared its bowels of the unwanted worms.

For want of better things to do, I climbed up to my bunk and, as expected, was back in the arms of Morpheus in a jiffy.

✳

2

Calcutta

I spent most of my senior school years in Calcutta, surrounded by various relatives. As a lower-middle-class family in India, our lifestyle was characterized by fun and frolic, balanced with strict discipline and orthodoxy. Growing up among approximately 20 assorted relatives, including several cousins of similar age, naturally fostered a sense of competition—unspoken yet always present. This competition was healthy—books and notes were shared, ideas and thoughts exchanged—all contributing to a harmonious learning environment that encouraged excellence and focus.

My youngest uncle, who served as a role model for us children, was a lean and taciturn young man with a remarkable aptitude for mathematics, bordering on genius. His expertise, coupled with his ability to teach effectively and his unwavering dedication, played a crucial role in our success in various entrance examinations. His commitment was evident in the meticulously preserved notebooks from his Class XII days. He had four notebooks filled with answers to all the questions from the mathematics book we used for exam preparation.

The first notebook contained his initial attempts at

solving problems, full of comments and slashes, showcasing his thought process. The second notebook presented the same problems solved in the ideal textbook manner. The third highlighted his attempts to solve those problems using unconventional methods. Finally, the fourth notebook was a clean compilation of solutions, demonstrating unique methodologies for tackling the same problems. This achievement was pretty impressive, considering the question book he worked from contained over 5,000 problems covering topics ranging from algebra to integral calculus. And this was just one of the many books.

Such a role model inevitably inspired all of us to strive for excellence. Now, more than a decade later, all four of us cousins have become successful professionals in our respective fields. We owe an immense debt of gratitude to our uncle for his guidance and inspiration.

I lived with my parents until I was 13. It was then decided that the advanced schooling at my father's workplace would not be suitable for a young boy. Thus, by consensus, it was determined that I would be admitted to St Lawrence High School in Calcutta. I had previously studied there around the age of seven, before my father's transfer to a small town in western Uttar Pradesh. Thanks to my granduncle's charm and gift of persuasion, he managed to sweet-talk the school's rector into granting me admission with slightly less stringency than usual.

St Lawrence remains a fine educational institution with a well-established reputation for fostering all-round growth in children alongside academic success. We were encouraged to participate in activities like quizzes, and the school boasted one of the finest football and hockey teams in the city. The image of a student in the dull grey uniform carrying a hockey stick and a canvas bag full of books remains deeply ingrained in my memory.

I believe that the environment, place of birth, people around us, and overall culture play a key role in shaping our upbringing. I have met several people from Calcutta over the years, and all of them have fond memories of the city—its unique heritage, focus on art and culture, overall outlook towards life and its passion for sport. Like so many others, Calcutta has had a profound influence on my life. It was a place I considered home. While some may have deemed it dirty, uncouth, polluted or slow, to me, it was the finest place in the world.

In terms of geographical area, Calcutta is relatively small. Even when including the suburbs surrounding the core metropolitan area, the city stretches approximately 40 kilometres from Bagbazar in the north to Garia and Kudghat in the south. Its east-west span is a maximum of about 10 kilometres, from Beliaghata in the east to the Hooghly River in the west. In fact, in the northernmost of the city, such as Sinthee More, the east-west distance is less than 4 kilometres.

We lived in the heart of south Calcutta, near one of the city's landmarks—Deshapriya Park—where I learnt and honed my cricketing skills. This is not intended as a travelogue or an attempt to extol the city's virtues, but it is important to understand how Calcutta's influence, particularly its people, left an indelible mark on my development.

My quirky sense of humour, for instance, is a direct result of the people I grew up with—their ability to produce witty remarks during a hot, sweaty and uncomfortable bus ride or amid an engrossing play in one of Calcutta's many theatres. Finding something to laugh about and not taking oneself too seriously is a distinct Calcuttan trait that endures despite the changes that have occurred.

Additionally, the average Calcuttan is proud of their remarkable heritage; they are often knowledgeable, erudite and deeply family-oriented. It is common for them to engage in long monologues on eclectic subjects, especially with lifelong friends. Holding differing opinions on a similar subject and arguing both for and against them with equal conviction is another hallmark of a Calcuttan. This is likely influenced by the city's environment—hot and humid during the day but pleasant and vibrant in the evenings; often polluted and crowded, yet always spirited and passionate. It is an intriguing dichotomy that I have never experienced in any other city in the world.

As the archetypal average boy, shaped by the eclectic mix of a South Indian Brahmin family upbringing and growing up in Bengali Calcutta, I naturally became the target of some teasing at school. To make matters worse, my cousins, who also studied in the same school, were far superior to me in academics, sports and extracurricular activities. My stammering while speaking was another source of amusement for my classmates. However, except for one particular boy and his clique of followers, the teasing was rarely offensive.

Kartikeyan Grover, in particular, seemed to derive immense pleasure from mocking me—be it for my stammer, my awkward appearance or my unremarkable upbringing. He came from a wealthy family and always appeared smartly dressed, exuding an easy charm that only the truly privileged seem to possess. Unfortunately, behind that charm lay a vicious streak of cruelty, which he reserved for belittling his less fortunate and helpless classmates.

At times I wondered whether my pronounced stammer was a result of the deep sense of disappointment and disillusionment I experienced as the target of his verbal abuse. Kartikeyan was academically brilliant, the apple of the teachers' eyes and always surrounded by a large group of friends. He consistently ranked at the top of our class, and everyone blindly assumed he was destined to ace the IIT entrance examination.

I never knew what he did after school, and honestly, I had little interest in finding out. My circle of friends, consisting principally of studious individuals from middle-class and lower-middle-class families, was entirely different from his. Once we parted ways on the last day of school, I had little inclination to meet anyone from his group or even the curiosity to check on their whereabouts.

And yet, life has a way of surprising us. I encountered Kartikeyan Grover again on Day 81 after joining engineering college. But for that story, you will need to wade through a couple of hundred pages.

3

Calcutta Part II

woke up at 5 a.m. without the aid of an alarm. Silence was crucial—my plan to escape from the small two-bedroom apartment I shared with my grandfather, grandmother, uncle and aunt hinged entirely on my ability to leave without making the slightest noise. I crept to the front door silently, only to find the large lock on the inside of the wooden door tightly fastened, rendering my escape impossible without the key. For a moment, my brain, not at its sharpest in the early morning hours, was utterly befuddled. Why was the lock on the inside? Wasn't it supposed to secure the apartment from the outside? Was I still asleep? Was this a nightmare?

As I stood there, struggling to comprehend this surprising sight, it suddenly dawned on me: this must have been my grandfather's cunning plan to prevent me from sneaking off to play cricket and instead force me to use the time to prepare for the Class XII board exams and the IIT-JEE—the twin terrors every self-respecting lower middle-class family in India expects their children to conquer.

My suspicion was confirmed when I turned around to see my grandfather standing behind me with a triumphant look on his face. Without a word, I returned to my unmade bed and fell back to sleep.

The toughest years for any school-going child in India are Classes 11 and 12, dominated by the spectre of board exams and the entrance exams for universities. Due to unchecked reservations—implemented by politicians with limited historical understanding and driven by vote-bank politics—people like me, from the so-called 'forward castes' the competition is relentless, with only a handful of seats available in the general category.

The IIT-JEE is among the most challenging exams, and although I spent most of my waking hours studying, I harboured no illusions. At best, I could hope for admission to one of the lesser-known institutes rather than the prestigious IITs.

❋

I had been living with my grandparents and uncle since I was about 13 years old and starting Class 9. My performance in the Class X Board exams was disappointing, and my marks barely allowed me to continue in the Science stream at my esteemed school. My lacklustre academic results did not sit well with my family, most of whom were educated, enterprising and focused on improving their circumstances. Many viewed me as lazy and unfocused, lacking the drive to excel academically and secure a better future for myself.

Our family was not wealthy, and in the vitiated political atmosphere of the time, where members of certain communities—especially those from the priestly class— faced discrimination, academics were seen as the only viable path to progress. Sports, fine arts and other pursuits were not considered practical options for escaping the vicious cycle of a mundane lower-middle-class existence. Financial opportunities were limited, competition was fierce and jobs were scarce. Academic excellence remained the key to financial success, especially for those who did not belong to 'backward' castes or practised religions other than Hinduism.

The constant drive to excel academically was instilled in us from a young age. However, in my case, an imaginative mind, diverse interests and an ability to remember and recollect with minimal effort made me somewhat of a dilettante in my academic pursuits. My academic results reflected this inconsistency—one semester I would be in the top 10 per cent of the class, and the next, I would be close to the bottom. In some subjects, I performed exceptionally well, while in others, I struggled. Consistency was never my strong suit, and this pattern persisted through the initial months of Class XI.

My father visited on the day the results for the first semester of Class XI were announced. My school followed a system of four semesters per year, with each semester's results contributing to the final assessment at the end of the academic year. My results were typical—I excelled in a few subjects (notably Mathematics), performed reasonably well in others (such as languages), and fared poorly in some (particularly Physics). These results largely reflected the effort I had put into each subject, with the possible exception of English.

From childhood, I had been an avid reader, and my command of the language was evident in my writings, even in complex essays; I had a good understanding of grammar and could differentiate between literary nuances such as metaphors and similes. English was never a concern, and I generally found myself in the top percentile of the class despite my minimal efforts.

My father was sitting sipping a cup of coffee, chatting with my uncle and grandparents. From the staircase leading up to our first-floor apartment, I could hear my grandfather's deep voice complaining about my lack of sustained effort and attempting to convince the former to instil some sense into me. 'Raja is intelligent; he understands everything with just one reading. I hate to see all his intelligence going to waste because of his lack of effort. He spends more time on fiction than his schoolbooks—watching movies, listening to music, or God knows what else. The only time he seems to wake up early is to play cricket. Can you ask him to focus more on his school and studies?'

Oh, this crazy life,
Seemed so full of strife,
Play, fun, run, all gone,
Only academics, doggone.

As I walked in, my father caught sight of me and gave a reassuring smile that said, 'Don't worry. All is well.' I exchanged a brief hello with him and went into my room to change. Emerging a few minutes later, I felt excited to meet and speak with him. My father was my hero, the person I always looked up to, so when he suggested we go out for a walk and grab an early supper, I was stoked. We were soon strolling through suburban Calcutta in companionable silence.

'Dad, I received my first-semester marks today,' I ventured, breaking the silence.

'Are you satisfied with your results?'

I paused for a moment before replying, 'I'm not sure, Dad. I think I got what I deserved.'

'Life is often like that,' he said. 'We get what we work for. Ignore the outliers—those who win the lottery or stumble upon success by chance. For most people, our results reflect the efforts we put in. You are intelligent and curious. If you focus your curiosity on your current targets, you can achieve a lot.'

I reflected on his words. They made some vague sense at first, but I instinctively understood what my dad, in his usual understated manner, was suggesting: focus on the present, consider your options and make the right choices.

Was I good enough as a cricketer to play for Bengal in the Ranji trophy? Was I capable of building a career beyond academics? With my stammer, ordinary looks and lack of any obvious talent, what did the future hold for me?

These questions weighed on my mind, forcing me to ponder my next steps. I realized I had to determine what needed to be done over the next 18 months to secure admission to one of the engineering schools. It would not be an easy task, especially for someone from what, in India, was considered a 'forward caste'.

Over the next few days, I assiduously reflected on my own strengths and limitations. At first, I doubted there would be many strengths to note. But after about 20 minutes of reflection, I identified a few: I had a latent ability to work hard when needed, an intuitive understanding of numbers and mathematics, a broad interest in various subjects, and the ability to recall and express key concepts easily. I was fluent in four languages and understood a few more. I preferred chemistry over physics, and I grasped the first part of *Halliday & Resnick's* physics book better than the second. The first part dealt with mechanical physics, while the second part focused on light and electricity.

Despite racking my brain, I could think of little more.

As for weaknesses, there were too many to list, but one stood out: my inability to focus on any one subject for an extended period.

Whenever my cousins or my limited circle of friends discussed their study habits, I kept quiet, marvelling at their ability to spend an entire evening and night studying a single subject with almost no breaks. For me, it was impossible to concentrate for more than 30 minutes—or at best, an hour—before my mind wandered to something more esoteric.

I realized that effective time management was not something I was born with. Throughout school, I was consistently the last boy to enter the classroom. I wasn't late, but I would always arrive just seconds before the bell rang at 10 a.m. I knew something had to change if I wanted to make a real effort to work smart and succeed in the JEE. The next morning, I spoke to my dad and shared my strengths and weaknesses. He introduced me to the Pomodoro Technique.

For those unfamiliar, the Pomodoro Technique was created by Francesco Cirillo in the 1980s as a personal time-management system. The name 'Pomodoro' translates to 'tomato' in Italian, named after the tomato-shaped kitchen timer Cirillo used while he was a university student.

He released a white paper on the technique, which many found helpful in managing their time effectively.

The Pomodoro Technique is based on 'timeboxing', where you allocate a fixed amount of time to a task, and once that time is up, you stop working. This method is designed to minimize the effects of Parkinson's Law—the adage that 'work expands to fill the time available for its completion.' The technique is simple: tasks are broken into manageable intervals, usually 25 minutes, followed by short breaks. Some people prefer longer work sessions, but the flexibility of the method makes it adaptable to anyone's needs.

I decided to implement a similar approach. I started keeping a timetable, dividing my waking hours into 30-minute blocks. Each 30-minute block was followed by a 5–10-minute break, during which I would do something different from what I had been working on. Each 30-minute session focused on a single subject. Given the JEE's emphasis on mathematics and physics, I knew my preparation needed to prioritize those subjects. Chemistry was important too, but I felt my basic understanding of it was solid, requiring less effort than physics and mathematics. Although I could solve most maths problems well, I realized I wasn't fast enough to meet the time demands of the entrance exam.

Once a 30-minute session ended, I'd start a new one, usually focusing on a different subject. For example, after working on differential calculus, I would switch to mechanical physics, where some problems required knowledge of calculus. After each session, I'd take a 10-minute break—grab a coffee, read an essay, or do something else to reset. After every four sessions, I'd take a 20-minute break—go for a walk, talk to my uncle or listen to old Bollywood music—something I truly enjoyed.

The Pomodoro Technique worked because it combined time management, focus, and balance between work and rest. By breaking tasks into smaller intervals, productivity and creativity increased. It also prevented fatigue, burnout, and procrastination, and helped me build better habits for staying focused.

As the saying goes, productivity is about working smarter, not harder.

I started putting this method into practice. Initially, it was difficult, especially with my wandering mind and a small apartment filled with relatives. I often found myself distracted every few minutes, but I made a concerted effort to refocus on my studies. Over time, and with consistent effort, I found that I could concentrate for 45 minutes without being distracted. Within three months, I had developed a method and a level of dedication that I had never had before.

Unfortunately, it took less than 80 days in Varanasi for that dedication and focus to break!

4

Varanasi

It was late afternoon when we arrived at Varanasi Junction. Unbeknownst to me, while I had been tangled in the land of dreams, we had crossed the holy River Ganga about an hour earlier. I vaguely remembered waking up at some point, possibly at Gaya, for my morning coffee before drifting back to sleep. The sleep fairy's hold had weakened post-coffee, and I faintly recalled passing through Mughalsarai, the major railway junction where the principal tracks between Howrah and Delhi converge before branching off to different destinations.

From Mughalsarai, heading east, one could take the Grand Chord via Dhanbad and Gaya to Calcutta or follow the main line via Patna. Travelling west, there were three network options to Delhi; our train had taken the central route, crossing the Ganga before reaching Kashi Junction—the first of the three railway stations serving Varanasi. Despite being the smallest of the three, most trains stopped at Kashi. It almost felt as though the engines, having traversed the grandeur and sanctity of the Ganga, needed a moment's respite before entering one of the oldest continuously inhabited cities in the world.

Varanasi derives its name from the two rivers, the

Varuna and the Assi, which converge with the Ganga at this historic site. River Varuna, the larger of the two, meets the Ganga a few miles north of Assi, effectively forming the city's northern and southern boundaries. Assi, which also lends its name to a southern locality of Varanasi, boasts a significant bathing and boating ghat at the point where it merges with the Ganga.

Throughout its turbulent history, Varanasi has been known by various names, the oldest possibly being Kashi. The city's earliest concentrated habitation is believed to have started adjacent to this small railway station, which is situated at the point where the tracks cross the Ganga from the eastern approach. During the Muslim invasions, the city was renamed to the more Urdu-sounding Banaras—a name that persisted even when Madan Mohan Malviya founded one of the largest universities in the world, Banaras Hindu University.

Varanasi is steeped in antiquity, with a documented history spanning nearly four millennia. Stretching along the west bank of the Ganga, it occupies the only point where the great river flows from south to north, covering a mere 15 kilometres. The banks of Ganga have witnessed countless civilizations and serve as a holy crucible where Hindu philosophy and ways of life have been deliberated, ordered and practised. Just a few kilometres to the north lies Sarnath, the hamlet where the Buddha delivered his first sermon.

Varanasi's significance in India's often chaotic but invariably colourful history cannot be overstated. Even in the far south, a thousand miles away, a pilgrimage to Kashi and a ritual bath in the sacred waters of the Ganga is considered one of the holiest journeys. Millennia ago, the great southern ruler Rajaraja Chola travelled this vast distance to conquer this city and bring the holy water to his kingdom. He was henceforth honoured as *Gangaikondacholavaram*—the Chola who brought the Ganga to the Chola kingdom. Legend has it that Lord Shiva meditated in Varanasi and the great southern seer Markandeya built a subterranean passage from Thirukaddayur, near present-day Mayavaram, to Kashi for easier access during his meditation sessions.

My uncle and I disembarked from the crowded train and made our way out of the platform, eventually reaching the station gates. The first thing that struck me was the smell. It was unlike anything I had encountered before—a potent mix of cow dung, sweat and petrol fumes. Yet the breeze carried with it the sweet fragrance of jasmine flowers being sold nearby, which helped slightly mitigate the stench, preventing it from becoming overwhelming.

My initial glimpse of the city that would be my home for the next four years was from the grand lobby of Varanasi Junction. The space bustled with activity, crowded and polluted, reminiscent of Calcutta yet with subtle differences. It was much smaller, lacked the imposing grandeur of Howrah Station, and was painted a dull yellow instead of Howrah's iconic brick red.

Loud conversations surrounded me, primarily in Hindi, but the dialect had a distinct, sing-song cadence that set it apart from the Hindi I was used to hearing. The melodic rhythm of their speech was punctuated by the chomping of tobacco, their mouths stained red with betel juice. I also noticed how frequently people nodded their heads while speaking, often accompanied by graceful hand movements that emphasized their points with confidence and elegance. This was quite different from the animated and passionate gestures of a typical Calcuttan, who rarely used their arms while speaking and usually preferred to stand with their hands by their sides or holding a cigarette.

The atmosphere was alive with a different kind of energy, almost subdued. People moved with deliberate patience, often stepping aside with a courteous bow to let others pass. Despite the milling crowds, there was an unexpected sense of space, as if people consciously chose to be gentle, chivalrous and considerate in their daily interactions with strangers. This was a stark contrast to the busy streets of Calcutta, where such genteel behaviour would result in a walking speed of less than 10 metres per hour.

The attire of the people further set them apart from the average Calcuttan. Most men wore long, loose cotton shirts called *kurtas*, often in pale pastel shades, paired with loose trousers known as *pyjamas*, typically in pale yellow or white. There were very few women in the crowded lobby of the station, and those there wore the female version of the kurta-pyjama, rather than the saris commonly seen in Calcutta.

Amidst the typical chaos of an Indian railway station, a large cow stood serenely near the exit, oblivious to the commotion around it. The animal formed an impenetrable barrier, reducing the space available for entering or exiting the station lobby. I observed a few people pausing to reverently touch its forehead as they passed. I wondered at their courage—or foolhardiness—considering the cow's large, sharp horns that could easily gore a person.

As we ventured outside the lobby, I was greeted by a scene far removed from the stereotypical image of a small district town—which is what I had imagined Varanasi to be. A sprawling public vehicle stand stretched before me, teeming with at least a hundred autorickshaws—black three-wheeled vehicles legally restricted to three passengers but often accommodating up to eight. Scores of taxis, buses, and cycle rickshaws were also present. What struck me as unique about the parking area was the presence of numerous cows, all of them seemingly in good health and radiating contentment.

We approached the first autorickshaw in line, and before we could say a word, the driver eagerly exclaimed, '*BIT jaana hai, saab?* (Do you need to go to BIT, sir?) Come, come! *Sirf 25 rupees.* (Just Rs 25.)'

I was impressed by how he accurately surmised our destination, and my uncle seemed satisfied with the fare. The driver quickly grabbed our bags and secured them in the compartment behind the seats. Before I could even spell my first name, he zoomed off, manoeuvring through the narrow spaces between the other autos parked in the stand, leaving me in a state of mortal terror, wondering if I would safely reach the college and face the dreaded ragging ordeal.

A small part of me secretly wished for a minor mishap, one that might grant me a dignified escape from this arena and send me back to the safer pastures of Calcutta. (Yes, yet another bovine reference. Punning is indeed Hobbit-forming—a spelling mistake intended as a Tolkien reference).

The journey to the campus felt interminable. The air was

filled with incessant exhortations and counter-exhortations from the drivers of various vehicles, each vying for the right of way. Amidst this cacophony, cows and other bovine creatures ambled nonchalantly in the middle of the road, oblivious to the pandemonium they caused. People promptly made way for these majestic animals—sometimes out of fear, but mostly out of reverence. At times, the cows would squat in the middle of the road, leisurely flicking away the flies that sought to feast on the filth covering their bodies. Their presence unintentionally created a natural road divider, which seemed to make the journey safer.

The roads we traversed were narrow, flanked by ancient houses, some of which seemed to be centuries old. Many of these had small balconies, from which women chatted with their neighbours on corresponding balconies. The roads never seemed wider than 15 feet, and I shuddered at the thought of what would happen if two vehicles met head-on.

> *Oh! This is hardly the ideal place to be,*
> *As far or near as the naked eye can see,*
> *Only dogs, cows and goats—both she and he,*
> *For the fruit of my fervent prayers, I'll give a penny.*
> *And head back to Cal without wasting time any.*

The stench of cow dung pervaded the air, and the warm breeze created by the autorickshaw's motion did little to dispel it. The city exuded the aura of an 18th-century metropolis, where traders from the hinterlands would come to hawk their wares, hoping for quick sales before returning to the safety of their villages. Mirzapur and

Bhadohi, both renowned for their carpet weaving, owe much of their prominence to this trading post.

Clutching the overhead handle of the autorickshaw for dear life, I braced myself as the driver seemed to relish moving the vehicle sideways as much as forward, eagerly overtaking the car ahead of us. Autorickshaw commuting was a relatively new experience for me; only a few months earlier, these three-wheeled contraptions had made their debut on Calcutta's streets. Interestingly, Calcutta's bus drivers disparagingly nicknamed them '*peepde*'—the Bengali word for ant.

Suddenly, after about 30 minutes into the bumpy ride, the potholes vanished. The autorickshaw made a sharp right turn, and the road became as smooth as Hema Malini's cheeks—although this simile is perhaps geographically misplaced, considering we were in Uttar Pradesh and not Bihar, albeit barely 50 kilometres from the border. (One of the Bihar chief ministers once famously promised to make his state's roads as flawless as the actress' famed visage). Still, it was the first thought that crossed my mind.

The road also widened significantly, resembling an autobahn in Germany. This grand thoroughfare was lined with newly constructed buildings, their fresh coats of paint in a spectrum of colours lending the entire area an air of prosperity. It felt like I had just stepped out of the whitewashed simplicity of the 18th century and into the emulsion-painted exuberance of the 20th.

I later learnt that we had entered Lanka, the approach road leading to the university and the newly developed centre of Varanasi. Passing through a large archway at the university's entrance, I noticed a life-size statue of its founder, Madan Mohan Malviya. The road widened further and became even smoother as we entered the gates of the esteemed campus. Lined with shady trees that made the oppressive July heat more tolerable, the scene was alive with students walking or cycling, their animated conversations filling the air.

The stench of cow dung had disappeared, replaced by the fresh scent of leaves and flowers. The buildings around us were painted a deep shade of yellow with red accents on the corners and lintels, creating a striking contrast. The structures appeared newly painted and featured Gothic architecture, characterized by their wide and robust construction. The sight was incredibly beautiful and alleviated some of the heaviness in my heart as I anticipated my four-year stay in this charming environment.

A classmate had previously informed me that the campus was picturesque, but nothing could have prepared me for this breathtaking view. The university layout was semi-circular, with the entrance situated near one of the two corners, mimicking the curve of the nearby Ganga. Hostels were arrayed along the grand chord of this semi-circle, and our autorickshaw trundled along this route.

Turning his head slightly, the driver asked, '*IT jaana hai kya?* (Are you going to the IT campus?)'

I informed him that we had been instructed to report at Rajputana Hostel, which was located within the BIT campus. Nodding knowingly, he drove us for a couple of kilometres along the winding road, framed by the enchanting greenery I had been admiring, until we reached one of those remarkable Gothic buildings. Pulling up at a wide gate, the driver announced, '*Yeh hai hostel, saab.* (This is the hostel, sir.)'

I disembarked from the autorickshaw, surprisingly composed considering the tumultuous initial part of the journey, and surveyed my surroundings. The spot where we stopped seemed to be the hostel's lobby, a space about 10 feet wide, flanked by notice boards on each side. A flight of five steps on either side led to a ground-floor veranda, where the rooms were situated. The hostel's architecture formed a rectangular courtyard, with the rooms situated along the perimeter and a large grassy area in the centre. The grass was overgrown, and in the middle of the courtyard sat an empty tank, which I speculated might serve as a fountain during the rainy season. In one corner, a large cot was draped with a blanket, perhaps concealing its age. I carefully placed my luggage on it.

My uncle left me in the lobby, instructing me to guard our belongings while he located the office—conveniently positioned on the right side of the veranda.

With nothing else to do, I wandered to the notice boards. Most of the notices were from an association called the 'IT-Gymkhana Cultural Wing', signed by the General Secretary. Others were standard directives for freshers to report to their respective hostel offices upon arrival. The lack of activity around me was puzzling and I wondered where all the other newcomers were. I had assumed we would all be assigned to the same hostel.

Just then, a couple of students sauntered in. Sporting spectacles and short-sleeved shirts paired with shorts, their appearances were shabby and unkempt; it seemed they had not shaved in weeks. After observing them briefly, I returned to my desultory perusal of the notices.

✳

5

First Blood

I felt a hand on my shoulder and turned to find the two individuals I had noticed earlier staring at me.

Curious about their intentions, I waited for one of them to speak.

'*Abey, wish nahin karega kya?* (Won't you wish us?)' one of them asked.

Confused, I could not help but think that things were getting stranger by the minute—as Alice would say, 'curiouser and curiouser'.

Seeing my baffled expression, the other individual asked, 'Just arrived, have you?'

I nodded, confirming my recent arrival. The first one demanded, 'Start the intro.'

Realizing he was asking for my name, I began, 'Hi! I am Raja, and I just arrived from Calcutta,' while extending my right hand for a handshake. I stammered over the 'R' and 'C' as usual.

The first person looked horrified, staring at my outstretched hand as if he had just encountered Dracula in the flesh. He asked incredulously, 'Nobody taught you how to introduce yourself? Where did you go for counselling?'

Puzzled by their reaction, I wondered what was wrong with starting an introduction with my name and a friendly handshake. The second individual, who seemed to be from a small district town based on his attire and dialect, took it upon himself to enlighten me.

'First of all, you are supposed to greet all seniors with a "Good Morning" or "Good Afternoon", and address them as "Sir". Secondly, you have to mention the examination you cleared before joining this college and your "hawa". Thirdly, you should state the name of the school and place you are coming from, as well as the department you have joined here. And remember, address all seniors as "Sir", always wear full-sleeved shirts and formal shoes, avoid jeans. Now, start again.'

Although I did not understand what he meant by 'hawa' (which literally translates to 'air' or 'wind'), I took a deep breath and tried again. 'Good morning, Sir,' I said, relieved that I didn't stammer this time.

'Good morning?' the first person repeated sarcastically, adopting an exaggerated accent that sounded like Rajinikanth attempting to speak Bhojpuri in a Bollywood action film.

Realizing it was nearly four in the afternoon, I quickly corrected myself. 'Good afternoon, Sir,' I said, fumbling over the 'G'.

His face twisted into a threatening scowl. 'Don't you know that the plural of "Sir" is "Sirs"? Or do you only want to wish him?'

I instinctively shook my head in the South Indian fashion, which translated into a 'yes' in North Indian culture. Their astonished expressions made it clear I had committed yet another faux pas.

Before further interaction could escalate my already nervous state, I hastily started over. 'Good Afternoon, Sirs. My name is N. Raja Venkateswar, and I completed my Senior Secondary Examination from St Lawrence High School, Calcutta. I have cleared the Joint Entrance Examination and joined the Chemical Engineering Department of BIT.'

Reasonably satisfied with my performance, with only a stammer on the 'St' and 'D', I stood pleased with myself until the first person rudely said, 'You're not supposed to use any acronyms, you idiot! Next time you use one, I'll turn you into a *murga*.'

Murga—Handy Guide to IT Lingo

Having learnt enough Hindi in school, I knew what he meant—he intended to make me squat on the floor, holding my ears in the humiliating pose of a hen. No self-respecting person would want to become that.

I quickly backtracked. 'I have joined the Chemical Engineering Department of the Banaras Institute of Technology,' I clarified, ensuring that no acronyms were used this time.

'Start freshly, bugger,' the second one interjected with his rustic English.

My nerves were fraying, and the murderous look on the first person's face didn't help. He was now rolling up his sleeves, revealing forearms thick as logs—proof of more time spent in the gym than was healthy for me. I gulped and began again, stammering only on the 'I' in 'Institute' and the 'L' in 'Lawrence'.

When I concluded my monologue, the second person asked with feigned concern, 'And who conducts the examination, dear fresher?'

Remembering the admonishment about the use of acronyms, I replied, 'Indian Institutes of Technology.' I did not even stammer at the 'T', and I felt a glimmer of hope that this round of introductions was nearing its end.

I was amazed at the reactions on the faces of the two seniors to my simple and justified answer, which I knew by personal experience to be perfectly true.

'Idiot! The exam is conducted by the Banaras Institute of Technology, and the Inferior Institutes of Technology. Come on, start again.'

So, I began again, duly rectifying the mistakes I had made. I stammered only on the letter 'L' this time.

When I paused for a breath, the first person asked, 'What's your hawa?'

The word threw me. Should I mention the troposphere? My confusion must have been evident, as the second person kindly explained, 'Your All India Rank, *chirkut.*'

Chirkut—Handy Guide to IT Lingo

It suddenly dawned on me that 'hawa' meant 'All India Rank', which was often abbreviated as 'A.I.R'. There seemed to be no end to these acronyms. Nevertheless, I kept a straight face and continued, 'One thousand six hundred and eighty.'

'Didn't we ask you to address all seniors as "Sir" at all times?' the first person inquired.

'One thousand six hundred and eighty, sirs,' I repeated.

'What's your name again?' the first person asked.

'N. Raja Venkateswar, sirs.'

'I thought you said you're from Calcutta, right?'

'Yes, sir.'

'A Bengali with a South Indian name. That's interesting.'

I quickly clarified, 'No, sir, I'm not Bengali. I am indeed a South Indian.'

'But you said you're from Bengal.'

'Yes, sir, I am South Indian but was born in Calcutta and have lived there for most of my life.'

'So, your parents live in Calcutta. How long have they been there?'

'My parents don't live in Calcutta, sirs. My father works in Bokaro.'

'Confused man! A *makku* from Calcutta whose parents live in Bokaro. Just a minute—Bokaro is in Bihar, right? It's in Bihar, isn't it?'

Makku—Handy Guide to IT Lingo

'Yes, sir.'

He seemed to ignore my singular use of 'sir' this time, possibly weighing his options and trying to figure out where this 'confused individual' was from.

'You must have a passport then.'

Unsure why he would ask about a passport, I responded, 'No, sirs.'

'Then how did you come from Bihar to India? You do realize you crossed the border just before Mughalsarai, don't you?'

Baffled by the question, I remained silent while the two seniors burst into laughter.

The second one then asked, 'So, you speak Bengali?'

'Yes, sir.'

'What is your mother tongue?'

'Tamil, sir.'

'So, you're actually a makku?'

I wondered what 'makku' meant, but before I could dwell on it, I noticed my uncle descending the stairs, signalling that his office work was done.

My facial expression must have betrayed something because my uncle paused his stately progress and waited at the stairs.

'He's with you, is he?' the first person asked, nodding towards my uncle.

I nodded and replied, 'Yes, sirs. This led to a brief interrogation about our relationship. I replied truthfully, and the first guy turned on his heels with a 'see you soon' as he walked off, his friend trailing behind him.

I had no interest in meeting them again.

'What were they saying?' my uncle asked as he approached me.

I shrugged my shoulders and replied, 'Nothing much.'

'Your room has been allotted. It is Room 150, on the first floor,' he informed me, pointing to the row of rooms directly above the ground floor lobby.

'Come, let's go see what it's like,' he continued, picking up one of the bags and heading towards the opposite side of the hostel.

I followed him, the overnight bag slung over my shoulder. The hostel was large, painted a dull yellow with mahogany-brown stripes on the balconies. It was a rectangular structure, the longer sides measuring approximately 200 metres, with the shorter sides about half that length. The entrance was at the centre of one of the longer sides.

To reach our rooms, we had to walk across the courtyard along a narrow pathway bordered by lush green lawns. As we made our way down the pathway, I noticed that no other students crossed our path.

We soon found ourselves on the opposite side of the hostel's entrance, where a set of stairs leading to the first-floor lobby awaited us. Standing on the stairs was a peon, holding a bunch of keys.

'Room 150?' he asked.

Confirming with a nod, my uncle and I climbed the stairs to the first floor. The stairs were made of cement but polished from extensive use, with a wide balustrade for support and safety.

The room, in front of which we waited patiently as the peon stooped to unlock the door, faced the main entrance of the hostel. It was separated from the balcony's edge by a lobby that ran along its length. To access the lobby, we had to climb a wide set of stairs from the ground-floor veranda.

The room itself was roughly eight feet by ten feet, with a small window on the wall opposite the door. The window overlooked another hostel, separated from ours by a large open area covered in grass, shrubs and trees. The walls were freshly painted with white plaster, and two closets had been carved out of the wall—one covered with greyish plywood, the other left bare. Several cement shelves were built into the wall; I assumed the uncovered shelves were meant for books, while the covered ones were for clothes.

The peon waited expectantly for his *baksheesh*, glancing first at my uncle and then at me, much like a well-trained dog waiting for a bone after performing a task. He accepted the amount my uncle offered, sniffing at it with ill-concealed distaste, clearly dissatisfied with the sum. Without a salute or a simple 'thank you', he turned and walked away.

'We need to go to the warden's office to complete some paperwork. You need to sign a few forms before we settle in. Let's get that done before we find the toilets and grab some food,' my uncle said.

I nodded in agreement and followed him into the warden's office, which was located on the ground floor near one corner of the hostel. Inside, we found a short, dark-skinned man seated at a desk, poring over a thick file of papers. He had short, curly hair flecked with grey at the temples and wore a half-sleeved white shirt. Thick, black-framed spectacles perched precariously on the edge of his nose.

Noticing us at the door, he beckoned us in, closed his file and invited us to sit on rickety, uncomfortable chairs in front of his desk. The office was rather small and did not seem to align with what one might expect from an institution reputed to be the second-largest university in the world. My uncle initiated the conversation. 'Hello, Dr Kumar. This is my nephew, whose papers I submitted earlier.'

Dr Kumar nodded and said, 'Welcome to our institute, Raja. I hope you find it comfortable here and make our college proud. My name is Dr Sujoy Kumar, and I am the warden of this hostel. I am a Reader in the Mechanical

Engineering Department and live just behind the hostel. Tell me something about yourself.'

I began, 'My name is N. Raja Venkateswar. I come from Calcutta, where I attended St Lawrence High School. I achieved a rank of one thousand six hundred and eighty in the Joint Entrance Examination conducted by the Institute—'

Dr Kumar interjected, 'Well, it seems you have already met a few seniors, though I didn't think many would have returned to campus yet. Classes for senior students don't start for a few days. I assure you that the experience shouldn't be too bad.'

Before I could respond, he turned to my uncle and said, 'Don't worry about these ragging incidents. The seniors mean no harm. They usually ask silly questions and try to prove they are smarter than the freshers. I studied here two decades ago, and I look back fondly on my ragging period as a time of immense joy. Just relax and tell Raja's parents and others that he is well cared for. Leave him to us; we will take good care of him. Once he gets used to living here, you'll see a completely different person.'

It was kind of him to reassure us, although I don't think he could have imagined just how true his words would turn out to be within 12 hours.

Meanwhile, my uncle inquired about the scarcity of students on campus, as we had not seen many people around.

'Oh! That's because it is a Saturday. The institute officially opens for freshers on Monday; most of the new students will arrive tomorrow, and classes for seniors won't start until Wednesday. You'll see a different campus tomorrow when the overnight trains start arriving.'

His explanation did not satisfy my uncle, who looked indecisive as he stood up to shake hands with Dr Kumar. I wondered if I would be asked by my uncle to return to Calcutta and enrol in one of the other institutes closer to home.

6

The Makku Brigade

One of the first things that struck me about university life was the abundance of acronyms used in everyday conversations. Yet, as freshers, we were strictly forbidden from using any!

After returning to my room, we noticed that the door to the neighbouring room was open and the lights were on. A studious-looking person sat inside, engrossed in a thick journal. He glanced up when he saw us and greeted us with a pleasant 'Good evening'.

'You have the room next door, right?' he continued, getting up and walking towards us.

My uncle wished him a good evening in return, confirmed that we indeed had the room next door and introduced me as his nephew who had just joined the institute.

'Hi, my name is Ajai Kumar Gupta, but everyone calls me AKG. I am an MTech student here,' he said, offering an acronym of his own. *Another bloody acronym*, I thought.

Ajai stood about my height but appeared even thinner, his high cheekbones accentuating his narrow face. He wore a light blue kurta that reached his knees, over white pyjamas, his feet bare. His thin, friendly face sported a scruffy moustache, and his long, thick, jet-black hair fell untidily to his collar, covering his ears.

My uncle asked Ajai about the relatively quiet atmosphere, mentioning he had expected more students to join such a prestigious institution.

AKG smiled and assured us, 'Oh, don't worry about that. Just wait until tomorrow—you won't be able to hear yourselves think.'

Curious, my uncle asked if Ajai had completed his bachelor's degree at BIT as well.

AKG replied, 'Yes, I completed my bachelor's here and then decided I wanted to be a professor. So, I took my GMAT (Graduate Management Admission Test) and stayed on to learn more.'

'That's great to hear,' my uncle responded. 'Now, how about the ragging? Raja had a funny incident while we were waiting for the paperwork to be sorted. Is it safe?'

'I'm sure you're worried about leaving your kid here,' AKG said, pointing his thin finger in my direction. 'But don't worry. There is no physical ragging here, and the seniors are a friendly bunch. Plus, there are several MTech students in this hostel, and we will take diligent care of him. Come, let me take you to the mess for some food, which, true to its name, is indeed a mess,' he said, chuckling at his pun.

Regardless of whether his pun was funny, he was right about the mess. It was on the ground floor, right behind the veranda. A long passage led us to a spacious room with approximately 15 benches arranged inside. The walls seemed to have been painted nearly a decade ago, and the deep brown wooden benches and tables appeared ancient and could easily pass as antiques. There were two entrances to the mess—one from the corridor where we entered and another leading to the kitchen, which was barely visible from our position.

AKG led us inside, and we sat at one of the tables, with him and my uncle sitting opposite me. Observing the room, I thought to myself, *What a mess they've made!* Little did I know that this thought would soon take on a whole new meaning.

AKG called out to a boy named Chhotu, who promptly appeared from the kitchen entrance.

Chhotu—Handy Guide to IT Lingo

'*Teen chai lana* (Bring three cups of tea),' AKG instructed.

While my uncle politely declined any food, AKG ordered aloo parathas for himself and me.

AKG assured my uncle, 'Don't worry about the food. One of the things you learn in a hostel is that seniors are responsible for ensuring juniors are always well-fed. It's my duty to take care of Raja here,' he said. He then looked at me and said, 'If you need anything, just ask, and don't feel shy.'

Soon, my uncle and AKG were deep in conversation. I learnt that AKG hailed from a small town called Ghazipur, a couple of hundred miles north of Varanasi, where his father worked as a government official in the Public Works Department.

Chhotu soon returned with three glasses of tea, slightly darker than what I was accustomed to in Calcutta. To my delight, it turned out to be excellent—rich, sweet, hot and fragrant with the aroma of cardamom.

As we enjoyed the tea, the aloo parathas arrived, accompanied by pickles and curd, and I eagerly indulged in their delectable taste. Aloo paratha happened to be one of my favourite dishes, and I savoured every bite, never having tasted such delicious parathas before. Feeling content, I hoped that the other meals here would be equally satisfying.

AKG asked Chhotu if the Maharaj was around. When Chhotu nodded, AKG requested he bring the Maharaj over. I was perplexed by this exchange and even more so when a large, corpulent old man emerged from the kitchen. He sported a thick white moustache that contrasted with his bronzed chocolate-brown skin. The Maharaj, dressed only in a loincloth of an unusual colour, did not resemble the Maharajas I had read about in my history books.

Maharaj—Handy Guide to IT Lingo

As he approached us, AKG inquired if he could accommodate me in his mess for a few days until the first-year mess started operating. It then dawned on me that the Maharaj was the person in charge of one of the messes in the large dining hall. The Maharaj nodded in agreement with a 'Ji, sir', and proceeded to explain the meal timings: breakfast at 7 a.m., lunch at noon, and dinner at 7.30 p.m.

Later that night, as my uncle and I lay down to sleep—me on the bed and he using the travel gear on the floor as a makeshift bed—our conversation revolved around the scarcity of students. We debated whether it might be wiser for me to join Jadavpur University (JU) or the Indian Statistical Institute (ISI) back in Calcutta.

Eventually, we decided that if the student population did not increase the following day, we would leave for Calcutta and then decide between ISI and JU upon our return. Soon, I could hear my uncle snoring gently as I drifted into an uneasy sleep.

The next morning, we were abruptly awakened by a loud call of 'Machchan'. The word, Tamil for 'brother-in-law', surprised us. My uncle and I exchanged bewildered glances, wondering if we had misheard. However, more Tamil phrases followed, wafting through the door. I was astonished to hear my mother tongue spoken so far from Tamil Nadu.

Checking my watch, I realized it was already past 8 a.m. I opened the door to the balcony and was greeted by bright sunlight streaming in. My uncle joined me a few seconds later, and together we observed the bustling activity below in growing amazement. Dozens of students filled the green patch, some engaged in animated conversations, shouting choice phrases at each other in Tamil mixed with English. We exchanged glances, both thinking the same thing—there was no way I could return to Calcutta after witnessing this.

My attention shifted to a noticeably large, dark figure wearing a bright red round-neck T-shirt. His distinctive attire made him stand out among the crowd, but what captured my attention even more were his energetic, almost manic movements. He swung himself around as if bursting with excess energy that needed an outlet.

As I observed him, a lean guy in a black shirt shouted at the top of his voice, 'Hey, Pondy, stop the crap and come take a look here!'

Two students had climbed into the centre tank of the hostel and managed to on the taps, causing water to gush out and form a small fountain. Pondy cheered and dashed—rather, waddled—towards the tank. Upon reaching it, he stripped to his briefs, humming a Tamil song as he dove into the rapidly filling tank. A few others also joined the impromptu pool party. Soon, a dozen young men, in varying stages of undress, belted out Tamil songs at the top of their voices, creating an unforgettable scene.

This surreal spectacle was the last thing I expected on my first morning at the institute. It occurred to me that these could not be freshers, as my previous evening's experience had taught me that freshers could not be left alone for even a few minutes without interruption. They would not possess this level of exuberance, especially among South Indians, who were known for their studious and reserved nature. I considered quietly retreating to my room to avoid the usual round of questioning when something strange happened.

More people began entering the hostel, and it was clear that they were seniors. Their confident gait, unshaven appearance and 'uniform' of shorts or torn jeans, pastel T-shirts and Hawaii slippers set them apart. The uproar abruptly ceased, revealing that the guys revelling in the tank were indeed freshers. Seven seniors stood before the gaggle of boys who had been frolicking in the water. The crowd of freshers below seemed to disperse rapidly, seeking refuge in their rooms, the warden's office or the mess.

My mind oscillated between curiosity about the fate of the freshers and the urge to slip into my room before any senior noticed my presence in the first-floor lobby.

The brain beat the heart, and I ducked into my room. AKG, who had just stepped out, joined me shortly after. A couple of freshers, who had thought the flight of stairs to be a good escape route, nervously lingered near the entrance of my room, unsure if they had avoided one ordeal only to stumble into another. AKG invited them in and reassured us that no seniors would come up, since the rooms on the first floor of the hostel usually accommodated postgraduate students.

As I looked at the other two freshers—who had adhered to the prevailing first-year dress code of full-sleeved shirts, formal trousers and black leather shoes—they appeared less animated than they had a few minutes ago. To break the ice, I mentioned that I had overheard them speaking Tamil and informed them that I, too, was a Tamilian.

Soon, Bala, a short, stocky, bespectacled Iyer Brahmin from Madras with a perpetually sleepy look on his round face, and Sundar, a tall, dark and moustachioed Iyengar from Tiruchirappalli became comfortable in my room. They began sharing their experiences of the train journey from Madras to Varanasi. Their 40-hour journey unfolded as a source of free entertainment for the seniors on the same train. Sundar had been enlisted to sell tea to passengers, while Bala's notable accomplishment was singing popular Tamil movie songs and acting them out in front of everyone. In return, the seniors had been kind enough to cover all their expenses throughout the journey. Their admiration for the seniors reminded me of Stockholm syndrome.

They informed me that about 70 freshers had travelled on the same train, with approximately a quarter opting for Metallurgical Engineering. Sundar explained that Metallurgy (Meta, for short) was the most popular and renowned department at BIT, especially known for its students receiving scholarships to prestigious institutes in the US for further studies. Many students aimed to go abroad for higher education, with some eventually settling in the US or Europe after completing their studies.

In the next few hours, Bala, Sundar, Sridhar—a short and talkative guy with freckles covering his red face—and I became fast friends. My uncle left for Calcutta later that evening, far less apprehensive than when we had initially arrived.

The following morning, I was introduced to the other members of our group, humorously dubbed the 'Makku Brigade'. It included Bhoopathy, a dark and slim Tamilian known for his penchant for using the most challenging but fitting words from the English lexicon, as though he could not find simpler terms; Padmanabhan, a short and jolly guy who happened to be extremely overweight, earning the nickname 'Pondy' for obvious reasons; Ramnath, a short and dark guy who often wore tight and bright T-shirts despite his rotund figure; and the second Sundar—fair, of medium height, with thin straggly hair, which was cut short and neatly oiled—a complete opposite of the original Sundar.

Among them, Pondy was the most talkative and extroverted, never hesitating to share his longing for his girlfriend and updating us on their temporary separation.

Just to be in Madras at this time
When the sun beats down just fine

And the beautiful sweetheart of mine
In my ever-willing arms all the time.

It was also Pondy who brought about my first real encounter with ragging.

The incident occurred on Monday, the scheduled opening day of the university, when we were instructed to gather in the common hall, referred to as G11, for our formal induction. The Director addressed us for about 30 minutes, delivering the usual speech about hard work, honesty, focus and dedication. We also had the opportunity to meet several professors during the event, and were invited to join them for tea and snacks. Apart from a brief interaction with Dr Kumar at the hostel, this was my first encounter with professors, and they left a strong impression—friendly, treating us like adults, open and even exchanging jokes with us and among themselves. The brief program concluded before noon, and we returned to our rooms feeling elated; it felt like we had taken a significant step towards becoming successful engineers.

On our way back to the hostel, we spotted several senior students, a stark reminder of our status as freshers. Wisely, we opted to return discreetly to our rooms, devising strategies to avoid them. Our hostel rooms had two wooden doors that opened inwards, and with some deft manoeuvring, we discovered that we could lock the outer door from the inside.

We immediately put this plan into action, and soon Pondy, Sridhar and I were comfortably settled in Pondy's room, which was the first one on the left side of the lobby upon entering the hostel. We spent the afternoon anxiously conversing in hushed whispers to avoid arousing suspicion from any passing seniors, listening for footsteps echoing through the corridors. Our plan would have succeeded, but for Pondy's unfortunate habit of opening his mouth—he had a regular foot-in-the-mouth disease.

About an hour after our clever manoeuvre, we heard more footsteps outside and fell silent, waiting for the seniors to move on. Through the crack between the doors, we caught sight of two seniors strolling, one of them saying to the other, 'I could swear I heard someone talking just now.'

'Must have been a dream, you idiot!' the other replied.

As soon as they walked away, Pondy cheerfully remarked in his characteristic loud voice, 'The idiots are gone!'

No sooner had he uttered those words than we heard the unmistakable sound of running feet; a finger gleefully poked through the crack in the door, and a triumphant voice declared, 'Caught you this time! I was wondering about those noises. Now open the door, quickly! *Jaldi, jaldi! Pronto, Pronto!*'

Shortly after, we found ourselves standing in the lobby outside our room, feeling dejected and unsure of what awaited us. Two seniors loomed before us—one tall, thin and fair, sporting a straggly moustache, and the other of medium height, extremely dark, with a thick moustache. Both were dressed in the unofficial IT attire—funky-coloured T-shirts, faded torn jeans and Hawaii slippers. As I focused on the floor in front of me, I noticed that one of the seniors was wearing slippers held together with a safety pin. *What peculiar characters*, I thought, as they did not appear impoverished. *Eclectic fashion sense, perhaps.*

One of the seniors remarked, 'Looks like all are

makkus, *yaar.*' The other must have nodded in agreement. My gaze remained glued to the floor, preventing me from understanding their reaction to this Sherlockian deduction.

Yaar—Handy Guide to IT Lingo

'Okay, guys, start on your intros,' the first senior said.

When I began my introduction, the shorter senior found my initial 'N' particularly amusing. He asked me what 'N' stood for, to which I explained that it represented my father's name. But he persisted, adding an exaggerated South Indian lilt to the pronunciation of the letter.

Then it dawned on me that in Tamil, 'N' signifies 'belonging to me.'

He appeared in great humour, finding the weak joke tickling his poorly located funny bone. He asked me if I knew what makku meant.

I said, 'In Tamil, it means an idiot.'

He replied, 'Also, it stands for Madras, Andhra, Kerala, Karnataka union, he he he.'

When he had sufficiently recovered from the paroxysm of laughter his own jokes had reduced him to, he continued, 'Are you a Brahmin?'

'Yes, sir,' I replied.

'Iyer or Iyengar?' he queried, referring to the two predominant types of Tamil Brahmins. Incidentally, Iyer Brahmins believe in the supreme power of Lord Shiva while the Iyengars believe in the supreme power of Lord Vishnu.

'Iyer, sir,' I replied.

With exaggerated glee and emphasizing the lilt he asked, 'So, you only eye her, eh? Don't go around eyeing her, eh? Whom do you go about eyeing, eh? Tell the truth, or I'll start ragging you properly.'

The 'eye-her and 'eyeing-her' were drawn out to sound like Iyer and Iyengar (fun with a pun), respectively, leaving no doubt that he was attempting his silly puns on me.

'Nobody, sir,' I replied.

'No girlfriends, eh? You are from which city? Calcutta, you said, right?'

'Yes, sir,' I answered.

'Bong females are said to be fast and sexy. How come you have no girlfriends?'

'I was too busy for girls, sir. I had to focus on getting into engineering, after all.'

'What! Too busy for girls? So now that you are in engineering, you will go after girls, eh?'

'I don't know, sir. It depends on the courses here. But first, I intend to do well in my studies.'

'Fresh guy, eh! Remarkable. Someone who came to an engineering college to study, especially BIT—I have not encountered many like you!'

He turned to his friend and said, 'This guy is boring, seems naïve, and is only interested in studying. What should we do?'

The other senior replied, 'Don't worry; he'll be fine in a couple of weeks. But this fatty here is interesting. He claims to have something that you and I don't.'

'What is it?' the first senior inquired.

'A steady girlfriend,' came the response.

'Damn, that's great! Hey, Fatty! What is her name? And sorry, what was your name? I did not catch your intro because I was busy with this idiot,' he said, pointing at me.

Pondy, his eyes still cast downward, replied, 'Arundhati.'

'Arundhati is your name? You'll get in trouble here with a name like that, he he he.'

'No, sir. Sorry, my name is Padmanabhan Srivatsan. My girlfriend's name is Arundhati, sir.'

'Good, but let me give you some advice—don't tell the seniors about it. Some of them can get a little dirty. Just say what this guy said,' he pointed at me, 'though I don't believe a word he says with that innocent face. Bong females are HOT HOT HOT, man. You can't help but have a few girlfriends in Calcutta.'

I pondered his statement, the emphasis on 'hot' and 'Bong,' wondering where all these females had vanished during my years in Calcutta. The only 'hot' things I could recall were the scorching months of April and May before the monsoon arrived, and the flavourful *aloo dum* served by the local *phuchkawala*. For the uninitiated, phuchkawalas are roadside vendors selling spicy hot, deep-fried dumplings filled with all sorts of snacks—a Calcutta special.

Briefly lifting my gaze, I noticed Sridhar walking out of the hostel with the tall, thin senior, while the other one continued to look at Pondy with admiration.

'I think you and I need to have a chat, Fatty. I need to learn how to impress girls, yaar. I am absolutely hopeless at it. I haven't even managed to impress a GKW yet.'

Saying this, he draped his arm around Pondy's shoulder and led him to the mess, leaving me to contemplate the meaning of 'GKW'. Based on my experience, I was sure it was just another absurd acronym.

GKW—Handy Guide to IT Lingo

I looked around and found myself alone in the lobby. With a sigh of relief, I hurried back to my room; considering the likelihood of lightning striking the same place twice, I decided against locking the door from the outside. I collapsed on my bed and fell asleep.

> *To the welcoming arms of Morpheus, I go*
> *To escape the interminable ragging so,*
> *For the seniors always ask us to bow*
> *Before their wishes, treating us so low.*

7

Human Disgust

Not for long, though. My sleep was abruptly interrupted by a violent knocking on my door. Groggily, I asked, 'Who's there?'

'*Tera baap* (Your father),' came the sharp reply.

Half-asleep, I stumbled sluggishly to the door and opened it. Before me stood two seniors in their usual attire of jeans, T-shirts and dirty Hawaii slippers; behind them stood a stocky fresher. He had a dark, rough face that seemed made to smile easily, but presently wore a wretched expression, evidently due to the presence of two seniors. Each of them clutched one of his arms like handcuffs, reminiscent of a first-time convict being escorted by two large Jatt constables. The two seniors were tall, thin, clean-shaven, and had short-cropped hair. They looked as if they had just returned from a visit home, where a strict mother had ensured they re-appeared at the institute as cultured human beings.

One of the seniors commanded, 'Come with us. We are from the third-year Electrical Department. I am Nalin, and this is Rathi. How come you are in your room, sleeping? No classes, eh? Bunking classes on the first day?'

I mumbled something about there being no classes

on the first day, though I doubted they even heard me.

We embarked on a long walk from our hostel to another called Vivekananda, located at the far end of the campus. It appeared significantly larger than ours, freshly painted, with thick grass growing in the central area and a volleyball court in one corner. Vivekananda was one of the newer hostels in the institute, having been completed just a couple of years before we joined. Separated from the other hostels by approximately 200 metres, it overlooked the fenced boundary of the university.

As we silently followed the two seniors, we saw several women busily cutting grass near the fence. Upon reaching Vivekananda, we were ushered into a room roughly the same size as mine. However, that is where the similarities ended. The walls were plastered with numerous posters of someone named Samantha Fox in various stages of undress, with one corner dedicated to posters of curvaceous Indian women whose bare bosoms seemed to gleam more proudly than their cheesy grins and provocative poses.

Never in my life had I seen anything like this, and it was quite a shock. Interestingly enough, once the initial shock wore off, I found myself stealing glances at the posters a few times and even contemplating whether my bare walls could use similar decoration. Bare ladies for equally bare walls!

The Indian posters, with the exposed bosoms, were a bit too much for my taste, but Samantha Fox actually looked stunning. Although she appeared topless in the poster, her strategically placed white-gloved hands crossed over what seemed like an ample bosom, leaving room for serious imagination befitting a boy starting university.

My attention was diverted when I noticed a large corpse lying on a dirty, unmade bed. Suddenly, it came alive when Nalin loudly addressed, 'Nutty, bloody hell, wake up!'

The bed cover fell off his torso and legs as Nutty slowly returned to the land of the living. He looked around for his spectacles, which had thick black borders, and put them on. Nutty, wearing only shorts, had a chest covered in thick black hair. His swarthy countenance gave him an almost jovial appearance. His rotund stomach threatened to burst free, aided by the top button of his shorts, which was undone.

'Got only two today, eh?' Nutty asked the guys who had brought us in, still half-reclining on his bed.

Nalin replied, 'I wonder where the others have gone. I thought I saw several buses arriving with freshers today. Perhaps the director has decided to accommodate them in Morvi and DG as well.'

At that time, none of this made sense to me, but everything became clear in the days to follow as we started understanding the lingo of the institute. DG (Dhanrajgiri) and Morvi were hostels where freshers were not usually accommodated. Freshers, up until our batch, had been housed in three other hostels—Rajputana, Limbdy and De. Apparently, the director (referred to as 'diro' by Nalin and the others) had made some changes.

Diro—Handy Guide to IT Lingo

Nutty, with some difficulty, roused himself from his bed and sat up straight, making room for Nalin to sit next to him, while Rathi stood by the door as if guarding us from escaping.

Nutty asked me, 'Where are you from?'

'Calcutta, sirs,' I replied.

'And your name?'

'N. Raja Venkateswar, sir.'

'Makku, eh? From Calcutta, no less. Interesting. What is your frequency, bugger?'

This unexpected physics question amidst the light-hearted nature of the interrogation threw me into a quandary. Based on my previous experiences with ragging, I did not expect the seniors to ask anything beyond the usual introductions. Such a question, posed so early, left me puzzled.

Though I had learnt about the frequency of oscillating objects in my physics classes during secondary and higher secondary education, I could not comprehend the relevance of that concept in this context. Suddenly, it dawned on me that the senior might be asking about the speed of my speech, considering my tendency to talk faster than normal. I had been nicknamed Metro by the less friendly individuals at school, and I figured the senior wanted to know if I had ever measured the speed of my speech.

Thus, I sincerely replied, 'To the best of my approximation, sirs, it is about four words per second.'

My honest declaration was met with astonished looks from everyone present. Even my fellow fresher glanced up momentarily, wearing a bewildered expression, the aura of perplexity exacerbated by his rotund facial structure.

The bulky senior, who had risen by about seven inches upon hearing my answer, exclaimed, 'You masturbate four times every second! Are you a semen-making machine or what?'

Lacking a mirror, I could not determine the exact shade of red that flushed my face upon hearing this comment, but I am confident it would have been the deepest hue of red, bordering on black.

I remained silent, unable to utter a word, when Rathi, who had been leaning against the open door, spoke up. 'What did you mean by "four per second"?'

'I meant the number of words spoken per second, sirs,' I clarified.

A loud guffaw erupted from all the seniors present. Even my fellow fresher, I could swear, managed a quiet grin.

The bulky senior declared me 'crazy' and returned to his reclined position, shifting his attention to the other fresher. This fresher had walked the entire way from my previous to the present hostel—about a kilometre—without once, except for the aforementioned occasion, raising his head from his chest, which seemed to have been magically affixed. The bulky senior demanded the standard introduction.

'Sir, my name is Ranjit Dasgupta, and I am from New Delhi,' he began.

And that was my introduction to the person who would become one of my closest friends and go on to play a key role in my life over the next few years.

During the interrogation, I learnt that Rajnit had attended a school called Bal Bharati in Delhi, had spent most of his life in Armed Forces housing estates, and—crucially—did not have a girlfriend. His 'hawa' was a few digits more than mine.

Nutty handed me a dog-eared copy of a pornographic magazine. The cover depicted two generously endowed blonde women hugging each other and looking at the viewer with seductive eyes. Despite the circumstances, I could not help but feel a certain pleasure just from looking at the picture. It was yet another first for me, something I had never witnessed before.

The magazine was filled with letters from unknown individuals graphically describing their favourite sexual positions or fantasies to someone they all addressed as Aunt Nancy. I was instructed to open a specific page and asked to read aloud from it. It happened to be a particularly explicit letter from a woman describing her sexual encounters with animals. With a deepening sense of unease, I read about half a page, wondering why someone as amply endowed as she would engage in such acts. Just as I was about to continue, Nutty commanded me to stop. He swiftly turned to Ranjit and subjected him to cutting questions about the passage I had just read aloud—a sort of comprehension examination.

'The length of the dong—what was it?' he asked, followed by two more rapid questions. 'What was her initial feeling when she held the dog's dong?' and 'What kind of bra was she wearing?'

Evidently, Ranjit had not followed what I had been reading aloud, as he could not adequately answer any of the questions asked of him.

'Abe, don't you understand English, or are you a faggot?' demanded the senior. 'Think and answer, or I'll give you a good GPL.'

GPL? What on earth is that? I wondered.

'*Saale chaatu, bahut chaat raha hai* (The bugger's boring us),' the senior standing at the door commented.

GPL and Chaatu—Handy Guide to IT Lingo

Ranjit stood there with his head stooped, a position I figured he should copyright, quietly and seemingly oblivious to the questions from the seniors. Exasperated, Nutty told him to become a murga. It was a strenuous effort for the portly Ranjit, and he soon gasped for breath.

'Okay, Makku,' Nutty continued, turning to me, 'Did you understand the appropriate reading material for growing boys?'

'Yes, sir,' I replied.

'Okay, read this one now,' he demanded, handing over a thick magazine titled *Human Digest*. The bold black letters on the cover framed a young Indian woman staring directly at the camera. She was dressed in only a skimpy pair of black pants and a low-cut blouse that revealed ample cleavage. The magazine seemed new, its vibrant cover contrasting with the densely written text on the back. Rathi then seemed to take over the questioning. 'What do you think of this magazine?' He slid past me, turned a hard wooden chair around to face me and sat down. 'Have you ever read one of these before?'

'No, sir,' I replied.

'What do you like reading, then?'

'The last couple of years, I've been focused on my entrance exams, sir, and haven't read much for pleasure; usually it's been just newspapers and the occasional Agatha Christie or Doyle.'

'So, you've never read a porno in your life?'

'No, sir.'

'So, what do you do when you want to masturbate? Or are you a virgin there too?' The last statement was delivered with a sly look on his face, triggering peals of laughter from Nutty and Nalin.

Meanwhile, Nutty asked Ranjit to stand up and asked, 'So, what about you, Fatty? Do you masturbate, or don't you?'

Ranjit remained quiet and continued looking at his boots. That's when I noticed the size of his boots—they were huge. Ranjit wasn't a tall man, probably standing an inch or two taller than my five-foot-seven frame, but his feet were enormous—size twelve at least. *Strange indeed.*

Nalin, who had been silent until now, remarked, 'We have such boring guys here. I wonder what happened to the JEE. Why are they sending us the studious types?'

Nutty chimed in, 'Competition, man, competition.' Then he turned to me and said, 'Okay, read the first couple of pages and give me a summary of the story.'

I hesitantly opened the book and started perusing the initial pages. They contained a letter from Sue, a woman from Minnesota who claimed to be a blonde, blue-eyed, reasonably pretty woman with larger-than-usual breasts. Her letter described her fetish for having sex with strangers in hotel rooms—never at home, always in hotels. The explicit descriptions included her encounters with men, focusing on one particular part of their anatomy.

A few minutes later, Nutty demanded, 'So, did you like what you read?'

I wished I could have read it alone in my room, without the seniors and my batchmate present. However, I did not want to express that in front of them. I simply replied, 'It's okay, sir.'

'Okay, okay, *Goli kha ke aaya kya?* (Did you take a

pill before coming here?)' Nutty exclaimed, sitting up in justified anger, as if his sensibilities were affronted by my ambivalent approach.

Goli? I wondered. What spherical object is he referring to?

Goli—Handy Guide to IT Lingo

'What a nut,' he continued, turning to Nalin. 'He says *Human Digest* is okay!' he said, drawing out the 'okay'. 'Just okay,' he repeated, leaving nobody in any doubt what he thought of my opinion.

I stood silently, anticipating the storm of words that usually followed such moments of quiet contemplation. To my surprise, Nutty spoke calmly and evenly, 'Alright, perhaps you'd prefer to read it privately. Take it with you and read it. You can bring it back when you've had enough. Maybe if I see you somewhere, I'll ask for your opinion.'

This man must have had extrasensory perception.

I silently accepted the magazine, feigning reluctance, and stood waiting for the next set of instructions.

Exhausted from his attempts to instil some proper reading sense in us freshers, the overweight gargoyle (Nutty, not to be confused with Ranjit) leaned back on his bed and requested that I leave and shut the door behind me.

Leaving the hostel, I cautiously made my way towards the comfort of my room, intending to peruse the magazine Nutty had generously lent me, which I had hidden beneath my shirt. It was already dark, and as I approached the entrance of my hostel, I encountered two seniors who made a lasting impression. First, they were bald, unlike the rest of the seniors who typically had long, unkempt hair; second, they were dressed immaculately in clean white kurta-pyjamas!

The taller of the two introduced himself. 'Hi, I'm Prasenjit, a third-year electrical engineering student, and this is Rajesh. We're from the same hostel where you were just ragged. Did they physically harm you or force you to engage in any dangerous activities?'

I pondered the question for a moment. Aside from the discomfort I felt while reading the explicit passage about anal sex written by a woman described as 23, slim, with short blonde hair and large breasts, there was no physical danger involved. I dismissed the possibility of Ranjit suffering any harm from the intense exertion of being made to perform like a murga for a while.

So, I answered in the negative.

The shorter senior then added, 'If you have any problems, please inform us. Our rooms are 165 and 156 in Viveka Hostel. We're part of the anti-ragging team and want to ensure that nothing bad happens.'

With that, the peculiar duo trotted off, likely in search of other freshers to engage with, leaving me perplexed by the ways and means of the seniors. However, they did leave me with some quality reading material in the cool and comfortable confines of my ten-by-ten foot room.

8

The Batch: Making of the Brew

The next day was Tuesday, marking the beginning of our classes. The weather was scorching and the humidity made it feel like a sauna even at seven in the morning. The temperature had already surpassed 30°C, and I shuddered at the thought of wearing the fresher uniform.

While brushing my teeth at the washbasin in the lobby corner, I bumped into Ranjit. He had walked out of Room 155, looking drowsy and anxious, but his face lit up when he saw me instead of a nosy senior.

'Morning,' he greeted with a shy grin.

With my mouth full of toothpaste and the brush, all I could do was nod in return.

A few minutes later, as I wiped my face with a towel, I stepped aside to let Ranjit take his place at the basin. 'Your name is Ranjit, right?' I asked.

He nodded, filling his mug with water.

Continuing the conversation, I said, 'I'm Raja. Shall we go down for breakfast together? I am in Room 150. Let me know when you're ready.'

It was funny how living in a hostel could bring about such a dramatic change in a person's behaviour. This was the first time I had proactively introduced myself to someone!

Half an hour later, when we entered the mess, we were amazed by the bustling activity. The hall was filled with freshers dressed in their serious uniforms, busily eating bread and eggs while engaging in friendly conversations, creating a pleasant hum of chatter. The enclosed space only made the atmosphere hotter, and I could feel sweat trickling from my hair on to my collar.

As we walked in, a couple of guys sitting on the benches near the entrance turned around curiously; one of them asked, 'Which branch?'

'Chemical,' I replied. 'What about you?'

'Meta.'

Ranjit and I took seats next to the guy who had spoken to us.

'I met a few guys from Meta on Sunday. It seems like this hostel is mainly for the Meta students,' I said.

'Not really. There are plenty of Chem guys too. I met quite a few this morning,' he replied.

'By the way, I'm Raja, and this is Ranjit. We're both on the first floor of the hostel,' I said, introducing us.

'Oh, that explains why you guys missed the night ragging. I don't think the seniors realized freshers are also on the first floor. The ground floor is packed with freshers. By the way, my name is Bhuvan, and I'm from Bangalore,' he said.

'Good to meet you. I'm from Calcutta,' I replied.

'Delhi,' chimed in the usually taciturn Ranjit.

Just then, the mess Maharaj came out, asking us to sign our names in a register. 'Co-operative mess, saab,' he said in Hindi. 'The warden runs it.'

Ranjit and I thanked him, signed the register, and officially became members of the co-operative mess, which promised quality food at reasonable prices. As we ate, Bhuvan and I continued chatting, and I learnt that he came from a well-known convent school in Bangalore, and his father held a senior position in one of India's largest corporate houses. That's what made the institute remarkable—we had students from every stratum of society and every corner of the country. This created a diverse group where everyone could learn from and appreciate each other's unique cultures, philosophies and opinions.

While enjoying our aloo parathas—which quickly became my preferred breakfast—I met several other freshers, including some from the Chemical branch. Three of them—Surendra, Sushil and Vikram—sat next to Ranjit and began speculating on what our first day of classes would entail and debating whether we would make it to the Chemical Engineering department, considering the prowling seniors.

I had no clue where the department was located, but a few of my classmates, whose parents accompanied them, had taken the initiative to scout the area. I joined their group, and about a dozen of us who had met at the mess table eagerly set off towards the department, keeping a watchful eye for any lurking seniors. It was astonishing how quickly we had begun to get acquainted.

The Chemical Engineering department was approximately one and a half kilometres from the hostel gate. We crossed a large field flanked by football goalposts on two sides, the grounds now overgrown with tall grasses and weeds. Beyond the field, we passed a basketball court and soon spotted the Mechanical Engineering department—a striking brick-red building with a Gothic spire. Adjacent to it, separated by a wide road, stood the Chemical Engineering department; even to a casual observer, the building appeared grand, with its long façade of red bricks and a grand arched entrance that led to a spacious veranda accessible via eight polished stairs.

Later, I would learn that the department boasted one of the longest continuous lobbies in any educational institution, stretching an impressive 700 metres. As we entered the building through a side door closest to the road, we marvelled at the sheer length of the corridor. Soon, we realized that the room we were searching for was at the far end. We trooped along, attempting to remain silent and soaking in the awe-inspiring grandeur that surrounded us. The towering ceilings, more than two storeys high, were painted white and accented by the brick-red walls, creating a striking effect. The large open spaces around the institute, the massive edifices, the vast lobby, and the sense of quiet, repressed energy created an atmosphere that made us reflect on our own insignificance. Amid both synthetic and natural beauty, we walked silently, each lost in our deepest thoughts.

Finally, we arrived at the designated room, where a dozen or so freshers were already seated on the rough wooden benches. Ranjit and I found an unoccupied bench towards the back of the classroom, thus beginning our four-year association with the backbenches. The classes would change, the years pass and the subjects and teachers vary, but our spot in the back row remained constant, except on the rare occasions when we were asked by the professors to sit in the front row to prevent any mischief.

A few minutes later, a short and stout young man entered the room. His fair complexion was complemented by his white shirt, which was not tucked into his grey trousers, and leather slippers. Despite his small stature, standing at around five foot three, he exuded an air of confidence and power. Ranjit and I exchanged amazed glances—a fresher with an untucked shirt and leather slippers! What happened to all the ragging?

Sensing our curiosity, the person winked, gave us a broad smile, and said, 'I'm Nimesh Menon, but most guys call me Chaaku.'

Ranjit and I introduced ourselves, marking the start of a remarkably close friendship between three vastly different individuals.

Precisely at 9 a.m., a severe-looking individual with straggly white hair, which was cleverly combed to cover his receding hairline, entered the room. Even in the sweltering heat of July in North India, where temperatures frequently surpassed 40°C, he had chosen to wear a brown tweed coat with elbow patches over a pristine white shirt and dark grey trousers. His tall, lean frame and gaunt face only made him appear even taller. Reaching the podium, he theatrically cleared his throat, and the whispers in the classroom subsided.

Once he was confident that he had our complete and undivided attention, he began, 'Friends, my name is Professor Dr Y.D. Tripathi, Head of the Department of

Chemical Engineering. Welcome, everyone. I hope the next four years will be a time of great learning, forming new friendships and enjoying every opportunity this great institute has to offer.

'The first year is common, so you might not frequent this department often. However, from your second year onwards, you will come here daily, as all your classes will be held in this building. The curriculum is designed to give you a broad understanding of every facet of engineering in the first year. You will attend classes in the Electrical, Electronic, Civil and Mechanical Engineering departments, along with other first-year students. Once you successfully clear the second-semester examinations, you will officially enter this department.

'Now, I will not bore you with a long speech, but please be assured that we are here to assist you. You can find me on the first floor of this building, right next to the stairs. Your first point of contact, who will now guide you further, is Dr S.N. Bandopadhyay. Ah, here he comes.'

We turned to see a smart, young individual entering the room. Dressed in a white shirt, black trousers and shiny black boots, he could have easily been mistaken for one of us freshers.

Over the next couple of hours, Dr Bandyopadhyay expertly guided us through the courses and subjects for the eight semesters, emphasizing key areas to focus on and assisting with administrative tasks. It was an informative session, and in the end, each of us received a welcome kit containing practical information—directions to the campus bank (next to our department), lecture schedules and a list of professors for each subject along with their office locations.

The two professors then stood by the door, shaking hands with each student as we walked out of the classroom. All of us felt blessed and like true adults. No teacher had ever shaken my hand in school!

While I was shaking hands with the two professors, I noticed three young ladies jogging towards us. The one leading the way was rather short and reasonably pretty, with her long hair tied in a severe ponytail. She wore a neatly tucked white shirt and black flared trousers. Out of breath, she, followed by two others who were tall and thin reached us just as I stepped aside.

'Hello, sirs. My name is Meenakshi Murty. Sorry, I am late for this session—I got held up by some seniors who would not let me leave on time,' she gasped. 'I have enrolled in Chemical Engineering, sirs.'

'That's alright,' Dr S.N. Bandyopadhyay replied. 'Your classmates can give you a brief; here's your welcome pack.' He handed her the thick folder we had all received and passed one each to the two other girls. He asked us to ensure the three of them got up to speed and left with a friendly wave.

In the lobby, we ran into two more freshers—Vinay, a lanky guy, and Ram, equally tall but with an athletic build. They were examining the timetable in their folders, and had already met Chaaku earlier.

Ram started the conversation, 'Well, Chaaku, we don't have classes until 2 p.m. today. Our first class is in the Mechanical Engineering department. Should we go to the canteen?'

We exchanged introductions, shook hands and strolled towards the cafeteria. A short walk later, we reached the IT Cafeteria between the Chemical and Mechanical Engineering departments. We enjoyed samosas and tea, getting to know each other better.

For the first time, I was sitting next to a young woman without feeling shy or embarrassed. We engaged in idle, nonsensical chatter—a refreshing change from my previous experiences in Calcutta, where my all-boys school and strict upbringing had often left me tongue-tied around girls my age. It was an idyllic time, and we all felt accomplished and excited. Just being a part of the institute, with its rich history, prestige and beauty, was a fantastic sensation. The realization that I was now part of a hallowed tradition sent shivers down my spine.

As we conversed, we discovered that while half of our department's 30 students had been allotted residence in the Rajputana hostel (including me), the remaining were divided between the two adjacent hostels, Morvi and Dhanrajgiri. Also, several students had yet to arrive and were expected to reach the institute later that week. I was particularly inquisitive about Chaaku's attire and asked why he was not wearing the prescribed dress.

Chaaku explained, 'My elder brother is a third-year Chemical Engineering student here. I'm staying with him until I move into my room, which should happen today or tomorrow.'

After further inquiry, I discovered that Chaaku was my next-door neighbour in Room 151.

The first day of classes passed uneventfully. I spent much of it chatting with my new classmates, enjoying the peaceful atmosphere that came with the comfortable knowledge that we were all studying at a hallowed institution.

Our daily morning journey to the classroom, however, filled us with apprehension, as the grassy playground we crossed, usually in a large group, was a favourite hunting ground for seniors. We went in groups because we had some understanding of quantum mechanics. According to Heisenberg's uncertainty principle and Pauli's exclusion principle, a certain predetermined percentage of freshers would inevitably be accosted by seniors, though the exact individuals remained unpredictable.

These scientific principles, however, proved futile on a fine morning when six seniors targeted our entire class. All 29 of us boys were ragged for seven hours in their hostel. First, we were ordered to march past the seniors, pretending to be Hitler and his Nazi cohorts, raising our hands in a Nazi salute and shouting, 'Hail, Electro!'

They happened to be the second-year Electrical batch in Morvi Hostel, where five of my Chemical classmates were also staying.

If Agatha Christie were alive and spent a week at an IT, she would likely have written something like this:

Ten little ITians
Decided to go on a jaunt;
One had a sick aunt,
Calling on a telephone line,
And then there were nine.

Nine little ITians
Decided to catch a movie;

One caught an AIDS smoochie,
Being unable to refuse the bait,
And then there were eight.

Eight little ITians
Decided to go to class;
One had to attend mass,
For a stairway to heaven,
And then there were seven.

Seven little ITians
Decided to go to a temple;
One flicked a lab sample,
So got into a major fix,
And then there were six.

Six little ITians
Decided to go for an early dinner;
One deemed himself a sinner,
After having stolen a dime,
And then there were five.

Five little ITians
Decided to go riding;
One fell off his pommel horse laughing,
After having ridden for an hour,
And then there were four.

Four little ITians
Decided to learn swimming;
One fell ill after bathing,
After two hours, we agree,
And then there were three.

Three little ITians
Decided to row at the lake;
One tried to have the cake,
After having eaten it too,
And then there were two.

Two little ITians
Decided to meet the king,
To try to make him sing;
One had to stay back alone,
And there was one.

One little ITian
Decided to reach for the moon;
One fell into a deep swoon,
On hearing a remarkable tune,
And then there were none.

Our classes were typically held in large classrooms, akin to basketball courts, shared with first-year students from the Ceramics and Electronics branches. The lecturers, as a whole, seemed remarkably indifferent to the fact that 99 per cent of the students in attendance did not understand a word of what was being said. The lone per cent who did grasp something was invariably someone repeating the year. These classes, however, became excellent opportunities to meet and get to know freshers from other branches. Within a few days, we had formed a cohesive group of like-minded individuals from diverse backgrounds.

During this time, I managed to overcome much of my stammering and began speaking more fluently, stringing together long sentences with only the occasional stutter. Unfortunately, while my spoken words were improving, my comprehension during lectures remained frustratingly low. Most subjects did not make much sense to me, but the mathematics lectures stood out for the intensity of helplessness they evoked. While I could sometimes understand 20–30 per cent of the content in most subjects, I could make sense of almost nothing in mathematics. This surprised both Ranjit and me, as we sat together in the last row. We had been considered good at the subject in school, so our lack of comprehension was unexpected. The professors' monotonous delivery, devoid of passion and interest, did not help either. We wondered why they could not find a better professor, especially considering the abundance of mathematics professors. *Don't they multiply?* Puns not intended.

The hours after classes were equally tense as we often encountered seniors and endured ragging sessions. Fortunately, nothing serious ever happened; no anger or violence was involved, and some of these encounters even provided moments of humour. A few seniors had a good sense of humour, and I soon became less nervous in their presence than when I had first joined the institute.

The long walks to and from classes, though fraught with apprehension, also offered opportunities to bond with my group of friends. In addition to Vinay, Ram, Ranjit and Chaaku, we welcomed Amit Sharma, a short, fair and handsome Gurkha, and Rajinder Singh Popli, our institute's equivalent of Big Moose, into our group.

We formed a close association despite our differences in appearance, backgrounds, interests and opinions. The test of a first-rate intelligence is the ability to hold two opposing ideas in mind at the same time and still retain the ability to function. One should, for example, be able to see that things are hopeless yet be determined to make them otherwise. Our eclectic group excelled in this regard. We remained open to suggestions, thoughts and diverse viewpoints, and appreciated the exchange of ideas and opinions. Remarkably, considering the differences within our group and the broader batch, we managed to navigate four wonderful years without any major conflicts.

9

Far from the Maddening Seniors

The first week was eventful, and during those early days, Ranjit and I became inseparable—due to our remarkably similar tastes in movies—and we quickly devised ways and means to evade the relentless mental torment inflicted by our seniors, who would be waiting for us outside our classrooms.

While we never faced any physical harm, there was a constant desire to hit the seniors on the head to make them stop asking the same stupid, inane, burlesque and needless questions.

Twinkle, twinkle, old senior,
How I wish where you should be,
Up above the world so high,
Looking down at us with an envious sigh.

The first Friday of our first week in Varanasi dawned clear and sunny, and during our walk to the classroom, we decided to explore the areas outside the university gates over the weekend—if the weather held up. Ranjit, who had lived in Varanasi for a couple of years during his schooldays, knew a couple of spots, and we decided to spend the weekend roaming the areas of the old city he could recall.

Saturday morning was bright and sunny, promising a hot and humid day. We got up nice and early, and after a hurried coffee, we left well before 7 a.m., through the back gate of our hostel with extreme caution. Then we swiftly walked towards one of the side gates of the university, located beside a fourth-year hostel right behind ours. We knew that the fourth-year students famously followed the sleeping habits of well-behaved owls, so we did not expect any final-year student to accost us at such an early hour. With the coast clear, we took the back roads to Lanka and then to the Ghats at Godowlia, hailing a rickshaw along the way.

The Ghats, a defining feature of Varanasi, are broad stone steps and platforms used as bathing places along the Ganges. The Dashashwamedh Ghat at Godowlia is possibly the largest and often doubles as an open-air auditorium during music concerts, easily accommodating a couple of thousand people. The music festivals, typically held in February and March, are remarkable. During these, a large wooden stage is constructed on a raft beside the gently lapping waters of the Ganges, and the entire area is illuminated by brightly burning torches—a magnificent sight to behold.

During my four-year stay in Varanasi, I was fortunate to witness four of these festivals, called Ganga Mahotsav, where some of India's most celebrated musicians, including the inimitable Hariprasad Chaurasia, performed. Remarkably, the entry was free, and eminent artists considered it a great honour to perform before a packed, knowledgeable and appreciative crowd.

These concerts often extended into the wee hours of the morning, and there was hardly any standing space for the spectators. A few friends and I would generally hire a boat and watch the spectacle from the water, where the gentle rocking of the Ganges and the divine strains of Indian classical music combined to create a transcendental experience. It felt as though the waves themselves were in harmony with the melodies, carrying us into a state of serenity that lingered long after the final notes had faded into the night.

Upon reaching Godowlia—later nicknamed 'Gods' by us—we strolled into the Gali, a narrow lane leading to the Kashi Vishwanath Temple, dedicated to Lord Shiva. While the common noun 'gali' refers to any narrow lane, in this context, it specifically denotes the lane—Vishwanath Gali—leading to the sacred temple. This iconic lane lies to the left of a broad road that leads to the Dashashwamedh Ghat.

Godowlia, along with the surrounding localities of Luxa and Chowk, houses Varanasi's largest shopping area; the narrow streets are packed with shops in every possible nook and cranny. A few makeshift stalls even sprawled defiantly in the middle of the road. Our autorickshaw had to stop at a crowded junction, forcing us to walk the last couple of hundred yards, as all vehicles except bicycles were banned. The place was teeming with activity—women radiant in their bright sarees and men dignified in white kurtas, paired with pyjamas or dhotis.

At one corner, a series of tiny shops—no more than

holes in the crumbling walls—sold something called Mishrambu, which I later learnt was a milk-based drink that sometimes included a local variant of alcohol or other stimulant. To my curious eyes, seeing the city for the first time, it resembled a narrower, more crowded and rustic version of Calcutta's Burrabazar. Adding to the chaos were cows, buffaloes and other bovine creatures meandering with their stately indifference in the middle of the road or standing still with quixotic calm, undeterred by the traffic congestion they caused, aided in no small part by traffic constables intent on making a quick buck.

Ranjit led the way, using his considerable bulk to carve a path through the sea of humanity, while I followed closely behind, relying on my considerably thinner frame to slip through the gaps in the crowd. The din made any type of conversation completely impossible.

As we neared the Gali, the smells of the city shifted—a fresh breeze gently blew away the pungent mix of cow dung, urine, human sweat and jasmine flowers, lending much-needed succour to the olfactory nerves assaulted by the constant musky smell. Though I couldn't see it at the time, I realized the fresh scent could only be coming from the Ganga, a river I was quite familiar with, as it also flows through Calcutta.

Eventually, we reached the Gali, where Ranjit guided us to a small shop owned by a man named Ramesh. The shop, a literal hole in the wall, thrived on selling *suparis* in an array of colourful bottles. Well-regarded in the area, Ramesh was the chairperson of the local shop owners' association. This position gave him considerable influence and authority, and Ranjit mentioned that local politicians frequently sought his involvement, urging him to take on a more active role as a full-time activist for one of the leading political parties.

Ramesh sat on a comfortable-looking cushion, trying to entice a pretty young foreign lady into buying his suparis. He was endeavouring to give the lady a spoonful of his newly prepared mixture, declaring in his quaint English, 'Best supari madam! Try once, and you'll always want more! Try! It's top-notch!'

The lady tried to avoid the sales pitch by waving her arms with the universal gestures of tourists deflecting persistent vendors and street urchins commonly found on most Indian streets.

'No, no, thank you,' she said firmly.

Ramesh managed to thrust some supari into her palm and continued, 'Please try, Madam. It's good for health, digestion and diet control.'

The mention of 'diet control' seemed to catch the young woman's attention—not that she needed it, I figured, as an interested observer (No puns intended on the word 'figure'). She stopped resisting and sampled the supari Ramesh had so adroitly thrust into her palm. At first, she grimaced slightly as the taste hit her, but her expression brightened as the flavour settled. Licking her lips in obvious pleasure, she exclaimed, '*Sehr gut, sehr gut!* (Very good, very good!)'

Ramesh, not one to miss an opportunity, immediately switched to German. '*Sprechen sie Deutsch, Madam? Ich spreche Deutsch. Ich lerne Deutsch für zwei Jahre,* (Do you speak German, madam? I speak German. I've been learning German for two years)' he said, his German interspersed with English when he struggled for words, 'but no practice, so...' He paused, then switched back to German, saying, '*Ich vergesse alles.* (I've forgotten everything.)'

The woman nodded and replied in perfect English, 'Fine, how much is that?' pointing to a jar of supari. Finding the opening, Ramesh quickly completed the sale and stuffed the proffered money into his pocket. He then noticed Ranjit and me, as we had been patiently waiting for him to finish his transaction while contentedly observing the pretty woman in front of us.

'Ranjit *bhaiya*!' he exclaimed and immediately thrust some supari into our hands. '*Aap yahan kaise?* (How come you are here?)' he asked. Then he turned to the lady and exclaimed, 'My friend, my friend!'

Ranjit introduced me to Ramesh and explained that he had joined BIT for engineering, so they would now be meeting regularly. Ramesh excitedly turned to the pretty woman and said, 'My engineer friend, good boy!'

I shook hands with Ramesh and tried the supari he had given me. 'Fantastic,' I offered truthfully. It truly was splendid. I turned to the young woman, who was watching Ramesh's display of affection with amusement, and asked about her fluency in both English and German. The World Wars, combined with the minimal information Indian students received about the culture of different countries, had given me the impression that these two cultures mix about as well as vintage wine and club soda. I was naturally curious about her origins. The fact that she was easy on the eye probably had something to do with my curiosity, I suspect.

She explained that her father was English, from Doncaster, which explained her Yorkshire accent, and her mother was German. She had lived a large part of her adult life in Munich, where English was taught in most schools. She said she intended to spend a year in India and was fascinated by Varanasi. She had originally planned to stay for a week but now intended to spend an extended period here.

Andrea, the woman from the supari shop, and I met a few more times during her stay, and we had a wonderful time exploring Varanasi together. One memory from those outings remains vivid: her astonishment when I casually mentioned that I neither had a steady girlfriend nor any female friends, and was still a virgin at the ripe age of 18! Andrea replied that at least now I had a friend who happened to be a girl, if not a girlfriend.

Mustering courage, I asked her what it would take for her to become my girlfriend. She giggled and said, 'Well, you need to add a decade to your age,' and then laughed uproariously at her little joke.

I was genuinely pleased, not with the obvious rejection, but because I had managed to speak to a girl without stammering and even gathered courage to flirt with her, for the first time. *Way to go, man!*

After a pleasant conversation with Ramesh, we made our way to the temple and gained immediate access thanks to his presence. After a day of roaming the Ghats, we watched a movie at one of the numerous movie halls in Gods.

Speaking of movies, the posters in Varanasi struck

me as very odd. In Calcutta, we were used to high-quality prints, done lovingly in natural colours. But in Varanasi, the posters looked funny and garish, with a maroon background and an unnatural appearance. Ranjit attributed it to the quality of the walls, given their crumbling nature and washed-out, ancient look. A garish image would be more noticeable than a natural one. I reckoned it was more of a cost-saving measure since the posters seemed cheap and shabbily done.

Over the next few days, Ranjit and I escaped the monotonous college and hostel life to roam around the city, exploring its numerous nooks and crannies, savouring the street food and immersing ourselves in the city's vibrant atmosphere. We often returned to Dashashwamedh Ghat, descending the wide stone stairs to sit by the river. We enjoyed the cool breeze from the river and talked about ourselves, our likes, pet peeves, favourite actors and actresses, movies and girlfriends, although we did not have the guts to approach a girl. But one can always dream, can't they?

Sometimes, we took boat rides and soon befriended a young boatman named Ganesh, who claimed to own 11 boats, including two houseboats. Ganesh was an excellent raconteur with an extensive repertoire of anecdotes about eastern Uttar Pradesh in general and Varanasi in particular. He was a Hindu fundamentalist and a staunch believer that India should be declared a Hindu nation. There was no shortage of reasons Ganesh would list as he rowed along the Ganges, and many of them, Ranjit and I agreed, had their basis in logic.

Despite coming from a bucolic background with

limited exposure to current trends, Ganesh demonstrated keen intellect with some of his ideas. Though a thumbs-up (our lingo for illiterates), he possessed remarkable common sense and a sense of duty towards his customers and friends. His obligation and abiding interest in his friends came to the fore when approximately a dozen first-year students decided to celebrate the end of the first semester with an alcohol-laden party on the east bank of the Ganges a few months later.

Varanasi lies on the west bank of the Ganga, but the east bank, opposite Dashashwamedh Ghat, is a singularly isolated and deserted location frequented by jackals and other nocturnal creatures that prefer life away from teeming humanity. However, it boasts one of the finest river beaches in India, with soft yellow sand and clear, clean water—an eminently suitable place for swimming due to its weak current.

It was late in the evening when Ganesh, declining the proffered alcohol, set off for his residence on the Ghats, leaving around a dozen of us with about five litres of potent alcohol, a crate of beer and assorted foodstuffs thoughtfully prepared by our cook under the careful guidance of Amit, our self-appointed quartermaster, on the deserted east bank of the Ganga. Nicknamed 'Major' because of his education in various army schools across the country, his disciplined upbringing had instilled in him a deep sense of perfectionism, ensuring we had enough food and drinks for 12 students on a post-achievement high.

Soon, all of us were pleasantly drunk and feeling deliciously relaxed, except for Ranjit, who was a confirmed teetotaller and desired nothing stronger than Coke or

Thums Up, and Om Prakash Badri—a short, dark fellow whose claim to fame in the first semester was studying all night for the English examination. Badri preferred swimming in the cool waters of the Ganges and watching bubbles rise from the air released by farting underwater rather than consuming the alcohol or enjoying the excellent snacks.

I must have dozed off during the night in an alcoholic stupor, since it was around three o'clock in the morning when I awoke to a feeling of extreme discomfort. I found that a strong drizzle had started, leaving me wet and mildly cold. The chill soon turned into a severe cold as the rain intensified. We huddled under a banyan tree, which offered scant shelter on the open beach. Suddenly, our Major declared that he felt hungry, possibly due to a post-alcoholic hangover, and reached for the leftovers from dinner that he had so meticulously packed.

Water, especially rainwater, has a peculiar property of getting in precisely where it is completely unwanted. On opening the packets, he discovered that everything—chicken masala, paneer pasinda, chhole, tikkas and all the other items—had thoroughly soaked in rainwater. He threw everything away, uttering a string of oaths that could teach a few new and previously undiscovered blasphemies to even Sergeant Snorkel from *Beetle Bailey*.

As we debated whether we should walk across to Ramnagar and take the bridge across the Ganga, we saw Ganesh and a couple of his friends rowing a large houseboat with all their might towards us. Within moments, we were inside its warm confines, sneezing incessantly and battling runny noses.

Ganesh informed us that his grandfather had the ability to smell imminent rain and had instructed him to quickly row across the river to rescue us. It took at least an hour to row a houseboat across the wide expanse of water, and his grandfather's instinct had saved us from further discomfort. Ganesh had remarkable strength and could row the boat against the strong current without noticeable discomfort—something one would scarcely expect from somebody so thin and emaciated. He tried to teach me to row, but the current left me gasping for breath, making it impossible to lift my arms.

The times Ranjit and I managed to escape from the seniors, we watched a couple of films on average every week, usually Hindi potboilers. I have always been an avid movie watcher—I once spent a 75-day break after my secondary examinations watching 62 films. This desire to watch all types of movies often took me into peculiar nooks and crannies of Calcutta, to movie halls that most sensible Calcuttans would be unaware of. When I was only a 13-year-old lad still wearing shorts, I travelled 19 kilometres to Howrah to watch an old Hindi film. This interest had a positive outcome: whenever friends or relatives needed directions to an unknown place in Calcutta, they invariably turned to me.

> *When in doubt about Calcutta, they came to me,*
> *All flocked across to me in droves and droves,*
> *Wanting to reach the place they wanted to be,*
> *And took directions from me in scores and scores.*

I am certain that, in the coming days, the few movie theatres that Ranjit and I neglected during our four years in Varanasi could effectively advertise themselves with the tagline, 'The theatre not visited by Raja/Ranjit'. I imagine the paying public would flock to these establishments, curious to discover why we disregarded them.

The area around Godowlia boasted numerous movie theatres, such as the Saraswati and Mazda halls located near its western end. Further north stood smaller venues like Kanhaiya Chitra Mandir (KCM) and Radha Chitra Mandir, each capable of seating only a couple hundred misguided individuals. KCM was so tiny that its balcony comprised just four rows, accommodating a mere 40 people at most. Given our insatiable appetite for movies, it was no wonder Ranjit and I spent most of our time there.

In Sigra, a couple of miles west of Godowlia, we came across a roadside vendor selling splendid tikkis—spicy potato dumplings served with sweet and hot sauces—opposite a movie theatre called Saajan. On one occasion, we watched the same movie twice in a day as we found the lead female actor particularly appealing to our esoteric tastes, taking breaks in between for some heavenly tikkis.

There was hardly any opportunity to watch Hollywood movies in Varanasi, as no theatre showed any inclination to screen them—except for one. The owners of this particular establishment earned their livelihood by duping the gullible public, most of whom had little exposure to quality Hollywood movies. They enticed the movie-goers with cheap posters featuring scantily clad blondes, with a few large rifles thrown in for good measure, promising racy thrills but delivering low-grade, semi-pornographic C-grade thrillers instead.

In this theatre, we witnessed an interesting method

employed by the operators to compensate for the lack of 'interesting' footage in some films. A few minutes of XXX-rated footage—usually from Malayali films, featuring mammoth, dark-skinned Amazonian females in various stages of undress and well-built, moustachioed, dark and stocky men engaged in the throes of orgasmic pleasure— would be inserted into the main film around the time when the audience would start to grow restless. This occurrence was quite common, and during the first couple of times Ranjit managed to persuade me to watch one of these Hollywood films, I spent half the time anxiously waiting for a police raid on the theatre and the subsequent repercussions at home.

While exploring Varanasi within the first few weeks of hostel life, we discovered eating joints in locations most IT students who had spent four years in the city would never have heard of. At Hanuman Ghat, we stumbled upon a Tamilian eatery serving piping hot *idli* and *vada* with spicy and tasty *sambar*. We were so impressed with the food that, at the end of our eating binge, we realized we had consumed 46 idlis and vadas between us!

At Godowlia Chowk, we also found a Bengali eatery that served superb *kachodi-sabzi* and excellent *khoya sandesh*. The joint was open all night, a true 24×7 venture. In Sigra, we discovered a roadside vendor serving kulfis that melted in the mouth and another offering magnificent *chana bhatura*. We also found a vendor in Maidagin who made heavenly Indo-Chinese dishes. Our shared love for vegetarian food, despite Ranjit being a confirmed non-vegetarian, allowed us to sample the multi-cuisine delights of this captivating city.

The nightlife of this city could put any Indian metropolis to shame. Late in the evening, the narrow lanes of Varanasi would come alive with throngs of people. Men wearing loose, pastel-coloured kurta-pyjamas and women dressed modestly in salwar-kameez or vibrant sarees roamed the streets. Chewing betel leaf was a favourite habit of most Banarasis, and the tell-tale red stains of betel spit marked the streets—a less appealing aspect of the Banarasi way of life.

However, as Kishore—a Banarasi—argued with me, chewing *paan* was a better habit than smoking since it only harmed the user and not the general public. 'It is a paan-in-the-neck habit backed by extremely convoluted logic,' I informed him.

Despite its quirks, Varanasi captivated me. The ghats, the wide river, the activities and the colour all around us remained a divine sight and even now, I can visualize them, even two decades and more later.

The ghats of Varanasi, they beckon,
Look splendid for all, I reckon.
The water so blue, the sky so azure,
A definite lure, I am sure.

On the first Sunday after classes began, the skies opened up. I took the opportunity to sleep in after an exciting but hectic Saturday, and it was close to 10 a.m. when I finally mustered the strength to get out of bed. The weather had turned cool, with a thick cloud cover offering a delightful respite from the intense heat of the previous week. Drops of rain had just started falling from the dark, cloudy skies.

As I finished my morning chores, I noticed that Ranjit

and Chaaku were still in their rooms. The absence of the large Godrej locks on their door handles was a clear indicator. I tried to wake them up but without much success. Their doors remained stubbornly shut, and I could hear loud snores emanating from Chaaku's room.

Just as I was about to give up on waking Ranjit, I saw Popli walking towards me.

'Hoy'—Popli always began his sentences with a 'Hoy'—'let's go for a cup of tea and find some seniors to get ragged. I'm getting bored.' Popli never cared about being ragged and would perform any task asked of him without any embarrassment.

'Well, the tea sounds good; I wouldn't mind a cup myself. Plus, this weather is perfect for a hot cup of tea. But let me stay clear of seniors. I would rather head to the city and explore. The ghats would look lovely in the rain,' I replied.

By the time we reached the hostel gate to head to our friendly neighbourhood tea vendor, DG Corner, the raindrops had grown heavier, and we had to rush into the makeshift tea stall to avoid getting drenched. Soon, Popli and I were sitting in companionable silence, sipping our tea—tasty, hot and with just the right amount of sugar to add a tinge of sweetness.

DG Corner—Handy Guide to IT Lingo

However, our peaceful moment was interrupted by about half a dozen seniors, umbrellas in hand, who entered the small shack and requested tea. This group knew Popli as they had ragged him before, and one of the unwritten rules at IT is simple—never rag the same person twice.

Once ragging is done, it's friendship from then on.

One of the seniors, a tall and thoughtful fellow named Rakesh from the third year of Meta, insisted on paying for our tea and invited us back to their hostel to meet his other batchmates. Little did I know I was about to witness the most grotesque event.

As I stood near the hostel entrance, answering questions from Rakesh's batchmates ('ragging' would be too strong a word), an altercation broke out a few yards away between two individuals who had been speaking amicably until then. A dark, stocky senior dared the other—a tall, fair, robust-looking fellow—to perform a certain task for the royal sum of Rs 10.

Accepting the challenge, the tall senior dashed into the pouring rain, ran after a large frog in the swampy, muddy area and jumped around for a few minutes, searching for something in the steady rain. After a series of amazing displays of dexterity that would put Jane Fonda's aerobics to shame, he triumphantly held up a large frog in the same way Kapil Dev held up the Prudential Trophy, a wide-mouthed, cheesy grin spreading across his face. I casually pondered who was dirtier—the senior or the frog he clutched tightly between his fingers. After displaying his 'trophy', he invited us to the mess with a courtly, old-fashioned bow, holding the frog against his stomach.

Upon reaching the mess, he called Chhotu and instructed the cook to boil water in a large vessel. We waited in companionable silence, wondering what was about to unfold. When Chhotu emerged from the inner recesses of the mess and declared that the water was ready, we followed the senior into the kitchen. The senior unceremoniously dumped the frog into the boiling water and closed the lid. After a few minutes, he fished out the frog, which had reduced to a colourless, soggy mass. He sprinkled salt and pepper on it and proceeded to eat it with obvious relish, in front of our stunned and unbelieving gazes.

Seeing my incredulous expression, Rakesh gravely explained that this behaviour was normal for this remarkable individual. Some misguided folks seem capable of doing anything for the sake of a wager. At that moment, one of the seniors—the dark fellow who had initiated the bet—posed a riddle to me. 'Hey, fresher; what's green but turns red at the flick of a button?'

I shook my head in confusion, prompting him to reveal the answer. 'A frog in a mixer.' In response, the room erupted into a cacophony of hearty laughter mixed with groans.

Somebody declared, 'Kaushik and his *shick* (pun intended) jokes. *Ajhel* stuff. They give a new meaning to the term PJ.'

Ajhel—Handy Guide to IT Lingo

Walking back to my room later in the evening, at the end of what had indeed been an interesting weekend, I thought to myself, *Welcome to the strange world of the seniors.*

10

Graffiti

One fine morning, a loud, authoritative knock on my hostel door startled me awake. It was about 10 days after I had settled into life at BIT. When I opened the door, I found myself face-to-face with a broad, dark fellow who was almost as wide as he was tall—a truly immense figure. His stature and appearance made him hard to miss around the campus. He was often seen chatting with everyone and seemed quite amiable. He bore an uncanny resemblance to Papa Bear from *Goldilocks and the Three Bears.*

I wished him a good morning, to which he pleasantly replied, 'What's so great about this particular morning? Seems the same as every other day. No rain for three days, making the heat unbearable. *Hajaar* homework, full classes, no *chhutti.*'

Hajaar and Chhutti—Handy Guide to IT Lingo

'Since when do you make it to classes, Fatty?' countered a thin, dark fellow of medium height, approaching us lazily. 'The day you attend two classes in a row, the Director will declare a medical emergency.'

He turned to me, extending his hand. 'Hi! I am

Funny, fourth-year Mining. Has this gargoyle here,' he gestured towards the broad fellow standing at my door, 'introduced himself yet?'

I shook my head, and Funny continued, 'This is Fatty, alias Venky; he's a Tamilian like you.'

I surmised that 'Venky' probably stood for Venkatraman or Venkateswar—both common in South Indian naming conventions. Sherlock Holmes would have scoffed at my deduction, arguing that guessing is a shocking habit, destructive to the logical faculty—but at that moment, I had little choice. I lacked the courage to ask him for a more precise introduction—or, for that matter, to probe into Funny's real name.

I couldn't imagine someone going through life with a name like his. People are usually sensible once they become parents and rarely would they willingly name someone 'Funny'. Later, I discovered that Venky stood for Venkataramani and Funny's given name was Phaneesh Sriram, both hailing from Madras.

I wished Funny a good morning but avoided shaking his outstretched hand; I could still recall the first morning and countless days of ragging with striking clarity. Seeing my obvious discomfort, Funny patted me on the shoulder with the same hand and said, 'Relax, Raja. No ragging business here. Fourth-year guys like us have had enough of that nonsense in the past three years; we have no desire to continue it.'

Venky, who seemed interested in classes—and evidently hadn't tired of ragging after four years—demanded, 'Not attending classes? You've just been here for a week and are already acting like a true ITian—no classes, sleeping till 10. Early learner, eh?'

The previous night, I had been ragged by two idiots from Morvi Hostel who had devised new and harrowing ways to bore me to death. As a result, I missed the early morning deadline to either escape from the campus or to the classroom.

It was one of those occasions when this late bird did itself a favour by not catching the symbolic worm attuned to escape by late morning, since I met a group of individuals who would shape my life at the institute in ways I hadn't anticipated. They would also go on to create the finest humour magazine I have ever had the privilege of reading or being associated with.

Funny continued, 'Adesh Pandey from your school—a close friend of mine—asked me to keep an eye on you. You know he graduated earlier this year and is now working with Levers?'

I nodded and mentioned that I had met Adesh's younger brother—a classmate of mine back in school—the day before I left for Varanasi. He informed me that his brother had spoken about me to his college friends.

'I was told you used to write for the school magazine, Raja,' Funny said.

I nodded again.

At this point, Fatty interjected, 'Aren't you going to invite us inside?'

Apologizing for my oversight, I hastily invited them in, standing at attention while they made themselves comfortable on my unmade bed.

Funny continued, 'We are starting a campus magazine— but not the usual kind you come across. This will be a full-scale humour magazine, and we need input from people like you. If you're not doing anything particular, come to the hostel with us, and we can introduce you to our gang.'

I agreed to accompany them to their hostel, though my heart hesitated. My head tends to rule over my heart, after all.

The apprehensive look on my face must have been obvious, as Funny laughed and said, 'Don't worry, we're not interested in ragging you.'

Fatty got up, threw his beefy arm around my shoulders, and declared in the best imitation of a Tamil villain, '*Machchan*, act smart, and I shall finish you. Ha! Ha!'

'Show me some of the articles you wrote for your school magazine,' Funny requested.

I rummaged through my overnight bag and handed him the last two issues of our school magazine. He browsed through them for a few minutes while Fatty amused himself by pulling strange faces in the mirror, trying to decide in which pose he looked most handsome.

'Do you think a moustache would suit me?' Fatty asked me with utmost seriousness. 'It will make me look rakishly handsome, don't you think?'

I mumbled a yes, as one could not afford to antagonize seniors, no matter how unattractive they might be.

Funny looked up from the magazine and remarked, 'Pretty good, but we're looking for something different. Get ready and come over to my room. I have some stuff you might find interesting.'

We walked over to the fourth-year hostel, Vishvesvaraya (Vish, in short), my head held high. My nervousness disappeared when Fatty started cracking jokes and stopped behaving like an overgrown eight-year-old. My sense of humour came to the fore, and for the first time in a week, I laughed heartily at the jokes cracked by these two characters. Funny inquired if I knew the name of the new unit of weight adopted by scientists after they met Fatty. I answered in the negative, to which he replied, 'New-Ton.'

Then he pointed to our right, where a four-foot-tall wall stood, desolate and forlorn, looking much worse with a large crack in one corner. 'Do you know what happened to that wall, the crack in the corner?' he asked.

'No,' I replied.

'Fatty sat there last summer. Ha ha!'

We soon entered their hostel, which was considerably larger than mine—about the size of Vivekananda hostel—and we walked into a room next to the entrance, climbing four steps on the right of the main gate. I later learned that this massive hostel contained 300 rooms.

Inside the room, a thin, dirty-looking individual wearing a blood-red T-shirt and torn jeans reaching up to his ankles, which on closer inspection appeared to be the remnants of a full pair torn down to fit his spindly ankles, was scrutinizing a large foolscap screen. He had thick, unruly hair falling in waves over his forehead, an unseemly stubble and an altogether unkempt appearance.

Without looking up, he said, 'Abey, let's go to Sinha. We have some composing work to get done today.'

'Das, meet Raja,' Funny informed Das, who then deigned to look up and gave me a cursory glance. Muttering 'Hi,' he resumed his work.

'Do you know anything about printing?' asked Fatty.

I informed him that I was actively involved in publishing my school magazine and had a working knowledge of dry-letter transfers, offset printing and the works.

At this, Das looked up and shot me an interested look.

'Hi,' he said, waving his hand. 'I am Sukumar Das, third-year Mining. I am a Bengali but from Ranchi. What about you? Where are you from?' he asked.

'Calcutta, sir,' I replied.

'*Abey, ye sirf sir nahi hai, ek lamba sa body bhi tere saamne hai!* (Hey, there's not just a head, but a whole body in front of you!)' Waiting to see if I understood the bilingual *phatta*, he continued, 'Which school did you attend?'

Bilingual Phatta—Handy Guide to IT Lingo

'St Lawrence High School.'

'Do you speak Bengali?'

'Quite well, sir.'

'Who speaks Bengali here?' inquired the frog-eating senior, Kaushik Chatterjee, who had just entered the room right on our heels.

Das pointed towards me and informed him that I was from Calcutta and could speak Bengali.

'Bengalis, being of the same flock, stick together,' a voice wafted in from just beyond the door. The speaker was a thin individual resembling Funny but taller, and even more emaciated. He entered the room, which quickly began to feel like the Black Hole of Calcutta, where 143 Englishmen were interned, leading to claustrophobia and the deaths of around 120 people.

'When two Bengalis meet...' he started before being rudely interrupted by Funny.

'Enough, Pods. You do not even require a prod to get started. Here, meet Raja, a Tamilian from Calcutta, who is proficient in both Tamil and Bengali. Try some trilingual phattas with him. And he writes well.'

Pods extended a bony hand with a friendly grin on his cadaverous face. 'Hi, I am Potluri Krishnan, a third-year Ceramic student from Gwalior—but a Tamilian.'

I wished him a good morning in return.

'You are from Bengal, so you should be aware of this—do you know how many Bengalis it takes to change a light bulb?'

Kaushik turned a deeper shade of brown, while I shrugged, unsure of the answer.

Potluri, at my negative sign, continued, 'I don't know, but will this question come in the exam?'

Everybody collapsed with laughter, including the protesting Kaushik, when Das, suddenly transforming into a born-again Bengali, interjected, 'How does a Greek makku say "Mary had a little lamb"?' When nobody could answer, he declared, 'Mary had a little lamb-da.'

'How does a makku make dal-fry?'

Seeing blank faces, he answered, 'With dal-da.' He then pressed on, 'How does a makku make love?'

He answered his own question, 'With Lav-da.'

I mustered up the nerve to ask a riddle and said, 'What does a chemical engineer write in his New Year greeting card?'

At the blank looks of the *junta* around me, I answered, 'May your New Year be phosphorus.'

'And what do you do with dead chemical engineers?'

When nobody answered, I said, 'You...barium.'

Loud guffaws followed my snappy answer. Kaushik slapped my back and exclaimed, 'Welcome to Graffiti—the mag that will revolutionize all humour mags!'

Das declared that he was going to get some alcohol and was leaving the room when another thin, spectacled, fair individual of about my height—whose very demeanour suggested the archetypical studious Tamilian—entered.

He chimed in a singsong tone, 'Das, get some whisky for me if convenient; if inconvenient, get me some all the same.'

I murmured, '*The Adventure of the Creeping Man, Case-Book.*'

The spectacled one looked at me in complete astonishment.

'What! Who are you? A Holmes fanatic, eh?'

I answered, 'I could probably recite the *Hound's* first chapter verbatim.'

At this, he thrust his skinny hand forward and declared, 'I am Krishnan Kalyanasundaram—Krish to everybody here—third-year Electrical, and, dear boy, ecstatic to meet a fellow Holmes fanatic.'

I had gathered enough strength from the events of the past hour to shake his hand, albeit not as enthusiastically as Krish, but with a friendly smile. I told him that, I too, was delighted to meet a fellow Holmes lover and somebody with whom I could discuss Sherlock Holmes. I had sorely missed one during my school days, when my friends invariably preferred discussing Halliday and Resnick over Doyle.

Funny handed me a stack of papers with pencilled notes for *Graffiti*. As I flipped through, my eye caught a scribble: 'Space for a spoof on Sherlock Holmes & PGW.' I asked Funny if anyone had shown interest in writing the spoofs on the two authors whose works I never seem to stop reading.

'Krish here is our resident Wodehouse & Doyle fanatic. You may help him write the spoofs,' Funny said. I looked up with joy in my heart—at last, I had someone erudite to talk about Emsworth, Uncle Fred and Jeeves.

Krish and I became fast friends over the next two years. The day before he left BIT after graduating to join IISC as a research scientist (a position in which I understand his creative writing talents are suffering from stagnation, except during March when he helps in squaring up the yearly accounts and applies for new budgets), we spent seven hours in my room reminiscing about the terrific times we had and wondering if we would ever meet anyone else in the years to come to discuss the nuances of Sherlockian deductive genius and Galahad's ready wit.

It is quite remarkable that in all the years since, I have yet to meet anyone with the same interest in Doyle as I have. However, while working in a small town in England a few years ago, I encountered an oddity—a PGW fanatic who did not care much for Doyle. We thoroughly enjoyed each other's company for three years before he left to pursue further studies.

I soon realized that Das and Funny were the nerve centres of *Graffiti*. Das looked after the core content of the articles and provided razor-sharp humour, while Funny handled the more practical details of the entire production process. This is not to say that Funny lacked any of Das' cutting wit; rather, it was more logically thought out, with phrases and complete sentences geared towards authoring a short article suitable for publication.

Funny's personality mirrored his work ethic—clean, organized and methodical—while Das was a whirlwind of chaotic genius. Das' observations were spontaneous and brilliant but often lost in the ether because he rarely wrote them down. Funny, on the other hand, acted as a project manager, gathering the scattered gems from Das, introducing structure, and tracking the magazine's progress meticulously.

Das' wit was spontaneous, and an example of this occurred when Krish and I were discussing the best way to spoof *The Hound of Baskervilles.*

Das interrupted us and asked, 'Do you know what promises Doyle would have made to the poor junta had he been a politician?' Seeing our blank expressions, he answered, 'Holmes for the homeless. Ha ha!'

Fatty, who had been sitting morosely in one corner, looking at the articles already written, assumed the role of the salesperson. He conceived the idea for the cover page, featuring cartoons that bore a remarkable likeness to Das, Funny and Fatty, along with a balloon imploring: 'Please buy this magazine and save us from bankruptcy.'

Funny was an excellent cartoonist and could draw caricatures of anybody with a remarkable degree of resemblance. It was he who drew the cover page. It is said that genius is an infinite capacity for hard work, and we proved that publishing a humour magazine like *Graffiti,* which achieved considerable success, required such dedication. Das created the mascot for the magazine, naming him 'Abdul Peter Iyengar' as a tribute to India's multicultural roots. Funny, within minutes, scribbled the cartoon representing Abdul Peter Iyengar, complete with a cross on his neck, a *sef* on his head, and a vertical *naamam* on his forehead.

That memorable morning, I met the other members of the *Graffiti* gang—Ramulu, a nearly bald boxer who claimed he had lost his hair watching Das mess up his room, which he had lent for six hours due to the accumulated filth in Das' room; Amit Mangotra, who was as taciturn as an English Earl with his mouth full at the banquet table, and an even better cartoonist than Funny but without his biting humour; and Nikhil Pandit, a seemingly perpetually drunk and carefree classmate of Krish who informed me he was high because he had just consumed milk, a whole litre of it. Seeing my blank expression, he gravely explained that cows, buffaloes and other creatures consume grass, and therefore, milk makes us high.

Grass—Handy Guide to IT Lingo

Ramulu had a colourful vocabulary and had devised remarkably original words to describe simple, everyday events. He had no hair around his temples, and Das once asked me if I could figure Ramulu's motto in life. When I replied negatively, he quipped, 'A hair on the head is worth two on the brush.'

I witnessed Ramulu's outstanding vocabulary and unique choice of words one fine evening, a few weeks later, while watching a semi-pornographic movie at Shilpi. A young lady wearing dark sunglasses was referred to as the 'smuggler female'; a 'karra' female was a young, well-endowed nymphet and 'malty' referred to the mother or older women in the movie, typically large and buxom.

Ramulu delivered these descriptions excitedly, with

exuberant Gaelic shrugs, rapid hand movements and a face reflecting the animation of a young Indian boy watching his first international cricket game, with Sachin Tendulkar batting in all his glory at the crease.

Ramulu was an excellent raconteur, a skilled boxer and a loyal friend. Fatty and he were chosen to arrange for the requisite funds—beg, borrow or steal, as Funny succinctly put it—from shops, restaurants, hotels, or anyone who showed the slightest inclination of parting with a farthing. Ramulu had commented with a straight face that a man and his farthing are not easily parted.

11

Ladies Only

My experiences with the *Graffiti* gang, coupled with my daily interactions and questioning by fourth-year students, soon made me a well-known fresher in the IT set-up. I took pride in my sense of humour, which I believed was well above average, and it improved considerably thanks to the likes of Das and Funny. I was constantly looking for puns in simple words and testing my newfound lateral thinking on my classmates, much to their inevitable groans.

About three weeks after I arrived in Varanasi, I realized I was running short of cash. Plastic money was still an unknown entity in the city, and I needed to cash a demand draft worth the princely sum of five thousand rupees that I had brought with me. This epiphany struck me while I was with the *Graffiti* team, busy working on the artwork for the front cover and exchanging our usual one-liners. We were contemplating getting coffee from DG Corner when it hit me and I exclaimed, 'Bloody hell, I have to open a bank account! I'm down to my last hundred-rupee note.'

The ever helpful Das offered, 'If you need money, just let me know.'

'Thanks,' I replied, 'but I have a demand draft that

I need to encash, and I think I need to open a bank account for that.'

Indian schooling rarely prepares you for the basics of adult life; I had no clue how to open or operate a bank account, having been completely dependent on my parents and relatives, with the occasional pocket money my dad would leave for me.

Krish interjected, 'Come on, let's go and get that done. I need a break anyway, and a walk would do me good.'

As we stepped out, we spotted Fatty and Ramulu entering the hostel gate, and they immediately joined us, as if sensing that I needed the company in case we encountered more seniors.

Ramulu explained, 'At this time,' (it was about 11 a.m.) 'there will be a lot of guys at the bank, and you'll get caught in ragging. We'll lose time, and we need to get the artwork completed today. Sinha is waiting for it; I just met him.'

'Thanks,' I replied, 'but who's Sinha?'

'Rohit Sinha is the printer for *Graffiti*,' Ramulu explained. 'He's an alumnus from the 1980 batch, Mechanical Engineering. He now runs two newspapers in Varanasi.'

'And this fat slob here,' Krish pointed to Fatty, 'managed to persuade him to print the magazine for free. He's only asking for the cost of the paper. But we have to handle the typesetting and artwork. Anyway, you'll meet him tonight when we go to him with the draft pages. He's a great guy.'

When we arrived at the bank, as Ramulu had suspected, the place was crawling with freshers who had realized they were running low on cash. And where there were freshers, there were bound to be seniors—the area was crowded with second- and third-year students engaged in the usual ragging sessions.

As I was filling out the form to open an account, I was approached by a few second-year Chemical Engineering students, and the typical introductory session commenced. These sessions, which would have filled me with horror and trepidation a couple of weeks ago, now lulled me to sleep. I had grown accustomed to a more intellectual line of questioning from the fourth years in general and from the Graffiti gang in particular. Returning to mundane topics after the hiatus of the past few days bored me to no end. However, I bravely answered the same old preposterous questions with as straight a face as I could muster, occasionally adding 'Sir' to appease the seniors and their overinflated egos.

An hour or so later, after a couple of appearances by Fatty to cut short the ragging, I finally completed my bank work. Just as I turned to leave the crowded place, a lady with an impressive figure—who could have won any beauty contest where height and body structure were the sole criteria (and I later realized, brains)—walked up to me, flanked by two seniors, whom I deduced could only be her bodyguards or admirers. As Woody Allen might have contemplated, her figure described a set of parabolas that could give a yak a cardiac arrest. However, her face could induce a nervous child to have a few nightmares.

I figured her companions valued figure over face. *Figure that out*, I mused wryly.

As the trio neared, I greeted them, 'Good morning, madam. Good morning, sirs.'

The lady demanded, 'Your name?'

'N. Raja Venkateswar, madam,' I replied.

'Which branch?'

'Chemical Engineering, madam.'

'Meenakshi studies with you, doesn't she?' she practically shouted. The lady seemed to think I was half-deaf. The one-room bank branch was crowded and filled with a constant din, making it difficult to speak at a normal volume. However, there was no real need for her larynx's volume control to be set to maximum.

I looked at her blankly for a moment, wondering whom she was referring to, before realizing she meant one of the three girls in my class. Meenakshi—the stocky-looking individual with whom I had never exchanged pleasantries since the first day of classes. I had little recollection of her or the other two girls—Sonal and Priya.

I had nothing against Meenakshi or the other girls in my class, but it is quite difficult to strike up a conversation with people you've hardly met—especially since I had not been to my classroom for the past week, having been completely involved with *Graffiti* work.

'Well, you know Meenakshi, don't you?' she repeated, some asperity evident in her tone.

'Yes, but I have not really met her or know her,' I responded.

'That's precisely what I want to know. Why don't you guys communicate with her? She is treated like a leper in your class. She is your classmate, and I want you to take an interest in her, talk to her and treat her properly. I will handle the situation myself if I receive further complaints about you.'

'Yes, madam,' I said.

'"Yes" to what, you idiot?'

'Well, madam, I shall definitely look her up in class, madam.'

'What do you mean, "look her up"? I need you to tell me that you will become friends with her pronto.'

'Yes, madam.'

'"Yes, madam", what?'

Her two escorts, taking cues from her last statement, theatrically rolled up their sleeves—a remarkable feat for seniors (since no self-respecting seniors wore full sleeves), I idly wondered—and gave me a murderous glare. I realized that the lady treated her admirers as if they were still freshers.

'Hey, are you dumb or what?' the taller and stouter of the two demanded. 'Treat the lady here with deference. Answer her properly.'

I mumbled, 'Yes, sir.'

The other one, thickly moustachioed, dark and well-built, asked, 'Hey, bugger, what do you think of this lady? Do you know her? She is famous in BIT as the prettiest woman around. What do you think, eh?'

I stood there dumbly, uncomprehending, and wondered how to respond. For the first time during my time at BIT, I was scared of physical harm.

Meanwhile, the lady was preening under all the adulation.

Fatty came to my rescue at this juncture, followed by Krish, who had been engrossed in a conversation with someone he had met in the bank. Ramulu was nowhere to be seen. Fatty whispered in my ear, 'Don't worry, just carry on,' and moved a few yards away to observe the affair unfold.

I could see the two cohorts of the dynamite lady looking slightly uncomfortable with this turn of events.

Nevertheless, the lady continued. 'Are you dumb or something? You don't know how to talk to a lady. Behave properly and don't try to be insolent.'

I responded, 'Yes, madam.'

'What do you mean by "Yes, madam"? Say, "I shall do as Your Majesty says."'

'I shall do as Your Majesty says, madam.'

'That's better. Do you see the girl standing at the counter with her back to us?'

I replied, 'Yes, I see her.'

'Have you met her before?'

'I don't think so, but I cannot be sure as I do not have the advantage of seeing her face-on.'

'Go up to her and ask her out to dinner. If she agrees, I shall leave you and even pay for your dinner. I might even honour you with my company. And if she refuses, you will have to come up to my room and help me clean it up.'

I had no intention of sharing any meal with this lady, especially when I was enjoying my meals with the *Graffiti* gang, nor did I want to help her with her spring cleaning in early autumn. Nevertheless, a fresher's life is like that. I proceeded towards the young woman in question.

'Excuse me, madam,' I said to her.

She turned around and looked at me inquisitively.

I was quite in control of my senses, feeling deliciously comfortable at the sight of Fatty, with his immense bulk, watching over me, prepared to interfere in case of any trouble.

'You must have heard this opening sequence before, and many Hollywood actresses down the annals of movie history insist that it is pretty dumb, madam,' I began, 'but haven't we met before? I would generally remember meeting someone as pretty as you, if not for the circumstances of the past few days that have not been very conducive to remembering incidents, even supremely remarkable ones such as meeting pretty ladies.' I managed to say all that with barely a stammer. This realization hit me a nanosecond after I completed my spiel, making me feel almost cocky.

She gave me a wide smile and said, 'Hi! I am Prasanna, a third-year Electrical student, and your approach is new and unusual—quite different from the run-of-the-mill propositions I get. By the way, I know I am not pretty, so don't try any fast ones on me.' She then asked, 'What is your name?'

'I am N. Raja Venkateswar, madam.'

'Who sent you to speak to me?'

'The lady over there, madam,' I said, pointing to the lady flanked by her bodyguards standing about 10 yards away.

Prasanna snorted, her expression twisting into one of unmistakable dislike—some might even call it revulsion or hatred—and declared, 'Reema is mad, with all her antics,' her tone brimming with intemperance. 'Did she ask you to do anything else?' she inquired after recovering from her snorting fit.

'She asked me to ask you out for dinner, madam,' I replied. Sensing that the two of them didn't exactly set the Ganga on fire, I added, 'And she threatened to accompany us if you agree. Of course, she did say she would pay for it.'

'That's interesting. Come, let's have a word with her.' She walked purposefully towards Reema, with me following her at a respectful distance.

'Hi, I've agreed to accompany Raja here for dinner. You're going to pay for it, I trust?' Prasanna said.

'Cut it out, Pras. This is just to test the smartness of these young boys who will grow up to be engineers,' Reema countered, emphasizing 'engineers' with a snort.

Prasanna turned to me and said, 'Raja, nice meeting you. Our dinner is due, but I'm stuck today. However, I shall meet you again soon.' She asked for my batch and room number before walking away without a backward glance.

Reema turned to me with distaste and said, 'So, you think you're smart, eh?'

I kept my mouth tightly shut and focused on a point approximately six inches to the left of her left eye.

'So, what happened? What did you tell Prasanna to make her agree to dinner so quickly?'

'Nothing really, madam. I just asked her, and she was nice.'

'Oh! She was "nice", huh? So, what about me? I'm not nice, am I?'

'Oh no, madam. I would never say that, madam.'

And so, it continued, with Reema doing her best to taunt me, while I, with a straight, stoic face, gave equally inane answers to inane questions. After about 30 minutes, my patience began to wear thin, especially as I had a fair amount of work for *Graffiti* to complete before the evening and the proposed meeting with Sinha.

Meanwhile, a small crowd had gathered around us, watching the ragging continue interminably. By the time the taller bodyguard asked me a question that brought the ragging to an inglorious but entertaining halt, I was at my breaking point and utterly exhausted.

He asked, 'Reema is quite pretty, isn't she? Can you suggest any other ideas to make her even more beautiful?'

I looked at Fatty, who sensed something was up and came to stand just behind the tall idiot.

'Off with her head,' I replied, letting my guard down for a moment.

It might sound clichéd, but in the instant that followed my retort, one could have heard a pin drop in the crowded room. Then thunderous silence gave way to a deafening guffaw as the entire bank erupted in unrestrained mirth. One could blame it on my exasperation and newfound cockiness, but the deed was done, and I realized, too late, that I had made a huge error. I stammered an apology, explaining that I didn't quite mean it, but I doubted anyone heard my entreaties.

The two bodyguards and the lady so eager to enhance her physical charms with free opinions and postulations from young, impressionable freshers, stood transfixed, hardly believing what they had just heard.

It was quite unthinkable for any fresher to speak to a senior the way I had, and there could have been significant repercussions, all quite unhealthy for me. Fortunately, I was spared for a couple of reasons.

First, I was lucky enough to get into an altercation with a group of students who were disliked across the institute.

Second, there had been several complaints to the seniors about their behaviour, as their ragging of freshers lacked the friendly treatment one usually associated with ITians. Many third- and fourth-year students felt that someone was bound to put her in her place sooner or later.

Third, and what I considered the most important fact, was Fatty standing beside me with his immense bulk, leaving everyone in no doubt about where his loyalties lay.

This incident went a long way in making me popular among the ITians. Some seniors meeting me for the first time solicitously inquired whether I had indeed answered Reema back. Mostly, I got friendly pats on the back and was offered tea and snacks. The speed with which the story spread proved that truth, however fantastic, travels faster than rumours. *Sic.*

One of the key lessons I learnt from this experience was that whatever the circumstance, pressure rationale or provocation, it's best to keep the old trap shut. Words once spoken cannot be taken back, and have a habit of returning to haunt you at some point in life.

That evening also marked my first meeting with Sinha, an excruciatingly thin and bespectacled individual with an overgrown beard and a thick moustache. He wore an old shirt, rolled up to his elbows, and a smouldering cigarette rested beside him in an ashtray filled with cigarette butts. He sat with his shoulders stooped, a careworn look about him, and moved with measured deliberation. When he saw us entering his chamber—he had been expecting us and his peon had waved us in with a friendly gesture—he gave us a broad, welcoming smile that lit up his face with obvious pleasure.

He shook my hand with his bony grip, introduced himself as Rohit Sinha, and raised an eyebrow upon hearing that I was from Calcutta. Removing his spectacles—a habitual gesture, I would soon discover—he polished them vigorously while chatting. Mentioning that his younger brother was a well-known journalist at *Ananda Bazar Patrika* in Calcutta, he wished me all the best for my new life and welcomed me to BIT and Varanasi.

Das and Sinha were soon engaged in an intricate discussion about the merits of using a particular stencil or font for the articles. Their animated debate lasted nearly 20 minutes before they reached an agreement. Meanwhile, I found a comfortable chair and used the time to take in my surroundings.

Sinha's office was large and painted in an off-white colour that felt clammy and claustrophobic, almost as if the windows had never been opened. Sure enough, when I looked at the windows, a thin layer of dust around the panes confirmed my suspicion. The room was dominated by a huge desk, behind which Sinha sat in a thick, leather-upholstered chair. In front of the desk were three equally comfortable chairs where Funny and I sat, while Das hovered behind Sinha, poring over the initial designs.

The walls of the room were lined with open bookshelves filled with newspapers, books, journals and assorted reading materials. The wall behind Sinha featured a floor-to-ceiling bookshelf filled with an ancient-looking edition of the

Encyclopaedia Britannica and other thick reference books.

Funny noticed me marvelling at the literature around me and whispered, 'Sinha is the printer of the two principal daily newspapers here in Varanasi—both are vernacular, with a combined circulation in millions.'

We spent the next several hours discussing the magazine's layout—the front page and its advertisements, and the back page with its unique graffiti-wall design. It was a remarkably interesting introduction to the world of printing. Those few hours gave me newfound appreciation for the work involved in creating a professional publication at a leading university—so vastly different from the simpler school assignments where all you did was write or edit the content, leaving the rest to professionals or teachers. Here, we had to do everything ourselves.

We returned late that night. On the way back, Funny treated us to *launglatha,* an incredibly sweet Banarasi delicacy, and *malai dhoodh,* a thickened milk preparation served with a generous helping of cream on top, at Assi Ghat. It tasted like heaven!

A couple of days later, I ran into Meenakshi. It was one of those rare occasions when I found time and respite from the seniors to attend classes. As I walked to class, Meenakshi hailed me from the wide field just opposite the mechanical engineering division, where the morning classes were held.

Meenakshi and I had exchanged pleasantries since the bank incident, but we hadn't had any real conversation. So, her enthusiastic wave and fervent shout from about 50 yards away took me by surprise. I waved back and approached her at a gentle, leisurely pace. She wore black trousers and a light blue, full-sleeved shirt, buttoned almost to her neck. The rules of severe attire applied to women freshers too!

'Hi,' I said as I reached the edge of the road.

'You really talked to Reema like that?' she asked without any preamble.

'Like what?' I retorted, struggling to maintain a friendly tone.

It was her voice—thin and high-pitched, rather nasal and remarkably similar to the meow of a hangry cat denied its rightful saucer of milk for the past 17 hours—that put me off, much like how spectators would feel at the prospect of watching Babu Nadkarni bowl to Chris Tavare on the fifth afternoon of a dead rubber at Faisalabad! (What a pun! *Faisla* and a result? It would be interesting to find out how many Test matches at that venue actually produced results)

'You know very well what I mean.'

'Then why ask for confirmation?'

'What really happened there?' she pressed, emphasizing 'really' in a coquettish lilt that some misogamists liken to the mannerism of women trying to sound overly charming.

So, I recounted what had transpired in the bank, concluding with the lamentation that while I managed to open the account, I missed depositing the demand draft, which was still tucked away in my trouser pocket.

She graciously offered to accompany me to the bank during the 20-minute break after the second period.

'So gracious of you,' I replied, thinking that if one could get over the initial squeak, her voice wasn't so bad, and she seemed to have a heart of gold. Very few freshers would want to accompany another fresher to the bank, knowing it as a hotspot for senior encounters. I was delighted with her offer and equally pleased that I had spoken to her freely and without a noticeable stammer.

Meenakshi had learnt cycling only recently, after reaching Varanasi. As one would know, achieving the necessary balance to become an adept cyclist is quite challenging, given that she had picked it up at a relatively advanced age. However, her newfound skill came with challenges. To maintain balance, she had to pedal at breakneck speed. Slowing down invariably led to mishaps.

After giving it some thought, one of our classmates reasoned that her inability to balance, despite significant effort, could be attributed to her physique. He clearly understood physics well. Meenakshi had a stocky build and stood barely above five feet. Even in her sensible two-inch heels, which she usually wore, she was top-heavy due to the remarkable development of her bosom. It was said that Gina Lollobrigida envied Zeenat Aman's mammary development, but my classmates were positive that Zeenat, in turn, would be amazed at Meenakshi's remarkable development in that regard.

This imbalance, combined with the vigorous motion of her upper body as she pedalled furiously, likely explained her difficulty maintaining equilibrium. Some rather nasty folks from other engineering disciplines made several jokes about Meenakshi, which I dismissed as jealousy—we were one of the few classes with three good-looking girls in a university filled with young boys!

Here are a few samples:

'What did General Sam Manekshaw declare on

witnessing Meenakshi? "What a pair of booby traps!"'

'Who is Meenakshi's boyfriend? "Meh-boob Khan."'

But let's not digress. Back to the day Meenakshi accompanied me to the bank.

I borrowed a friend's bicycle for the short trip. It took us a few minutes of cycling to reach the bank and about 10 minutes to deposit my demand draft. Strangely, the branch was empty, devoid of any seniors. As we cycled back, with me trying my best to keep up with Meenakshi's breakneck pace, she lost control of the cycle and made a not-so-dignified landing on her ample backside.

Meanwhile, the cycle seemed to have developed a mind of its own, embarking on a three-act performance that was uncharacteristic of a well-trained bicycle. I watched the mayhem unfolding in front of me with idle curiosity.

First, the cycle refused to obey Meenakshi's commands, choosing instead to display an unruly streak rather unbecoming of a well-mannered cycle.

Second, with a sudden, vicious jerk—courtesy of the front wheel's inexplicable decision to aim exclusively for the very top of a large, battered pothole (eschewing the relative attractions of its sides or bottom)—it ejected Meenakshi from her seat. Freed from her grasp, it meandered aimlessly, entirely unbothered by the fate of its unfortunate ex-occupant.

Third, after a few seconds of aimless movement, it decided to return to its moorings, possibly feeling guilty for having treated its rider poorly, and parked itself on Meenakshi's still supine form. Meenakshi then gingerly attempted to lift herself, leaning on her right hand while vigorously rubbing her left knee.

I had fallen behind, unable to match the speed of Meenakshi's initial acceleration, so I was not close enough to offer immediate assistance. However, I increased my speed and soon found myself beside her as she struggled to extricate herself from the cycle. Acting like a knight in shining armour who regularly assisted damsels in distress, I removed the stubborn cycle from Meenakshi's recumbent position and helped her to her feet.

'Nothing broken, I trust?' I asked with concern.

She dusted herself off and asked, 'My dress isn't too dirty, I hope?'

Trust her to think about something as trivial as her attire at this time!

I assured her that she and her dress looked fine, and asked if she was all right. She confirmed that other than a slight pain in her knee and ankle, she was as good as new. I then suggested that we better move on since it was close to lunchtime, and seniors would soon be around trying to act superior.

No sooner had I spoken those words than a couple of seniors appeared beside us, leaning on their cycles. To my horror, I saw Reema walking towards us. I must confess that the fact that the two gentlemen were not the roughnecks who had accosted me at the bank a few days ago but two clean-shaven individuals who were remarkably well-dressed by senior standards brought a sigh of relief to my heart. In fact, I had even met one of these seniors at Fatty's mess a couple of days earlier and deduced that they were both from the fourth year.

'What happened?' the familiar senior asked anxiously.

'The lady here just had a fall from her bicycle,' I replied.

Reema walked the remaining distance and stood glaring at me with ill-concealed distaste. 'So, have you started talking to each other?' she snapped.

Some people never learn, do they? I wondered.

'Yes, madam,' I responded. 'In fact, Meenakshi found my company rather pleasant and accompanied me to the bank.'

'Why did you make her fall off the cycle, then?' she asked me crossly.

'I didn't, madam. The cycle performed a rather un-cycle-like manoeuvre and deposited my lovely classmate on her posterior. I had nothing to do with the unfortunate incident. I came to assist Meenakshi in getting up as quickly as I could, and was just asking her if she was feeling fine.' Looking at Meenakshi, I said, 'Do you agree with my observation?'

Meenakshi nodded silently in response, doubtlessly shaken by the fall and unclear about the impact the incident had on her appearance.

At the end of my monologue, the two gentlemen were grinning at me, while Reema's face was a study in contrast. It had turned a deep shade of purple and she stood rooted to the spot, presumably struck speechless. Her hands were clenched, and her bosom (not as well-endowed as the one standing next to me in heels) heaved with suppressed rage. It was evident that she hadn't forgotten the earlier incident at the bank, and my recent monologue had brought all her repressed anger to the surface.

The other senior, the one I hadn't been introduced to, interjected, cutting off any retort from Reema. 'Give us your introduction, chirkut.'

So, I began again, 'Sirs, my name is N. Raja Venkateswar, and I am from—'

I had barely begun when the other senior asked me to stop and commanded me to follow him. He bid goodbye to Reema, who remained rooted to the spot with a murderous look in her eyes. He instructed her to ensure Meenakshi reached her hostel safely and recommended that she accompany her to the medical centre for a quick check-up.

When we were out of earshot, the senior I had met earlier but whose name I did not know, said, 'Raja, I'm Steven D'Souza, a fourth-year Mechanical student. We met earlier at my mess. And this is Jayant Kriplani, a fourth-year Electrical student. Reema didn't take your digs at her too kindly, and you are in some trouble there. Don't underestimate her; she has a couple of cohorts who don't have the foggiest notion of culture or manners, and we could have had a bloody situation on our hands.'

So, my incident with Reema had reached their ears too!

'Thank you, sirs, for getting me out of that situation,' I said gratefully, fully aware of the predicament I was in. Steven and Jayant were good friends of the *Graffiti* gang, and they soon led me to Das and Funny, who were, as usual, poring over manuscripts containing the raw material for *Graffiti*.

Well, there went my well-intentioned efforts to attend classes, but what a relief!

12

Mess Food and Food
for Thought

Anyone reading this story might wonder if I ever attended classes or if my life revolved solely around working on *Graffiti*, wandering through Varanasi or occasionally encountering Reema. To be fair, they wouldn't be entirely wrong. While I did attend classes now and then, managing to grasp a few topics along the way, my attendance was about half that of my more diligent classmates. Though working with the *Graffiti* gang was enjoyable, and their disinterest in attending classes might have influenced me, in hindsight, it was my inherent laziness and growing disinterest in studies after years of monotonous academics at school that were the real reasons for my low attendance and subsequent subpar performance in weekly quizzes.

My struggles with the curriculum became glaringly evident when I reviewed my notebooks, which remained either empty or filled with doodles, in contrast to the meticulous notes my classmates diligently compiled. Yet, despite my academic floundering, several significant incidents contributed to my personal growth.

From being an innocent, stammering, anxiety-ridden schoolboy with a linear way of thinking, I transformed into someone who could communicate coherently, think laterally and engage with others confidently. While this change might sound dramatic, its subtler aspects will become apparent in this chapter, particularly in my newfound ability to lead and drive consensus decisions.

Food became a vexing problem after a few days of hostel life. The bland and tasteless dishes served in chipped and stained china were a far cry from the fiery South Indian cuisine I was accustomed to. The vegetable dishes or curries were usually deep-fried, floating in a thick layer of fat, often courtesy of *dalda* or some other budget-friendly alternative. The *dal* was tasteless, with not a hint of any spices other than the occasional green chilli, and the vegetable preparations left much to be desired. Soups, when served, were disappointments beyond description. They resembled water with a dash of chilli powder for a reddish hue but lacked vegetables or flavour. To describe the soups and other items on the menu aptly, one would have to turn to Lewis Carroll once again.

Drawing inspiration from Carroll's whimsical verse, here's my ode to the hostel soups:

> *Beautiful soup, so watery and red-dy,*
> *Waiting in a lukewarm bowl, mini,*
> *So bereft of tomatoes and carrots, any,*
> *Who for such dainties would not stoop,*
> *And avoid the food even when hungry?*

Such a tune deserves a rebuttal, and perhaps the mess Maharaj's reply could go something like this:

So like the consistency of honey,
Who wouldn't like to eat any?
It would be an event quite funny,
As boys eat bowls as many,
And stuff their bloated tummy.

Chhotu's chorus: *Beautiful soup, beautiful soup.*

The only palatable item on the menu, and something we all begged the Maharaj to cook daily, was aloo-fry— fried potatoes with onions and green chillies, served as an accompaniment to dal and rice/rotis.

Cut the potatoes and let them boil,
Peel the onions with some toil,
Make it into a spicy curry divine,
And we sit at the mess to dine.

While I was, and still am, a strict vegetarian, my friends were non-vegetarians and constantly complained about the absence of mutton in the biryani, chicken in the gravy, or eggs in the curry. After long days toiling in the fields, obeying the seniors' whims and fancies (or, rarely, attending classes), or enduring ragging in the seniors' rooms, we would be exhausted and ravenous. Even the bland food served in the mess seemed like a meal fit for royalty at those times.

Lunchtime at the mess was usually enjoyable since the seniors rarely bothered us then. We freshers used this opportunity to compare notes about the events of the past 24 hours, discussing the different ragging methods employed by the ever-inventive seniors. Those who knew me well were often curious about my experiences with *Graffiti* and whether the fourth-year guys usually ragged me or let me wander freely in their hostel.

Once, Rajeev Narayanan from Mining—a talkative and bespectacled fellow—claimed he spent seven hours cooped up in a senior's room, writing notes until his hands ached. Freshers with good handwriting were a prized commodity, often recruited to transcribe notes for lectures the seniors had missed. It was clear that attending classes was considered anathema for most of them.

Bala, the ever-mischievous imp, recounted how, when a second-year student asked him to copy some notes, he deliberately made numerous errors in the mathematics sections to create problems for the senior. With evident satisfaction in his voice and expression, he concluded, 'He will never ask another fresher to copy notes for him.'

Fortunately, I did not face such issues much after the first couple of weeks, mainly because my handwriting was only slightly better than that of a well-educated chimp.

Returning to the mess and the food served (if it could be called that), we frequently encountered dirty and stained utensils. The plates were seldom rinsed or washed properly and the water glasses were coated in a thick layer of grease, a result of being rinsed in plain water to save on soap.

> *Who cares for fish, eggs, or meat,*
> *To find any in the gravy is a feat,*
> *In the moment's hungry heat,*
> *I would eat anything while in my seat.*

Chorus: *Beautiful dish, beautiful dish.*

We soon realized that the issue with our mess was the lack of student control over the food and the daily operations. The hostel warden, usually responsible for the first-year mess known as the Co-operative Mess, had other significant teaching and research responsibilities, leaving little time to manage the mess' expenses and operations.

In contrast, some other messes, like the 'Munna Mess' at Vishvesvaraya hostel run by the fourth-year Mining and Chemical engineering students, served excellent food. It accommodated about 80 students and offered a variety of delicious dishes served on proper china with shining forks and spoons.

Munna, despite his name meaning 'young boy' in Hindi, was anything but that. In his late 40s, he was built like an ox, with an enormous, rotund stomach, a straggly beard and a generally unkempt appearance. Despite his appearance, Munna was extremely courteous and took great care of the mess members. Legend claimed that Munna was homosexual, and some envious individuals who did not have access to this exclusive mess suggested this explained his keen interest in the students' welfare. I had numerous opportunities to eat there, as the *Graffiti* gang often invited me to join them for lunch or dinner.

Aside from the Munna Mess, I dined at several other messes with my seniors. Balamurali, another member of the *Graffiti* gang with a low profile, was part of the Makku Mess where they served authentic Tamilian food with generous portions of curd, sambar and rasam—staples for most Tamilians. The food was delicious, prepared in true Tamilian style with coconut and fried yams. The abundance of curd was crucial to balance the spices typical of Tamil cooking.

One evening, I informed the Makku brigade in Raj

Hostel about our mess situation, and we all agreed that something drastic had to be done about the food quality. Despite numerous complaints to the warden, food quality remained poor, and the plates only seemed to get dirtier after each meal. Frustrated, about 15 of us decided to take matters into our own hands. The next morning, we approached the hostel warden, requesting permission to leave the Co-operative Mess and join a mess of our choice.

As news of our protest about the siege at the warden's office spread, dozens of other freshers joined us, having also reached their breaking point. Our numerous complaints about the unappetizing food and filthy utensils had yielded no results, leading some to suspect that the warden might be profiting from the mess, preferring to keep the food quality low to avoid losing any potential profits.

The Maharaj of the Raj mess,
He made lousy food much less,
Having sold all the green vegetables,
Bought with our dough for edibles,
While we played the games of chess.

Despite our pleas and heartfelt entreaties, the warden flatly refused our request. He cited hostel rules as the reason for his refusal, suggesting that our difficulties with the food were due to our inability to adjust to the North Indian cuisine as South Indians. His tone implied that we needed to 'co-operate'.

In response, we decided to remain officially part of the mess but implement a daily 'mess-off'. This meant we would not partake in meals and would only be charged a nominal amount for mess maintenance. The mess Maharaj had to be notified at least one day in advance, and the 'mess-off' needed to be documented in the mess register.

What followed was a heated discussion with the warden. Despite us being students and him being a professor, we stood our ground. Eventually, he agreed to consider our request, and those who wished to leave the Co-operative Mess were asked to submit their names and room numbers to his office peon.

'Well, it seems we got our point across,' the tall Sundar remarked as we retreated to our rooms.

'But what if he tries to create problems for those who submit their names?' asked the shorter Sundar, ever the cautious one.

This question dampened the upbeat mood, and we all worried about the possibility of trouble.

'Well,' I pondered aloud after working on my brain cells for most of the 22 seconds, 'he is a professor in the Mechanical department, and there are no Mech students in this hostel; so I suppose we're safe. What do you think?'

'I think Raja has a point,' Bhoops said, nodding sagely before lapsing back into his usual stony silence.

As we approached the centre of the hostel, heading towards the exit, we saw Das and Ramulu perched on the fountain's balustrade. Walking up to them, I said, 'Hi, what brings you guys here?' before sitting down beside them. The other guys who had come with me stood in front of us, as if at attention.

Das and Ramulu exchanged a glance and laughed aloud. 'Relax, guys, no ragging tensions here,' Das reassured them. 'What were you doing at the wardy's office? We saw a big crowd there.'

Wardy—Handy Guide to IT Lingo

Then, turning to me, he continued, 'Not been up to something funny, eh, Raja?'

'Nothing of the sort, Das,' I replied. 'We just tried to talk him into letting us leave this lousy mess.'

'The same problem occurs every year. These wardys never learn,' Ramulu said, shaking his head like a wise sage who had resigned to the futility of his efforts. It was as if he were failing, yet again, to warn his disciple of the perilous effects of watching Padma Khanna perform a particularly raunchy cabaret for Premnath—thereby breaking his silence, which rarely lasted more than seven minutes during his waking hours.

This reference is a nod to one of Irving Wallace's classics—*The Seven Minutes*. For those curious about why Ramulu could maintain silence for exactly seven minutes, they might find the answer within this path-breaking book.

'What happened? Did he agree?' Ramulu asked.

'I'm not sure,' I admitted. 'He asked us to leave the names and room numbers of those who want to leave the mess. He mentioned he'd sleep on the problem.'

'Sir, by the way,' the tall Sundar interjected in the wary manner of a deer asking for a favour from a hungry lion, 'is there any chance that the warden might cause problems when he gets the names of the freshers who want to leave the mess?'

'No, none at all,' Ramulu replied confidently. 'He can't do a thing. This happens every year. I'm sure the wardys are used to their moneymaking side business lasting for only a month or two. But it's probably enough for a holiday for two in Goa, right, Das?'

'Yeah, I am sure. I won't mind some dough right now. Don't have enough for a fag even,' Das replied in all seriousness.

Fag—Handy Guide to IT Lingo

'I'd never mind some dough, old boy. After all, dough is dear,' I declared, attempting to imitate Julie Andrews in *The Sound of Music*—a feat somewhat hindered by my masculine voice and a woeful lack of musical talent.

'Raja,' Das began, finally coming to the job at hand. He had to have come to me with some work in mind— after all, not even the prospect of meeting Madonna in the flesh (even in flesh, only in flesh, and in nothing else but flesh) would budge him from his room while he was working on a *Graffiti* project. 'You and Ramulu will do some fundraising for *Graffiti* tomorrow. Hit up the main restaurants in Lanka and Gadowlia, and beg, borrow or steal from the managers.'

'No problems, Das, CID,' I replied.

'CID? What is that?' Ramulu demanded.

'Consider it done.'

'Ha! A new one. Fresh from a fresher, ha ha! This bugger has learnt the IT way fast—already coming up with new acronyms!' Ramulu laughed.

The next morning, as I came down to the mess for breakfast, I saw the guys engaged in earnest conversation in small groups of three or four. I was as usual, in a truculent mood—the early morning air never did agree with me. It's probably why my grandmother, with whom I lived during my school days in Calcutta, called me the 'midnight ghost'. In my usual morning groggy self, I yelled for Chhotu to bring my coffee.

'What Chhotu!' Achintya, sitting beside me, demanded angrily. 'Thanks to you and your makku friends' antics yesterday evening, the wardy has decided to shut down the mess until further notice. Look at the notice out there,' he said, pointing a long finger at a piece of paper stuck on the door leading to the backyard.

I got up, disbelief written across my face, feeling dismayed and robbed, as though some cruel higher power had deprived a law-abiding citizen of their right to morning coffee and sustenance. I made my way to the door.

It was there all right; a rectangular yellow piece of paper, evidently torn hurriedly from a letter pad judging by the irregular tear on the left, with the following inscription on it:

> *It is hereby stated that the Co-operative Mess is closed till further notice.*
>
> *The advances given by the students may be collected from the warden's office between 4 p.m.–6 p.m. today.*

The notice from the Warden of Rajputana mess was written in longhand with straggling characters, and it seemed like the warden had written it himself.

Sundar, the tall one, standing beside me, studied the notice with great interest.

'What about breakfast? I can't think straight without coffee and something in my stomach,' I complained.

'Tell me about it. I can't even shit without a cup of coffee,' Sundar replied.

Caught between anger and bewilderment, we left the mess together. Popli, who had just read the notice and was unhappy, approached me from behind and exclaimed, 'Hoy! Hey, Raja! What's with the mess trouble yesterday? It is closed now, thanks to you guys. What do we do about food? You guys are nuts.'

'Relax, Popli,' I replied, 'there are plenty of messes around. You can always join one of them. And stop looking like a puppy denied a bone. Something will work out soon. Just relax, old boy.'

'But how will they take us on such short notice? You're fine—you can always eat with the fourth-year students. But what about me? I'm starving.'

'You generally are, Popli. It's not unusual. Anyway, it is your problem, old boy,' I said and walked off.

'But he's right, Raja,' Sundar said thoughtfully as he walked beside me. 'We need an alternative and fast. We can't last too long on empty stomachs.'

I spotted Mr Gupta, my PhD neighbour, walking towards his mess on the other side of the lobby. A flash of inspiration struck me, and I hailed him with sudden gusto.

'Mr Gupta! Mr Gupta!'

I reached him quickly and explained, 'We would like to join you for breakfast—my friend and I here—our mess is closed.'

'Your mess is closed? Why?' he asked.

I told him the whole story and sought his advice on what we should do next.

'You'd better join our mess for now. The food's not the best, but at least it's in this hostel, and the Maharaj makes a decent dal and a better-than-decent aloo fry.'

Following his wise advice, Sundar and I joined the

MTech mess that morning, and we never regretted it throughout the entire first year.

The mess imbroglio ended that morning. The Co-operative Mess never reopened in the hostel that year, and most of my batchmates joined their own messes. As the cliché goes, they ate happily ever after—at least for the first nine or ten months.

And yes, I did manage to go for the fundraising expedition that morning with Ramulu... But well, that, as they say, is another story.

13

Popli Kyon?

I have spent considerable time recounting the escapades of the first-year Makku gang and Ranjit. However, I have not given enough attention to my own engineering batch of remarkable individuals. This is partly because the batch was split across three different hostels, with the three ladies in our cohort housed in the women's hostel a couple of miles away. As a result, we rarely had the chance to meet except during our infrequent classroom sessions. Despite this, we managed to sail through four wonderful years together, finding harmony amidst our differences.

If there was one standout person in our batch of 30 during the first 80 days, it was probably Rajinder Singh Popli. While I was well known within a particular group, and Ranjit and Chaaku were popular among others, Popli was the one person who embodied our engineering batch—he was our mascot, capable of exhibiting 30 different traits in his massive body.

Physically, Popli was an impressive sight, just shy of six feet tall, with broad shoulders and massive, Charlton Heston-like forearms. However, beneath this Herculean physique lay a carefully curated façade of irreverence and buffoonery, as if his burly frame needed a joker-like spirit to remain relevant in a group of earnest boys. It didn't take us long to figure out that it was merely an act. Behind his vacuous-looking face, Popli concealed a razor-sharp mind capable of logical and analytical thought, which, combined with his exceptional capacity for arduous work, made him an outstanding student.

He often idled around the hostel entrance in the mornings, greeting everyone as they hurriedly rushed through their daily tasks before heading to class. Only at the last moment would he realize he hadn't brushed his teeth. Then, with a burst of energy that could rival a wild hound chasing an intriguing scent, he would rush to complete his chores and join the rest of the freshers on their journey to the classroom.

What set Popli apart, though, was his astonishing lack of shame. When any senior playfully asked him to undress, he complied without hesitation. Unlike most of us who would try to stall and avoid performing demeaning acts, Popli fearlessly carried out their requests. Even seasoned seniors like Das acknowledged that Popli was an utterly unique specimen, unparalleled in his immodesty, irreverence and sheer pig-headedness.

Popli was not only academically talented but also an exceptional athlete with remarkable stamina, strength and decent ball skills. He played football for the college as a centre-back. However, what truly made him stand out was his unflagging *joie de vivre*. He had an intense desire to live life to the fullest and taught me how to let my hair down and savour the beauty of life, embracing its unpredictability and cherishing every moment. It was a valuable lesson that only someone with an abundance of self-confidence, contentment in his being, and courage in his thoughts and actions could impart.

Popli also had a deep passion for singing, but unfortunately, his voice resembled a combination of a ship's foghorn approaching a crowded harbour and the grating sound of a speeding train passing over a rickety bridge. Adding to our woes, his repertoire of songs was limited to a few lines of a Hindi number and a Bruce Springsteen classic, which he insisted on singing alternately whenever the mood struck him—which was, unfortunately, quite frequent.

The English number always started with a booming 'Born', as deep and resonant as rolling thunder. The next word, 'in', would be rendered in a piercing falsetto, akin to the chaotic charm of a wounded dog in a skirmish with a much larger opponent. By the time he reached 'the USA', all semblance of musical decorum would be abandoned in favour of maximum volume, culminating in a slow crescendo with a boisterous sound at the instant of the 's'. The ensuing lines were sung in a faint, sotto voce, so low that one had to strain their ears to hear them, which, given the quality of his voice, did not particularly inspire enthusiasm among his listeners.

The Hindi song was an old Bollywood number, passionately sung as if it were a lament that the sky is home to a million stars, yet he could not find even one when required. The performance started with dramatic intensity but rapidly devolved into something resembling a poetry recital at a metal concert, complete with pregnant pauses and heavy breathing to emphasize the supposed pathos. For those familiar with Hindi music, the song

Popli used to butcher was 'Lakhon Tare Aasman Mein, Ek Magar Dhundhe Na Mila'.

On these disconcerting (pun intended!) occasions, he would aimlessly patrol the hostel lobby, singing the same lines repeatedly, with intermittent cries of 'Shut up, Popli' emanating from behind closed doors. Of course, given his thick skin—which would have given a particularly obdurate rhinoceros a rapid run for its horns—the reprimands from exasperated licentiates had the same effect on him as rainwater on the wings of a cavorting duck.

Popli's room was located on the ground floor near one corner of the hostel. A narrow corridor led from this area to the Warden's quarters, where Dr Kumar resided in opulent splendour with his family. His wife, an overbearing woman in her 40s, believed she was God's gift to humanity, and their two teenage daughters, thin and severe-looking, firmly believed that their beauty could launch a thousand ships.

The toilets were situated in the middle portion of the lobby, and to reach them, Popli had to pass about 20 rooms and the entrance to the aforementioned corridor. Every morning, he would undertake this journey with clockwork precision for his morning ablutions, wearing nothing but a straw-coloured towel with a black border draped around his shoulders, a pair of blue Hawaii slippers, a toothbrush lodged in the corner of his mouth and a bucket containing soap and shampoo—and nothing else. Yes, nothing else.

Some of the more naive freshers, still enduring the pangs of homesickness, were mercilessly ragged by Popli, who forced them to salute his dong, which he grandiosely referred to as 'Guruji', as he strolled past their rooms. I watched these occurrences with a hint of abstract interest and amusement, usually with Ranjit standing beside me, from the first-floor balcony. While watching a naked man parade around was not my preferred morning activity, it could take some very comical turns, as happened a day or two into our *sine die* (see Chapter 17) vacation.

One fine morning, as Popli carried on with his usual routine of displaying his generously endowed attributes, the Warden's wife and their daughters entered our lobby, presumably intending to go to the Warden's office, which was located near the other corner of the hostel. Upon seeing Popli's resplendent nudity, highlighted by a blue towel that broke the monotony of his usual straw-coloured one, the wife reacted in a series of actions, which can best be described in chronological order:

1. She widened her eyes in horror.
2. She then staggered back a couple of paces, as if she were punch-drunk.
3. She dramatically raised her clenched fist to her gaping mouth.
4. She then attempted to usher her daughters out of the corridor to shield them from the improper and untimely sight of a naked man strutting about the lobby.

The daughters, though, made of sterner stuff, widened their eyes, albeit lasciviously, and deftly evaded their mother's outstretched arms, which were vainly trying to guide them inside the corridor. They managed to get a full view of the incredulous sight before them. It was somewhat challenging for the mother to steer her daughters away from the lobby and back to the confines of their residence. The daughters cast one last longing look towards Popli before disappearing into the darkness beyond.

Throughout this spectacle, Popli stood with his hands on his hips, Hawaii slippers adorning his outstretched legs, wearing a gentle and mystified smile on his countenance as if failing to comprehend the reasons for the outrageous reactions of the individuals described earlier.

Ranjit and I could not contain our laughter as we watched this episode unfold from the first-floor balcony. We decided to go downstairs to talk to Popli and advise him to dress properly while heading for his bath. As we made our way down the stairs, Popli spotted us and plaintively cried, 'Hoy!'—as I had previously mentioned, Popli always began a sentence with 'Hoy'—'Hey, guys! Did you see what just happened?'

Before waiting for an answer, he continued in the same melancholy tone, 'You would think they had never seen a naked man before! They reacted as if they had just seen a UFO or something.'

With that statement, which left Ranjit and me speechless, he proceeded, shaking his head as if exasperated by the illogical actions performed by the women, towards the toilets.

A few days later, on a splendid evening after a spell of thunder and rain, Popli visited my room, where Ranjit, Chaaku and I were engrossed in casual conversation. Our discussions usually revolved around weighty topics such as the greatest footballers ever (on one occasion, we spent the entire night devising the Dream 11), the chances of India winning the upcoming cricket World Cup, and most crucially, whether or not we should attend classes the next day.

Invariably, we would decide to attend classes the next day by the time we parted ways for the night. The next morning, Ranjit and I would awaken and begin our daily routines. Then, we would try to wake Chaaku, which proved to be about as challenging as rousing a slumbering elephant that had just consumed several litres of pure alcohol. After 15 minutes of knocking on his bolted door and offering a barrage of curses to the unresponsive Chaaku, we would abandon our futile endeavour and decide against attending classes. In truth, we were not particularly keen on attending classes in the first place!

As Popli approached us with his peculiar shuffling gait—the one he usually adopted when he felt particularly intelligent—I greeted him with, 'What ho, Popli?'

'Yaar, I am feeling disgusted, demented, upbeat, ebullient, reckless, morose and effulgent,' he announced. 'Come, let's go for a walk, and I shall shake off my invigorated, debilitated, enervated and bored self.'

With an exasperated sigh, Chaaku demanded, 'Popli, please tell me in plain Hindi what's wrong with you.'

'Yaar, nothing. I was mugging up Norman Lewis's *Word Power Made Easy* and decided to test what I had learnt today on you guys. You think my words are getting better and better, eh?'

Chaaku, more skilled at containing his laughter than Ranjit or me, got up and put a kindly arm around Popli's shoulder, asking him in a syrupy voice, 'Are you feeling fine? You did not get wet in the rain, I hope. These preseason showers can be particularly dangerous to one's well-being, leaving them with a terrible fever and unknown treacherous diseases that make them feel miserable. Let us go for a hot cup of tea.'

'Tea,' he continued, ignoring Popli's frantic attempts to interject, 'is an excellent antidote to the clammy feeling one gets after drenching oneself inadvertently in a thunder shower.'

By this time, Ranjit and I had regained our composure after the stomach-aching laughter and followed Chaaku and Popli to DG Corner, our friendly neighbourhood teashop, the institute's answer to Pop Tate.

Feeling a second wind, Popli asked Chaaku, 'Abe yaar, how do you speak English so well? I want to learn new words, and Saurabh told me the only way to improve my English is by using them.'

Chaaku, with a sigh typically reserved for children with particularly poor comprehension skills, explained in a gentle tone, 'Popli, you are supposed to use the right word at the right time. If you are feeling morose, it means that you are unhappy. If you feel ebullient— although ebullient is not the right term to use in these circumstances— it means you are elated. How can you use these two words at the same time?'

Popli nodded as if comprehending completely, only to spoil it all a minute later by exclaiming, 'Hoy, there goes the sexy, beautiful, perilous, nugatory, latest female I told you about yesterday!' He pointed towards a well-endowed young lady walking with a deliberate, duck-tailed motion to attract attention just ahead of us.

Chaaku let out another world-weary sigh, shaking

his head in the manner one does for individuals who persistently make the same mistakes despite extensive counselling. He said, 'Popli, please tell me plainly, in Hindi, what's wrong with you.'

Popli declared, 'I am going after her. It would be interesting to find out where she lives. I can even *patao* her mother and get something to eat.'

Patao—Handy Guide to IT Lingo

We watched in wonder, trying to comprehend how this esoteric specimen had managed to crack the JEE, considered the exclusive privilege of the highly intelligent, as Popli trotted off after the female he had so uniquely described.

He caught up with the lady and exchanged a few words. She laughed at something funny he must have uttered (Beauty × brains = constant works like clockwork, we decided) and then they walked away from together.

Later that evening, we spotted him back at the dinner table and Chaaku asked, 'Where did you suddenly disappear to?'

'Freak-out female, yaar,' Popli declared. 'What a cook!'

Freak-out—Handy Guide to IT Lingo

I looked at him blankly and asked, 'Did you follow her for a date or dinner?'

'I was feeling hungry after I finishing the first chapter of the *Word Power* book, so I thought I could get some good food for free at her place.'

'Did you fix up a date with her or not?' I inquired.

'What for? I will have to spend for both of us then.

There is more pleasure in dining alone—I can eat a lot more for the same amount,' Popli explained.

Staggered by this response, I collapsed on to my chair and beckoned the mess boy for my evening nourishment, feeling disoriented.

As you will see shortly, it did not take me too long to realize that there are better ways to interact with girls than to leverage their culinary skills for a free meal!

Whew!

14

Achintya and His
100-Metre Dash

If Popli was the beloved mascot of our batch, Achintya Sinha was the furthest from being one. Sinha was a unique character, even in appearance.

Towering well above six feet, he had a lean, scraggy build and a fair complexion, with a face that could be termed handsome where it not for a rather weak chin. His noticeable stoop gave him an air of perpetual introspection, and his eating habits bordered on eccentric. Occasionally, he would go off food, not to lose weight—he never had much to lose, to begin with—but simply because he didn't feel like eating. At such times, his appearance would become even more gaunt and ghost-like.

Achintya had a penchant for laying wagers, once even abstaining from talking for an entire day in pursuit of a few rupees. Although some might not consider this a significant achievement, anyone who knew Achintya would agree that it was a feat worth celebrating, ranking alongside Lindbergh's crossing of the Atlantic.

His vocabulary of expletives was intriguing—not the typical ones referencing immoral relationships between family members. They involved various Hindi names for commonplace vegetables and assorted culinary preparations.

His room was a few doors down from Popli's on the ground floor, leading to amusing situations throughout our first year due to their drastically different sleeping patterns. Achintya passionately believed in the adage, 'Early to bed, early to rise, makes a man healthy, wealthy and wise.' The problems arose when Achintya attempted to awaken Vicky, whose room was in the lobby perpendicular to his, a few yards away. He would persistently scream the following lines (sometimes interspersed with more 'abes') until he got a response from the just-awakened Vicky:

1. 'Abe'
2. 'Khotte'
3. 'Vickeeee'
4. 'Abe'
5. 'Khotte'
6. 'Baingan ke bharte (A spicy dish made from roasted eggplants)'
7. 'Get up'
8. 'Abe'
9. 'Paanch baj gaya (It's now five o'clock!)'

Abe, Khotte—Handy Guide to IT lingo

Vicky would eventually wake up due to Achintya's boisterous cries. His screams would often be joined by rhyming protests from Popli, who had barely fallen asleep a couple of hours earlier, yelling at Achintya to shut up.

A word about Achintya's voice. Legend has it that the doctors had to slap the newborn Achintya rather harshly to coax his first cry. The resulting wail was a good exercise for his vocal cords, which became remarkably well-developed. We jokingly referred to him as 'mic-ka-lal'—a nod to his ability to address crowds without needing amplification.

I once quipped that if he ever became a politician (as he had the prerequisite of demonstrating a beautifully vacuous look that concealed his razor-sharp brain), he could save money for his party by not requiring a microphone to address rallies. His mental acuity was a bit like Popli's—sharp but esoteric, and we often wondered who would win a chess competition between them, provided they could master the basic moves. I guessed it would end in a stalemate, as they would perpetually ponder their next moves without actually making one.

Achintya, however, was extremely diligent in attending classes and had developed a foolproof technique for passing exams: 'If you can't understand something, memorize it.'

After a few instances of being woken up by Achintya's foghorn-like voice, Popli asked the more 'sensible' folks among us to talk to him and help resolve the issue. So, one evening, Chaaku and Ranjit went to Achintya's room one evening for an intervention. I had been sitting with Popli in his room and strolled in after them.

After exchanging pleasantries, they requested Achintya to kindly refrain from waking up Vicky early or, if he had to, walk those 50 yards or so and wake him up without waking up the entire lobby. This, Chaaku argued in his smooth and personable voice, would create a better living environment for all of us in the morning and require less effort on Achintya's part.

'But I want to wake up all the boys. It is a good habit

to wake up early. My kindergarten teacher taught me that early to bed, early to rise, makes a man healthy, wealthy and wise,' responded the obdurate Achintya.

'Achintya, waking up early might be good for you, but everyone has their own biological clocks. Some people, like Popli here, prefer to sleep late and wake up late. The "early to bed" philosophy made sense in times without electricity when people relied on sunlight but, now, not so much,' the logical Chaaku argued.

'But I am doing a good deed by waking up Popli, and I was thinking of waking up the entire class at five in the morning starting tomorrow. You all will thank me in six months for leading you towards a healthier lifestyle.'

'Spare us, Achintya. We prefer the "late to bed" philosophy, so please keep the early morning stuff to yourself. No more early morning screams, all right? We need a good night's sleep to face ragging and lectures with stout hearts.'

With that, we left Achintya's room.

A roar erupted from the ground floor the next morning, jolting me awake. I checked my bedside clock and realized it was exactly five. Peering out, I discovered that Achintya, Vicky and Arun—the trio of early morning enthusiasts—were bellowing at the top of their lungs:

'Early to bed, early to rise,
Makes the first Chem batch
Healthy, wealthy and wise.'

When they noticed an angry audience on the ground and first floors—with Ranjit, Mr Gupta and others on the balcony—they laughed jeeringly, as if they had achieved their life's greatest desire, and retreated to their rooms.

As a parting shot, Achintya exclaimed, 'I told you it feels good to wake up early.'

Ranjit and I exchanged glances with consternation. Suddenly, Ranjit asked, 'Where's Chaaku? Don't tell me he slept through all that commotion.'

We looked at Chaaku's room, which was shut tight, realizing that he had, incredibly enough, slept through all the noise.

That evening, we called a meeting of all like-minded classmates frustrated by the early morning disruptions. Ragging fever among the seniors had subsided after four weeks of unrelenting action, leaving us mostly at peace. However, we were still required to wear full sleeves, trousers and leather shoes to distinguish ourselves as first-year students.

The meeting was attended by Popli, Chaaku, Ranjit, Major (Amit Sharma), Vikas, and a couple of other like-minded individuals. We all had one thing in common—a grievance against being awakened before 8 a.m. The incident with Achintya highlighted the lengths to which the other group, promoting early awakening, was willing to go to prove their point. After careful deliberation, we devised a plan and resolved to put it into action that very night.

We went out to watch a movie and returned to the hostel around midnight, when the 'early-to-bed club' rooms were already dark. Earlier in the day, we had secured an electric heater from Funny—who wholeheartedly supported our effort to curb early morning activities that spoiled the IT culture—and a high-powered amplifier and speakers from Steven, a fourth-year guitar player and another sensible member of the 'late-to-bed club'. We believed that if executed correctly, our plan would deter such misguided activities and prevent this detrimental epidemic from spreading to other lobbies and hostels.

Gathering in Popli's room, we put on a kettle to brew some coffee and brought out snacks we had purchased earlier. Ranjit had an impressive collection of rock cassettes, and we started by playing Dire Straits at maximum volume. 'Sultans of Swing' reverberated through the hostel, attracting other night owls to Popli's room like moths to a flame. Within minutes, a sizable crowd had gathered, dancing and screaming at the top of their lungs.

The impact was immediate—Achintya, Vicky, Arun and a few others who had enthusiastically participated in the early morning revelry appeared, looking dishevelled and bewildered. When Ranjit noticed them, he turned off the music and we chanted in unison:

Early to bed, early to rise,
Makes the first Chem
Unhealthy, poor
And definitely not wise.

This was met with raucous laughter from all the night owls, with pointed fingers directed at the other cabal.

We continued:

Late to bed,
Late to rise,
Ensures first Chem
Along life.
Late to bed,
Late to rise,

Ensures first Chem of
No classes and no lectures.
Late to bed,
Late to rise,
Makes first Chem
Fit, fundu and fabulous.

Fundu—Handy Guide to IT Lingo

Ranjit then played Tull's 'Aqualung', and we all chanted along to the song:

Sleeping well till the late morning,
Dreaming of sexy girls to our hearts' content,
We first Chem.

Even Popli, shaking off the lethargy of singing only two songs for several years, sang with gusto, and for once, we did not mind that he sang out of tune, as his voice sounded melodious to our thrilled ears.

The 'early morning club' slunk away without a word—they had received the message loud and clear. Our batch endured no more early morning disturbances for the next four years.

Achintya's predicament that night became a source of much amusement in the institute, and he gained popularity among the seniors, who often took him to their rooms for fun. People who adhered strictly to proverbs were rare in IT, and the students were genuinely intrigued by Achintya's unwavering commitment to that particular adage. 'Far-out' was one phrase that often escaped their lips when hearing about Achintya's early morning activities.

Far-out—Handy Guide to IT Lingo

Once, the third-year Chemical batch intercepted him on his way back from classes and brought him to Rajeev's room. Rajeev, a decent and serious individual, soon put Achintya at ease. As they chatted amicably, strange noises emanated from the adjacent room—heavy banging on the wall with a wooden object.

Curious, Achintya asked Rajeev about the noises.

'Mangotra must have had one of his attacks, I fear,' replied Rajeev.

'Attacks? What attacks?' inquired Achintya.

'He suffers from a type of schizophrenia. Sometimes, during an episode, he starts banging whatever he can lay his hands upon. I think he is presently slamming the chair against the wall.'

'Is he dangerous?'

'Not always, but he can be quite unpredictable. The other day, we were ragging someone when Mangotra suddenly had one of his attacks. He went after the hapless fresher and slapped him resoundingly. If we had not restrained him and locked him in his room, he might have caused serious harm. His episodes seem to grant him remarkable strength.'

'Oh my! He should be kept under lock and key. What is he doing here?'

'He is undergoing treatment, and the doctors believe he'll be fully cured within the next few months.'

'Still, it's dangerous to have him around.'

At that moment, Mangotra appeared at Rajeev's door, fixing Achintya with an intense gaze. Mangotra had a penetrating pair of eyes that seemed to see through lead and into the depths of one's thoughts. Slowly, he walked toward a terrified Achintya, picked up a thick book from the table, and brought it down with all his might on the wooden table next to Achintya's chair. The complete procedure was made with those mesmeric eyes fixed on Achintya in an unrelenting stare. He gave one last look, abruptly turned his heels and walked towards his room.

Rajeev exclaimed, 'My God, it seems the disease is upon him again. Achintya, you just wait here. I will call Vinay and a few others for safety, as we shall be powerless when he is in this mood. He becomes strong as a bull, you know.'

Rajeev hurried out of the room, closing the door from the outside, while Achintya waited in mortal terror hearing the thud-thud from the next room. As abruptly as they had begun, the sounds stopped, leaving behind an eerie silence. A couple of extremely silent minutes later, Mangotra opened the door to Rajeev's room, walked in again, then closed and bolted the door behind him. He stood against the door and fixed Achintya with his unblinking gaze.

Slowly, he walked towards Achintya, who was cringing in the chair, and picked up the chair recently vacated by Rajeev. He gave the chair one vacuous look, picked it up and brought it down with a resounding crash on to the cement floor.

Mangotra stared at Achintya with a sickly smile and then lifted his arms to the ceiling, flexing his muscles. He picked up the chair again and hefted it in his powerful arms, as if testing its strength. Giving Achintya a long piercing stare, he brought down the chair with all his strength on the floor, this time near Achintya's feet.

Achintya, losing the last vestige of self-control and strength, sprung from his chair, opened the door and ran out of the room screaming at the top of his voice. 'Help, he is going to kill me, help!'

Ranjit, Chaaku and I, with some third-year Chemical seniors, burst into laughter as our plan had worked like a charm.

Tag two for the 'late to bed' gang!

That evening, we learnt from our batchmates that Achintya had run into the hostel at top speed, screaming incoherently. He was terrified for the next couple of hours. When asked about the reason for his panic, he informed them, with horror evident on his clean-shaven face, that a mad third-year student had tried to kill him, and he had saved himself through sheer running speed.

The prank left such an impression on Achintya that he avoided Mangotra for the next few semesters, despite our reassurances that it was all harmless fun. Only after Mangotra personally visited his room a few months later and apologized did Achintya finally believe in his sanity.

15

The Raj of Rajputana

Rajputana Hostel was one of the prettier hostels on campus and home to students from three different engineering disciplines—Metallurgical Engineering, with several members from the Makku gang; Civil Engineering, with an eccentric assortment of primarily low-profile students; and my eclectic batch of budding Chemical Engineers.

As one entered the hostel from the main gate, the ground-floor lobby on the left was the domain of Metallurgical Engineering students, and the remaining section housed Chemical Engineering students. The first floor comprised about 10 rooms allocated to Chemical Engineering students and approximately 30 rooms for Civil Engineering, with the rest occupied by postgraduate students, like my neighbour AKG. With around a hundred first-year students, Rajputana was among the larger hostels in terms of freshers' allocation.

It is now time to turn our attention to some of the unique individuals from the Civil Engineering department, starting with Shashank.

While most freshers arrived at the institute wearing trousers or jeans with a shirt or T-shirt and closed-toe shoes, Shashank walked into the campus wearing a pair of shorts. He joined us a couple of weeks after classes had begun, by which time most of us had had our fill of ragging and it did not make us as nervous as it had when we first arrived.

Shashank's shorts, draped over his corpulent figure, were so distinctive that they deserve further description. His Bermudas were rather long, reaching his knees, with his thick, fair and hairless legs sticking out obscenely from underneath the loose cloth. The shorts were toned in two distinct colours—the right side was a dirty grey—dull and melancholy, while the left side was a bright, vibrant blood red. Topping off this ensemble was a black round-neck T-shirt a couple of sizes too big, making his flab appear even more unsightly.

He stood a little under five feet in height and preferred casual loafers, which made him appear even shorter. His waist size must have been close to five feet as well, making him look like an overblown balloon.

Shashank had a fair, ruddy complexion, with a beard on his face that defied the natural rules set by nature. It grew in uneven patches all over his cheeks, jawline, behind his ears, and even on his neck, but strangely not on his rounded chin. I once advised him in the second year to shave against the grain—i.e., with the razor blades facing upwards—and he diligently followed this technique until the third year. He later complained that his beard growth had not improved, and only the thin strands looked thicker now. I had to remind him that different people have different beard growth patterns.

Last I knew, he still shaves upwards and hopes his beard

shall rectify itself and follow established norms of growth.

✳

Back to his arrival. Shashank came to the hostel directly from the railway station, dragging a battered suitcase. He addressed the first person he saw in his unique manner, 'Hey, old man, could you direct me to the bloody warden's office? I bloody well intend to take a bloody room before the bloody hot day gets even hotter.'

Chaaku and I were sitting on the balustrade when Shashank entered, and we exchanged looks of surprise, raised our eyebrows, and shook our heads in resignation, thinking, *Well, this poor guy is in for it now.*

Unbeknownst to him, Shashank had addressed a third-year student, whose eyebrows went up in proportion to the monologue's progression.

'What is your name?' the senior demanded.

'Bloody hell! Shashank, dear chap. I presume you are staying in this bloody hostel. You see, I need help to find the blasted Warden's office.'

Ignoring Shashank's not-so-unreasonable request, the senior demanded, 'You are from which place?'

'Delhi, old boy. And bloody hell—'

Rudely interrupting Shashank's next request, the senior demanded, 'Which school are you from?'

'Hey man, I am just a low-profile guy from Modern School, New Delhi.'

This time I could almost imagine the senior's eyebrows shooting off his forehead in shock at the answer.

'What? Come again!' the senior demanded, aghast and quite unable to believe that Shashank had indeed uttered those words so flippantly.

'What's the problem, old chap? You don't know where the office is? No reason to get upset. I shall find it myself.'

With that, Shashank hefted his luggage and lumbered towards the stairs. By the time the senior had recovered from the conversation, Shashank had made his ponderous way to the lobby and located the office.

He emerged from the office a few minutes later with the keys to his room, ambling at his tortoise-like pace. As he passed by, the senior he had previously sought assistance from called out, 'Hey, fresher! Hey, Shashank!'

But by then, Shashank was already well on his way to his destination, completely oblivious to the world and all the assorted seniors in it.

'Hey, old chap, the office is there. I managed to find it all right. And the warden seems to be a nice enough fellow. It didn't take him a minute to fill up the requisite stuff and find the keys.'

The senior responded angrily, 'Nobody taught you to talk properly to seniors, fresher? You are supposed to talk with respect.'

'Well, I thought I did pretty well here. I spoke with a friendly enough tone and did not say anything wrong or irreverent to anyone assembled here.'

'You go up to your room and wear proper attire. Come down immediately after you freshen up. Looks like we have to teach you some fundamentals of life here. And remember, a senior is always right. Come over to the teashop outside the hostel in 15 minutes.'

Shashank came down a short while later, wearing a flaming red T-shirt with a large eagle and 'U.S.A.' printed in deep brown, paired with dark blue jeans. On reaching the hostel entrance, he saw the senior who had talked to him sitting at DG Corner, drinking tea. With a friendly wave, he walked up to the assembled caucus.

'Hello, there,' he wished on approaching them.

'Look fatso,' one of the seniors began, 'you are a fresher here, and for the next three months or so—until the end of the ragging period on freshers' night—you are supposed to follow certain rules and regulations. These include wearing only formals, with the shirt sleeves rolled down, no belt, and proper brown or black leather shoes. You are expected to wish all seniors with deference and adhere to the dos and don'ts of IT life for freshers.'

'I have a small problem,' Shashank said. 'I do not own any formal trousers or leather shoes.'

'You better get them pronto, or the consequences shall not be pleasant. We excused your impertinent behaviour earlier as you were unaware of the rules, but no excuses now. Borrow something—though I doubt if anybody would have a size fitting yours—or buy some, get them from home, whatever. Tomorrow, I shall come back, and if I see you in anything obscene, God save you.'

The last statement was made in sotto voce to terrify and throw a chill in Shashank's heart, and one could progressively visualize the effect of the monologue on Shashank. The friendly face had lost its inquiring and amiable look, replaced by a worried expression.

'And, by the way, why are you taking admission now? It's more than three weeks since the first day of classes.'

'Well, I had previously thought I would check out the colleges in Delhi where I got admission too, to avoid moving out from home. Then my parents suggested I should check out BIT too.'

'"Check out BIT too?" What impertinence! You will pay for such behaviour. "Check out" the finest engineering college in the country! Do you realize you are insulting the institute, the alumni and all the seniors here? We can take you apart in five minutes. After you have finished checking out BIT, your parents will wonder what happened to their son.'

Shashank's face became smaller and smaller as the implications of the words, the tone, and the suggested alterations in him became apparent.

'Sorry, I didn't mean it that way—'

'What did you mean then? Do you think we are all stupid here? That we don't know what you think? That we have all come to this institute by cheating or some computer glitch? Well, for starters, we need to teach you a lesson so that you know how to behave with seniors. Say "BIT is the best institute in the world, and I am privileged to be here" a thousand times. Every time you finish, bend down before us. That would perhaps teach you to respect the college and seniors. Start. NOW.'

The rotund Shashank was panting with the obvious exertion of bending—by his own admission, he had never exercised, never played any games, if one ignores chess and bridge for the moment, and his lack of physical activity made his face red, sweat dripping from it within a few seconds of commencement. He had barely completed a dozen repetitions when one of the other seniors asked him to stop.

'Bugger will die of a heart attack, I think. He better

stop. Look at him heaving, panting and sweating.'

Shashank stood upright, trying to get his breath back in vain when the senior continued, 'What's your weight, fatso?'

'About 90 kgs,' Shashank stammered between deep breaths.

'You end every sentence with a "sir" while addressing seniors. We just informed you, didn't we?'

'About 90 kgs, sir.'

'And your height?'

'Five feet one inch, sir.'

'Interesting… Haven't met anybody quite as round ever before; you are an eyesore to IT. We'll have to slim you down before the ragging period ends, or you will never have any girlfriends. Ha ha! You will slim down, won't you?'

'Yes, sir.'

'Now off you go. I will see you tomorrow in something less objectionable, or you will face the consequences.'

The next morning found Shashank struggling in a pair of trousers clearly stitched when he had been several inches less rotund around the middle, a pair of shoes borrowed from one of his fellow freshers and a plain white shirt, which, on closer inspection, still retained the price sticker found on new clothes; his face was freshly shaved, and hair neatly combed.

He came down to the mess table, anxiety written large on his fair features. I hailed him and inquired why he looked like a homeless mouse with the sword of Damocles of the resident tomcat hanging over its head. Having been in the hostel for over three weeks, we had slowly gotten used to the seniors and the ragging, which no longer held any terrors for us—anxiety perhaps, even discomfort, but terror—no. He tearfully proceeded to elucidate the reasons for his appearance and, horrors of horrors, refused the breakfast dutifully offered by Chhotu in the same old chipped china, which by common consensus was the only decent meal the cook could rustle up—one can't do extensive damage to two eggs, four slices of bread, and a dob of butter, can they? My incredulous face must have sent some signals into his head, and he turned towards me to state, 'I won't be able to fit into my trousers, you see. These actually belong to Ranjit, and I am, as it is, at least six inches too fat for them.'

With a sympathetic shake of my head, conveying in the fullest sense my unwavering loyalty to the thus misunderstood Shashank, I demolished his share of eggs, butter and bread. One could always do with extra nourishment, after all.

As we exited the mess hall together, Shashank suddenly went rigid. Following his unwavering gaze, I could see Nilesh, a third-year electrical student, lounging in the lobby with a couple of his classmates.

'So, you managed to antagonize Nilesh, did you?' I asked him.

'Who is Nilesh?'

'That tall chap in the brown T-shirt.'

'Yes, that six-foot gorilla is the one who terrorized me yesterday.'

'He is six-foot-three. I was informed when I was being ragged in his room. He then measured his height right before me to prove his contention and tell me I wouldn't last too long if I ever got on his wrong side.'

As we spoke, Nilesh and his classmates approached us and asked me in mock soliloquy:

'Baa Baa
Little fresher
Have you any periods free?'

I replied in the same mock-serious tone,

'No, sir, no, sir,
All three full.
One for the Shames guy,
One for the fuddy dame,
And one for the spoof
Who teaches down café lane.'

(Shames referred to the author of a Mechanics textbook that was the bread, butter and jam of the studious first-year students.)

Nilesh tilted his head back in a style that reminded me of Dev Anand in a movie I had seen some time ago (probably *Kala Pani*, when the ever-stylish actor turned around during the lovely duet 'Achha Ji Main Haari' to give Madhubala a glimpse of his enormous charm) and roared with unrestrained mirth. 'No wonder Funny saw something in you,' he said.

After he had had his fill laughing, he turned towards Shashank and demanded, 'So, bugger, you managed to dress properly, but how about wishing us?'

'Good morning, sirs,' Shashank replied.

'That's better. Now we have a job at hand—to reduce you to human proportions. You are a disgrace to the human race, looking more like an overinflated balloon than a person.'

I stood around watching with disguised interest (well, I needed to learn all the tricks of the trade if I was to rag freshers the next year!) as Nilesh proceeded to fish out a five-paise coin from the inner recesses of his jeans pocket. He handed it to Shashank and instructed him to measure the size of the lobby with the five-paise coin.

'You better complete it by the time I return for lunch,' he instructed.

The lobby was approximately half a kilometre long, and the five-paise coin measured a half an inch on each side.

'Good exercise, one would imagine. What do you say?' Nilesh asked me as Shashank looked first at the coin, which he held in his numb fingers, and then at the lobby. His expression was one of extreme bewilderment, as if he were wondering where the seniors got these crazy ideas.

I nodded dumbly and saw Nilesh raise one threatening finger at Shashank's face and remind him that he would return in a few hours. With a brief wave at me, Nilesh was gone.

I commiserated with Shashank, who, to an Asterix fan, looked increasingly like a smaller Obelix, with the sky rapidly closing in on his helmet-less and therefore noticeably exposed head.

Half an hour later, as I returned after a cup of tea at DG Corner and enduring ragging by a couple of second-year students, I saw Shashank still at his job, diligently working on measuring the lobby. He had perhaps progressed a hundred yards when I walked to him and said, 'Well, Shashank, there could be an easier way of doing this. The entire floor is covered with square tiles; perhaps you could measure one tile with the coin and count the number of tiles. That should take a few minutes, and you could do the arithmetic, right?'

Shashank looked at me, initially in confusion and then in disgust, before theatrically slapping his right hand on his forehead and exclaiming, 'Bloody hell! What is happening to me? What the f... am I doing?'

I consoled him by saying, 'No sweat, Shashank; often happens when one is tense.' I then helped him with the measurement and found a friend for life!

Nilesh made it a point to meet Shashank every morning, and at the end of the ragging period—80 days and plenty of exercise later—Shashank needed a belt to keep those once-too-tight trousers up. It is a different story altogether that Shashank, on the eve of graduating college four years later, weighed 117 kgs, standing just (about two-fifths of an inch) over five feet in his stockings.

Fat, rotund and round he was,
Weighing over a hundred kilos, alas,
Always doing thorough bakwaas,
And putting on hajaar hawas.

The seniors made him run,
No metaphors here or pun,
Never letting him have any fun,
Soon he lost kilograms many,
Making him look almost skinny.

All this changed at the end of ragging,
When he went greedily back to being
A glutton without working hard any,
And put on the lost kilograms many.

Pastries, chocolates and cakes he ate,
Without realizing his diet was at stake,
And became fat, rotund and round again,
All the weight he had lost, regained.

A scenario where well begun was not half done. People change rapidly given the right impetus, in the presence of the right catalyst, and under circumstances conducive to personal improvement.

The difference three months in BIT had on my mental makeup reflected in no uncertain terms on my physical appearance and was quite remarkably noticeable. A lovely lady, who happened to be my cousin's close friend and with whom I had perhaps exchanged a dozen sentences spoken with my usual stutter, hesitance, and incoherence before I left for Varanasi, put it quite beautifully.

'Raja went to Varanasi as a wide-eyed young boy, painfully shy and introverted. He hardly spoke unless spoken to, stuttering and stammering hopelessly with a panicky appearance on his painfully thin, pink countenance. He spoke with remarkable passion and speed, probably thinking that listeners would not wait to hear his opinions. To be fair, his ideas and opinions were often original and dynamic.

'After 80 days, when he returned for the first time after being admitted to BIT, he was a different young man. Physically, from afar, he hadn't changed much; he was still painfully thin and lean, which made him appear taller than his five feet, seven inches. However, his walk had changed considerably. Gone was the shuffling gait employed by the diffident individual that he was before his departure; he now walked with the swagger of a person suffering from supreme self-confidence.

'Looking into his eyes, one could swear they were of a different person. The wide-eyed, innocent look, displaying an overwhelming curiosity to observe and enjoy had vanished, replaced by half-closed, twinkling eyes that conveyed a know-it-all look, perusing the world with the supreme poise of an individual who has seen and heard everything and has an unspoken comment for everything observed and scrutinized.'

In hindsight, the change in me was predominantly beneficial and essential to my development as a human being and as a working professional. There have been other cases of change brought about by the impetus of hostel and engineering life that were not so beneficial to society.

A case in point is that of Nitin Iyengar, a Tamilian Brahmin like me, but that was where the similarities ended. He had taken admission in Civil engineering and was allotted a dozen doors down from mine. He was a devout Brahmin, performing the daily rituals prescribed by the sages of yore with religious intensity and regularity. He used to chant the *Vishnu Sahasranam*—praise of Lord Vishnu—twice a day, and performed the *Sandhi* puja thrice daily as laid down by the holy Hindu scriptures.

He was God-fearing and mortally terrified of only one living creature—flying cockroaches. When he first came to the hostel, he was extremely pious, and on any day he missed a particular chant or meditation, he was terrified that flying cockroaches would invade his room that night! On such nights, he would inform me with fright writ large on his cherubic face that he was going to sleep with the lights on and place a large towel under the door to block any chances of entry for the dreaded creatures.

He would rise in the morning complaining of a sleepless night and throw himself into the rituals with even greater intensity. This devout individual was always ready to help others in times of need, and I doubt I would have passed the first-semester exams without the aid of his notes, carefully copied with religious fervour and written verbatim as the lecturer delivered the principles, in his neat, well-spaced handwriting. Ranjit, Menon and I photocopied them a week before the exams and memorized them the night before.

After our first year, we moved to different hostels and classes. While we still met often, the closeness we had enjoyed when living in the same hostel diminished over time. By the beginning of the fifth semester, I could finally discern a change in his behaviour. His cherubic face, once so easily given to smiling, became pinched and careworn, as though the entire onus of the class' collective marks rested on his slim shoulders.

He became increasingly taciturn, speaking to no one in his class except in an acerbic tone to discuss ways to make money by any means—fair and foul. His obsession with the green stuff became all-consuming, and he cut down on food and movies to save money and, ironically, spend far more on alcohol, to which he had grown addicted.

A couple of years after we graduated, I was informed by an acquaintance, a serious chap called Nagarajan— who hailed from the same district as Nitin—that he had become a moneylender in a small town in Tamil Nadu. He had amassed a fortune by lending money to the impoverished and landless, who paid preposterous sums as interest on their meagre borrowings. If they failed to repay the accrued sum on time, Nitin would seize their possessions and auction them at great profit.

Nagarjan mentioned that there had even been a couple of attempts on Nitin's life by those of the grievously wronged gentry, whose money he had swindled through these unfair means. According to Nagarjan, Nitin had risen from extreme poverty, which had plagued him in college, to a position of immense wealth, and he was the proud owner of three large farmhouses besides four imported cars and all the trappings of luxury. Nagarjan concluded that despite all the wealth, power and prestige Nitin enjoyed in that small town, he never had a moment's respite and seemed to be always tense.

I considered what Nagarajan said and thoughtfully remarked that this was perhaps a case of changes brought about by the negative influence of some condescending and snobbish colleagues in our batch.

Pradeep Kumar was at the other end of the spectrum in terms of transformation. A bucolic simpleton from a village in central Uttar Pradesh located close to the famous tiger sanctuary, Dhudhwa National Park, Pradeep joined our institute to study Civil Engineering. His easy-going nature, pragmatic approach and captivating simplicity soon endeared him to all of us.

Pradeep's father was a poor telephone assistant in the village government office, and Pradeep had made it to IT through sheer hard work. When he first arrived, he could barely string three words together in English that made sense; yet, he possessed a deep and abiding interest in learning the language properly and speaking it fluently.

We soon became good friends, and Ranjit and I spent time in his clean and sparsely furnished room, enjoying his company and deep knowledge about his area and the wonders of the tiger reserve. We were ensconced in his room, a few weeks after we had been admitted to IT, when he asked us for advice on improving his spoken English.

Ranjit replied, 'Start by reading a newspaper regularly; mark the words you do not understand and look up their meanings in a dictionary. Keep a diary and record the same. Also, try to speak in English whenever you are with us. Do not worry if you are using the right words or not. We will correct you, and before you realize it, you will be fluent.'

Pradeep took Ranjit's advice seriously and worked diligently. At my suggestion, he began reading *The Statesman*, following the advice my father had given me a decade and a half earlier to improve the quality of my English. Every evening, while the rest of us took a break from the monotony of classes, Pradeep could be found engrossed in his newspaper, carefully noting down words and their meanings.

The improvement was dramatic; by the third year, his English was fluent enough for him to speak in forums. Pradeep remained one of the finest examples of positive transformation I have ever seen in a human being—the transformation came about by following some remarkably simple principles—hard work, dedication and the support of some good friends.

16

Budding Romances

As I mentioned earlier, the university was an exceptionally enchanting place. When I first arrived at the institute, the weather was hot and humid, punctuated by monsoon rains every fortnight or so. July and August mark a period of transition in Uttar Pradesh, as monsoon clouds form over the Bay of Bengal and sweep westward, blanketing the state in the refreshing aroma of rain-soaked earth and lush greenery.

After four months of relentless heat, dust and extremely uncomfortable weather, the temperature would suddenly plummet, and the fresh fragrance of rain would wash away the stench of sweat, magically transforming the world. The grass, which had appeared parched and lifeless during the summer, now gleamed in vibrant shades of green. Fields were dotted with water patches, and birds could be seen preening contentedly by the edges of ephemeral puddles. The monsoon brought with it a captivating and somewhat melancholic metamorphosis, evoking memories of Calcutta.

After the initial few days when I was not accustomed to staying alone in a room or enduring the repetitive ragging, I gradually relished my life in the hostel, and my longing for Calcutta, along with my old friends and relatives, faded. However, this sense of comfort and routine changed entirely one fine evening early in August when the monsoon arrived in all its grandeur.

Monsoon rains are distinct from the unseasonal nor'westers that occasionally punctuated the sweltering summer months. Until then, the rains had been brief and intense, lacking the continuous downpour characteristic of the monsoon. For those of us from Calcutta, the difference was unmistakable.

I stood on the balcony, watching the rain clouds darken the sky progressively, a mix of delight and melancholy in my heart. My thoughts wandered back to my hometown—its narrow streets where I grew up, the ancient movie halls where I sought refuge from monotony, and the school grounds where we played football amidst mud, slush and lush greenery.

Suddenly, Ranjit interrupted my daydreaming. 'What happened? You look glum.'

Shaking my head, I replied, 'Nothing, yaar. Just thinking of Calcutta. The monsoons are breathtaking there; back home, we used to run out and play football in the rain. I am just overwhelmed with nostalgia. And feeling a little sad, I suppose.'

'Well, we can do the same here, can't we? We can enjoy the rain too!' Ranjit responded with a twinkle in his eye. He walked over to Chaaku's room, and found him, as usual, fast asleep.

'Hey, wake up! Raja is feeling down. Let's go out in the rain and enjoy ourselves.'

Surprisingly, Chaaku woke up immediately, and they

both dragged me down the stairs to the central open area in the hostel to revel in the rain. Chaaku went to Popli's room and started playing some old Hindi film songs. Before long, dozens of us were outside, dancing in the rain with exuberance. The sadness in me, though not entirely dispelled, diminished to remain as a faint trace of nostalgia.

As we danced and sang in the rain with joyful vigour, something extraordinary happened.

A car pulled up along the road leading to the hostel. From it, I caught sight of a lithe figure hopping out and elegantly taking refuge in the foyer to escape the rain. The sky had grown dark by then, and the lights in the foyer flickered on just then, illuminating the hostel entrance and the lobby in blinding white light.

Mesmerized, I watched the graceful figure transform into a young woman dressed in dark-coloured attire, holding her dupatta protectively over her face to shield herself from the rain. Oblivious to everything else, I found myself walking towards the entrance as if in a trance—something about the young lady had utterly captivated me.

She stood in the foyer, observing a bunch of mud-splattered boys dancing and jumping joyfully in the rain with wide eyes that seemed both amazed and amused. It was at that moment I experienced my first crush.

I was so distracted that I failed to display the chivalry I prided myself on as a Calcuttan. I just stood there in the pouring rain, staring at her. Meanwhile, a couple of my friends, having noticed her standing in the foyer, approached her out of curiosity, while I remained rooted to the spot, utterly engrossed. It indeed would be an unusual errand that could have brought a young lady to a boys' hostel in such inclement weather.

'Sorry, can we help you?' Sridhar's words suddenly brought me back to reality. He had addressed the lady, rescuing me from my reverie. Bala, too, stood beside him, equally curious.

The young lady turned to them and said, 'Yes, please. I am looking for Ranjit from Chemical Engineering. I was told he is staying in this hostel. Do you know him?'

In that instant, I realized this angel was seeking my friend, Ranjit. I hastily stuttered, 'Yes, please wait a moment. I will fetch him for you.'

I ran back to the group, calling for Ranjit, and we walked back to the foyer. When he saw her, he exclaimed, 'Moon! What a surprise! What are you doing here in the rain?'

'You idiot,' she retorted with a hint of annoyance. 'Mom and Dad are extremely angry with you. You promised to come home as soon as you arrived in Varanasi, but you did not even call. Your parents are worried about you—you have not called or written to them for weeks. Your mother called my mom today, asking us to check on you. So, here we are... Father is waiting in the car.'

Muttering a sheepish 'Oh, shit!' Ranjit hurried to the car. The back door opened, and a distinguished-looking gentleman stepped out, embracing Ranjit under the shelter of the foyer.

My eyes returned to the young lady, and I felt an intense desire to speak to her, to ask her a thousand questions. I simply wanted to hear her voice and peer into her eyes. She gazed back at me, and I sensed something extraordinary—a feeling entirely unknown to me.

My mind flitted to a Katherine Hepburn statement—
'Plain women know more about men than beautiful ones
do. But beautiful women don't need to know about men.
It's the men who have to know about beautiful women.'

At that moment, Calcutta and the accompanying
melancholy faded from memory; nothing seemed more
important than speaking to this beautiful woman, ensuring
that this man knew all about her. I barely noticed when
Sridhar and Bala walked away; I no longer heard the
singing, shouting and dancing that continued with
undiminished vigour behind me. With a start, I realized
she was still staring back at me, amusement written all
over her pretty features.

'Hi,' she said.

I mumbled a weak 'Hi', realizing it was bad manners to
stare—even at someone as pretty as the angel before me.

'My name is Moushumi, but everyone calls me Moon;
perhaps because they think I have a scar like the moon,'
she said, letting out a lovely giggle that carried a hint of
self-deprecating humour.

Normally, a giggle from a girl would have irked me,
but with this angel, even a girlish giggle was music to
my ears.

'Hell, no! That can't be the reason—it's probably
because you brighten up the darkest nights with your
august presence.'

I don't know how I managed to string together such a
sentence without a stammer, or how I found the courage
to say something like this to a girl I had met barely a
couple of minutes back. Emboldened by the reckless surge
of confidence, I added, 'Or perhaps your friends consider

you to be the most beautiful being in the universe and, thus, call you by that endearing name.'

Suddenly, the horror and embarrassment of what I had said washed over me, and I fell back into my trance-like state, dumbfounded and stunned by the realization that I might have said something inappropriate.

To my immense relief, Moon responded with a full-throated laugh. 'My God,' she said, 'I thought you guys were here to study engineering, not flirt with every girl you meet.'

I must have looked like a mess under the bright lights of the hostel foyer, and her comment left me oddly embarrassed. This was the first time I had ever said anything remotely out of context to a girl. To add to my discomfort, a cold rivulet of water chose that very moment to trickle down my back. I was wearing an old pair of mud-splattered trousers, a white buttoned-down shirt clinging to me like a second skin, and my long unkempt hair, untouched by scissors for over two months, looking dishevelled and wet, falling over my face and collars, leaving rivulets of water running down my unshaven face, rough with the stubble of a four-day-old beard.

'And you haven't even told me your name,' she continued, looking more like an angel than ever before, a gentle smile now playing on her lips.

'Raja,' I replied, wondering if I could gather the courage to stretch my arms to offer a handshake when she extended her arms first.

I shook her hand, holding on for a couple of seconds more than necessary, revelling in the feeling of softness and comfort her fingers and palm exuded, reluctant to let go. Strangely, I sensed a similar reluctance from her.

Ranjit's voice broke our moment. 'Raja,' he said rather loudly, for the din from the rain made conversations beyond 10 metres impossible. Moon and I disengaged our hands, feeling a little guilty and awkward, and walked to where Ranjit was standing, talking to a dapper gentleman dressed in dark trousers, black shoes and a check-patterned shirt—presumably Moon's father.

'Uncle, this is Raja,' Ranjit introduced us, 'my good friend and classmate. He is from Calcutta and speaks fluent Bengali. Raja, this is Ghosh Uncle, my father's cousin who lives here in Varanasi. You have met Moon, I see; she is his daughter and my cousin.'

I shook hands with Mr Ghosh and asked what had brought them here in such inclement weather. Mr Ghosh replied that Ranjit's mother had called him earlier in the day and asked him to check on Ranjit. There had been no calls or letters from him for several weeks, and they were pretty worried.

He also mentioned that he and Ranjit's family used to be neighbours when Ranjit lived in Varanasi, and Moon and Ranjit, being the same age, were fast friends. He then asked about me and my family. Mr Ghosh spoke Bengali in a measured tone and halting manner, as if he were carefully choosing his words, unsure if they adequately represented his thoughts.

He then complimented my proficiency in Bengali. 'Wow, your Bengali is certainly better than anyone in my family—except my wife. You should come home and spend time with us. Even though we are Bengalis, we have never lived in Bengal. My army life kept me in various parts of the country, and other than being born in Siliguri, I have no real roots left in Bengal,' he explained.

He turned to Ranjit, inviting him to come over for lunch the next day and asked me to join them.

Soon, Moon and Mr Ghosh bid us farewell and drove away. As soon as the taillights disappeared, Ranjit turned to me and said, 'Well, you seem to have hit it off with Moon. Don't fib; I saw how you shook hands with her.'

I think I turned beetroot, but Ranjit reassured me, 'Don't worry, she is a good girl,' and put his arm around my shoulders in a friendly gesture.

Walking back to our rooms, we found that the revelry had ended and it was quiet again. The downpour had dwindled to a steady drizzle, and the weather was strangely clammy. As I opened the door to my room, Ranjit broke into my thoughts, which were all about Moon, and said, 'Now, I need to ensure we visit Ghosh uncle often enough,' giving me a broad wink, and went off to his room, leaving me to my thoughts.

Ranjit and I had dinner together at the mess, but we carefully avoided discussing the events of the evening. Instead, we focused on eating our food quietly. The Maharaj had prepared something special, which was usual for Saturday dinners, and there were even sweets to top it off.

I went to bed early, tired from the dancing and singing, but sleep eluded me and my mind kept going back to Moon. I must have fallen asleep eventually, as I woke up the next morning later than usual, feeling refreshed from a good night's sleep. It was a bright and beautiful Sunday. The breakfast seemed to taste better than usual, and even the sunny-side-up eggs looked resplendent in all their yellow glory.

After breakfast, I brought out my shaving kit; Ranjit stood next to me, commenting on my sudden desire to look like a human being. For once, I was focused on getting the cleanest shave possible, and I didn't have time to retort to Ranjit's quips. After getting ready, I spotted Ramulu and Funny arriving at the hostel on Ramulu's motorcycle. An inspiration struck me at that moment.

Ramulu whistled upon seeing me all resplendent in my best blue-coloured shirt and beige trousers, paired with polished shoes, as I strolled down to meet them.

'What's up, Raja? You look like you've just walked out of a fashion studio.'

'I have a favour to ask,' I said, ignoring his question. 'Can I please borrow your motorcycle for a few hours?'

Ramulu and Funny exchanged knowing glances, and Ramulu said, 'Looks like something is brewing. What do you say, Funny? It seems our friend here has found someone to ride with.'

Funny nodded in agreement, and Ramulu parked the motorcycle before handing me the keys. 'Hey, take care, all the best. And, by the way, do you need any money or something? Let me know.'

'Thanks, Ramulu,' I replied. 'Money shouldn't be an issue. But what brings you guys here so early on a Sunday?' I knew full well Funny would not leave his *Graffiti* work unless something was important.

Funny explained that they planned to go fundraising that day to gather more cash for the magazine. He also invited me to join them at Sinha's place after, as Krish and I were elected to do the final proofreading.

I replied in the affirmative, and soon Ramulu and Funny left me with with the motorcycle and its keys. Brilliant!

The afternoon turned out to be the most delightful one of my life. Mrs Ghosh had cooked a whole array of delicious dishes, including my favourite *jhinger posto*, and I enjoyed home-cooked food after several weeks. Post lunch, as we sat sipping some well-made tea, I felt an indescribable joy.

As Ranjit and I prepared to ride off on the motorcycle, I got a few moments with Moon without her parents in the vicinity. I bravely asked her if she would like to meet the following Friday for a lunch or dinner date. She responded with a delightful giggle and said she was free that afternoon as she had no classes, but would need to be back home by four to avoid any questions from her parents.

Ranjit stood nearby, pretending to scrutinize the flowers, though his ears were undoubtedly waiting for her reply. Moon and I agreed to meet near her college at noon, which was a fair distance from ours.

✸

The motorcycle's roar was like music to my ears, and with Ranjit holding on behind me, I felt an exhilarating sense of pleasure as I twisted the throttle. After six weeks of living in Varanasi, I realized that my transformation had gained significant momentum, much like the pleasurable acceleration the motorcycle under me was providing me with.

That Friday morning, I borrowed Venky's motorcycle and waited outside Moon's college for a full 90 minutes, dressed to bits and chewing my nails in anxious anticipation. Funny enough, there was no doubt in my mind that she would come; somehow, one gets these feelings, and scientists give esoteric acronyms like ESP, but as far as I was concerned, I somehow knew she would make the time.

I thought about my first glimpse of her as I leaned on my parked motorcycle, looking through a pair of borrowed sunglasses (borrowed from Chaaku, who had similar face dimensions as I). She emerged from a small group of young ladies, scanning the crowd, trying to find me. When her eyes fell upon me, a broad smile broke across her face and she hurried to where I stood waiting for her. She looked as good as ever, in a bright yellow dress that hugged her slim form.

The first-time experience of riding with a pretty lady who is not a relative, sitting on the pillion of your motorcycle as you weave through the traffic, is quite indescribable and stays with you for a long time. 'Top of the world' would perhaps be an apt metaphor.

The lunch with Moon remains a watershed moment in my life. I have no recollection of what we spoke about, but throughout the lunch, we talked constantly, laughing at silly jokes and looking at no one else but each other.

I didn't know what was happening, but life suddenly seemed more complicated and, concurrently, a sheer bundle of joy!

❋

17

Sine Die

I returned to the hostel late in the afternoon having, missed—once again—an entire day of classes. As I peeped inside Chaaku's room, I saw Ranjit and him poring over the *Times of India* crossword. Funny that I rarely recollect anyone ever closing the doors to their rooms when they were inside, except for the seriously studious folks who presumably wanted to focus their minds on the work at hand.

Ranjit looked up to see me and commented that my face looked more radiant than ever. Chaaku, all agog with curiosity at Ranjit's statement, managed to coax out of him that I had been out for lunch with a young lady.

'F...far out, man,' was Chaaku's first response. Then he wanted to know who the person was and how I met her; soon, he had the entire story out of Ranjit and me.

Ever the practical man, Chaaku then asked, 'So where did you go for lunch?'

'Well, took her to Clarks in the Cantonment area.'

'How did you find it?'

'Thanks to Fatty, who managed to get an advertisement from them for *Graffiti* and a discount voucher, which he gave me, so the lunch cost me about a third of what it should have.'

'That's awesome,' Chaaku said, shaking his head and wondering about these strange seniors who on one hand ragged us constantly and on the other, were so generous when it came to providing us with all the assistance in anything we needed.

Suddenly, we heard a shout and then screaming wafting in through the open door. Curious, we stepped out to find almost the entire Rajputana gang standing around the fountain, discussing something about 'Sine die' in loud voices. We went down to join them, and I saw the ever-cool, nonchalant Bala sitting contentedly all by himself, watching the crowd with interest.

Walking up to him, I asked 'What happened? Something seems to be wrong.'

Bala looked up, squinting against the setting sun, and said, 'Well, looks like you guys didn't go to classes again today. The Diro has declared sine die.'

I exchanged a blank look with Ranjit and Chaaku, wondering what that term meant; I was thinking if movies could die and, more importantly, how that could possibly affect students so badly and, most importantly, why the director of India's leading engineering college was announcing it.

'What is "sine die"?' Ranjit asked, the first one among the three of us to come out of our wandering thoughts.

Bala didn't even deign to look up as he was engrossed in the frenzied activity in front of us. 'No classes till further notice; evidently the Diro and his staff are demanding better pay and facilities.'

'Let's check with the seniors on what this means,' I suggested.

Bala finally looked up and said, 'Are you crazy? The ragging will only increase now; the seniors will have nothing to do but make our lives miserable. At least we had the classes to escape the ragging before.'

I said, 'Bala, we need to figure out what we need to do; there could have been something similar that happened earlier. Let's perhaps check with the MTech guys if they experienced anything like this before.'

Suiting action to words, I sprinted towards the stairs, intending to put the problem at AKG's door, when I saw him and his friend, Swadesh, coming down the stairs.

'Hey Raja,' he exclaimed upon noticing me. 'Evidently the Diro has declared sine die—no classes then for at least four weeks.'

Panting from my impromptu dash, I asked, 'So what is this sine die? I was just about to come to your room to ask what we should do or what we can do.'

'Well, this means that the institute is closed till further notice, and by the decree, the Diro has to give at least one week's notice before the college can be opened.'

'Has this ever happened before here?' Chaaku asked, catching up and gasping for air; it was obvious he was even more out of breath than I was.

'Yes, this happened a few years ago when I was in my first year; the college was closed for six weeks. The first semester had to be extended, which ate up into the summer vacations at the end of the first year. Not good news at all.'

'So, what do we do then?'

'Most students head home. The institute will send a letter to your address when it's time to return. The weeks' notice is essentially for that.'

With a wave, AKG and Swadesh were off, presumably for evening tea, leaving Chaaku, Ranjit and I wondering about our next course of action.

We walked towards the crowd of students, who were excitedly discussing their plans in small groups; slowly, it became clear what they were intending to do. Most of them were planning to return to their hometowns, some even scheduling their departure for that very evening.

The three of us elected to walk to Vish and check out the fourth-year crowd on their plans, with me leading the way. Chaaku and Ranjit had met the fourth-year *Graffiti* gang, and they were no longer afraid of them. We reached the corner of our hostel and turned left, which would have led us to Vish, when we saw Krish walking just ahead of us. A loud call from me made him look around and he stopped while we caught up to him.

'You guys must have heard,' was his greeting, leaving no doubt that he was speaking about the sine die.

I nodded and said, 'Look, we are confused, and don't know what to do.'

'Yup, this is the first time this has happened during my time. I heard that the last time this happened was three years back, when our fourth-year friends were in their first; I was going to ask them what an optimal course of action would be to follow.'

We followed him into Vish and found Funny, Das, and a few others lounging in Funny's room. Das was flipping through a *Mad* magazine while Funny was fiddling with his radio.

'Hey, guys! Everybody ready to go home, eh?' Funny exclaimed as we entered his room. As I mentioned earlier, no one ever closed the doors to their rooms.

'No idea what to do, Funny,' Krish replied. 'We thought we could ask you for some advice.'

'Well, when this last happened when I was in my first year, I went home; we were informed that the college would be closed for at least six weeks. I am not so sure about this one; the government cannot afford an institute like ours staying closed for an indefinite time.'

Das turned his attention from the magazine he was perusing and laconically commented, 'Two weeks of closure at best; the Diro will ensure the biggies in the government agree to their requirements. After all, they are just asking for a raise. That should be easily justifiable.'

We chatted for some time and decided to stay put till we got further information. As we left, Funny called after us, 'Remember, the hostel messes will likely close as most students will be leaving over the next day or two. If you guys stay back, just let me know, and I shall organize your meals at our mess. The fourth-year mess will stay open since we're not going anywhere.'

With at least the plans for the next few days decided, we wandered back to our hostel.

Over the weekend, we saw a mass exodus from the hostel and by Monday morning, Ranjit, Chaaku, Popli, Pondy and I were the only first-year students left in Rajputana.

We walked around the campus that day and found less than a hundred students left on the campus, along with the fourth-year students for whom classes continued as usual. For the next four weeks, while the institute remained officially closed, we led a most idyllic life—no ragging, no classes, no studies—just sheer enjoyment.

The only dark cloud was that none of the messes in our hostel were operational and we had to trudge to Vish for our meals. The issue of coffee in the morning was solved within a day when I decided to invest in a small electric heater and, for the first time in my life, made coffee. To me, it tasted great.

Chaaku walked in while I made a second cup before I could face the world with equanimity and said, 'Well, looks like coffee is brewing—I wouldn't mind some.'

I generously gave him the cup where I had poured coffee for myself and proceeded to make a fresh one. *Rather unselfish of me*, I thought to myself, when Chaaku exclaimed, 'Yech, this is coffee? What have you done to it? How do you make it? It is terrible.'

I thought that was rather strange, as he should have thanked me for my capital gesture. Seeing my method of making coffee, Chaaku said, 'Well, let me make the coffee for you. I think you don't know how to make coffee with the instant powder you have bought.'

I moved aside and let him do the honours; he poured us two cups—I sipped mine and it tasted divine. 'Awesome, Chaaku; this is really good.'

'You need to take a spoon of coffee in a cup, add a little cold water and mix thoroughly until frothy. Then pour in boiling water, mix again and add milk. You are not letting the coffee settle in, so the aroma and flavour did not fully develop.'

Well, one of the best things to come out of sine die was learning to make good instant coffee, if that is not considered an oxymoron.

The other great advantage was my induction into rock—not the fossil kind but music. BIT had one of the finest and proudest rock music cultures across India, and dissecting the music of Pink Floyd was about as critical as discussions on weather to a Londoner.

It was pretty strange that this introduction happened well into my fourth week at the institute; in most cases, it should have occurred in the first week. This *faux pas* could be explained by my proximity to Das and company, as their interest in music was eclectic. While Pods loved old Hindi music, Das liked blues and jazz, while Krish was a die-hard fan of Deep Purple.

Over the next few weeks, I slowly got hooked on rock and learnt to distinguish between acid rock, psychedelic rock, and rock and roll, and even began appreciating some of the lyrics. Till then, I thought that most of the songs were nonsense-verse, as I had never understood the actual words amid all the music (cacophony?). Soon, I came to love Pink Floyd as passionately as I admired Shankar–Jaikishan.

The sine die weeks passed in a blur of inactivity; we often slept till noon, played table tennis in the common room or cricket on the floodlit basketball court with some of the seniors on most nights. We watched movies every day in the seedy local theatres, soaking in the sights, sounds and smells of Varanasi.

We became great friends with the few seniors who remained behind and grew extremely comfortable with them—even the severe freshers' attire changed to more casual ones. The normal IT attire—jeans, a loose T-shirt, and Hawaiian bathroom slippers—became our uniform. The jeans, once dark blue, had faded to a dull whitish-blue from numerous washings in the dhobi-ghats, while the slippers were often held together by a rusty safety pin, the heel worn out from constant use. The face rarely saw soap, especially in winter, and seniors who shaved regularly were viewed as outliers, adopting an alien culture.

Within a fortnight, we had transformed into typical ITians—scruffy, wearing faded clothes, our chins becoming progressively covered with an overgrowth of facial hair, and in some cases—like Popli, who shaved reasonably regularly—resembling a pigeon's half-made nest. We began addressing each other by shortened nicknames and occasionally by nauseating adjectives, keeping much in line with the 'culture' of the hostel. Soon, we were no different than the seniors in looks or language. This transformation from a clean young boy to a scruffy young man took less than a fortnight.

One great advantage of the break, which lasted four weeks, was the time it gave us to complete all the pending work around our labour of love—*Graffiti*.

We spent nearly six hours every day working on the articles, cartoons, layout, fonts and most importantly, on the wall itself—the wall was designed as a space where literally 'anything goes.'

The magazine was laid out as a newspaper, with newspaper-sized sheets folded in two down the middle. We designed two separate 'wall' sections—the centre spread and half of the back page—with the other half reserved for advertisements from our two key sponsors. The front page featured minimal content aside from a large cartoon of three monkeys urging everyone to buy the magazine and save them from bankruptcy. Below the cartoon, we signed our names, leaving no doubt in anyone's mind about who was going broke.

I must mention that, while I didn't have to contribute monetarily—and any suggestion I made was waved off—I still received a share of the profits. Funny mentioned, in his matter-of-fact way, that he expected us to uphold the proud IT tradition of never asking freshers for any money; he hoped this experience would stand the others in good stead to ensure they continued the *Graffiti* tradition, maintaining it as an enduring landmark in the IT community.

By the time classes resumed, we had completed all the articles for *Graffiti*, including two by yours truly, with no small assistance from the intelligent and erudite Krish. I proofread the entire magazine about a dozen times, and the layout was also finalized. The Saturday before classes began, we got our first look at the printed magazine. This involved numerous visits to Sinha's printing press, where I became friendly with his three-year-old spaniel, a cute, frisky thing called Sam, and I also met a lady who would go on to become one of India's most recognized actresses.

I met Moon occasionally through the sine die break, but not often enough—she was becoming far too busy with her studies and was unable to find time. My company was once again an almost exclusively male one, so I was pleasantly surprised to see a gorgeous young woman sitting in Sinha's office when I entered for the final review of

Graffiti with Das, Krish and Funny.

Caught off guard, I stared at her in a trance, though it wasn't the same feeling I'd had when I first saw Moon. This was more of curious interest. I wasn't the only one who got caught staring at her; even my companions, usually very level-headed, found their curiosity far too much to bear.

Sinha gave a knowing smile and introduced her. 'Guys, this is my cousin from Nepal. She has just moved to Varanasi to pursue higher studies at Women's College in Rajghat as part of her dream to become a scientist. Ritu, these boys are from BIT—Krish, Funny, Das and Raja. They are here for the humour magazine I told you about and which you praised.'

We all stood in a line as Ritu got up from her chair and shook hands with each of us, complimenting us on the quality of work we had put in on the magazine, confident that it would sell lots of copies. She then excused herself. A few years later she became one of the best-known Bollywood actors and we all knew even then that she was slated for bigger and better things in life—not a scientist living in relative obscurity.

When we finally held the first printed version of *Graffiti*, we couldn't contain our excitement. We repeatedly pointed out the jokes and rejoiced in the feeling that we had achieved something quite extraordinary. We bade our goodbyes to Sinha and left the press well past midnight, reaching the hostel around 1 a.m.

On the auto ride back, there was a sudden silence, all of us deep in our thoughts, until Funny piped up just as we neared the campus. 'She is easily the most gorgeous woman I have ever seen—she should be in movies or be a model or something.'

I was hanging on to dear life in the front seat of the auto and marvelled at how our thoughts had converged. Das chimed in and suggested that we should plan a trip to Nepal if *Graffiti* made any money. *Lateral thinking*, I thought.

We went to our respective rooms, comfortable in the knowledge that the first two thousand copies of *Graffiti*—at that very moment—were being furiously churned out in a small dingy room 10 kilometres from where we were, ready for collection in just six hours.

18

The First Daaru Party

The first edition of *Graffiti* was ready for distribution at 6 a.m. on Monday, 14 September. Classes resumed that day after a four-week hiatus, and students returned to their hostels, eager to be the first to buy *Graffiti* and save many of us from bankruptcy. I didn't know until the night before, at Sinha's office, that Das, Funny, Fatty and Ramulu were broke—Funny hadn't paid his mess dues for over two months. Despite their financial difficulties, they maintained a positive and humorous outlook, ensuring none of their woes became apparent to impressionable younger folks like me.

Suddenly, all the effort we had put in—going from shop to shop, establishment to establishment and restaurant to restaurant, asking for advertisements to fund the magazine—became irrelevant and nothing but a footnote in the story of launching the first humour magazine at the institute.

For me, it was a wonderful experience—walking into shops and pitching ad space in a magazine that had never been published, created by students without any background in publishing and, most importantly, without the support of the university officials. The latter is crucial, as an institute-sponsored magazine has good sales potential, making establishments more willing to contribute. Despite our efforts and hard work to raise funds, we were short of meeting the costs and selling enough copies to recoup the money invested became imperative.

Fatty and I took the onus of selling the magazine to the first-year students. We spent the next two days going from room to room, mess to mess and class to class, convincing everyone to part with the princely sum of two rupees for sheer reading pleasure. Soon, there was enough word-of-mouth publicity and palpable excitement among the students to possess a copy, and almost everyone who read it was impressed enough to recommend it to their friends. I recall one unique experience where a second-year student bought 200 copies to sell at his old school and through his elder brother, a student at IIT Kanpur.

Our efforts paid off, and besides the money it generated, *Graffiti* became a best-selling magazine. Subsequent issues sold approximately three times as many copies outside the institute as within BIT.

With the seniors back in the black and their dues cleared Fatty suggested a daaru party to celebrate *Graffiti's* success.

Daaru—Handy Guide to IT Lingo

Until then, I had only sampled beer a few times, and most of the *Graffiti* gang—other than Ramulu, Fatty and Das—didn't care much for alcohol. Krish was a confirmed teetotaller, as was Pods, and other than the occasional beer Ramulu or Fatty bought me in one of the seedy bars around Lanka after a hard day of fund-raising, I had little exposure to hard drinks or drinking. All this changed about 10 weeks into college life.

We spent most of the first week selling *Graffiti*, with Ranjit, Chaaku and Popli joining the efforts. By Friday morning, we had sold out the first batch of 2,000 copies. That afternoon, while we were sitting in Ramulu's room, basking in the warm glow of a job well done, Fatty walked in with a stack of rupees in his hands.

'Well, guys,' he announced, 'looks like we made a neat profit from the sales and the advertisements. The last one, from the Chinese restaurant, was especially good—they shelled out Rs 3,000 for the back page. We are close to Rs 3,000 in the black, and we should do something to celebrate.'

Das suggested, 'Well, let's get some marijuana.'

Funny offered, 'Let's go out for a splendid meal and invite Sinha as well.'

'Yes, and that gorgeous lady we met,' I added.

'Hey, Raja, be careful with that dame, eh—Sinha is influential in Varanasi. We don't want you to get into any trouble.'

Ranjit and Chaaku were also hanging out in the room, and the former piped up, 'There's not much chance of that happening. Raja has found someone else, I dare say. He he!'

I shot him a baleful glare, but Funny added, 'Indeed, Raja, we were curious the other day, but I didn't want to embarrass you by asking questions. We are all eager to hear about your experiences. It is rare to see freshers adapt to college life as effortlessly as you have. Now, who was that girl? In the three to four years in Varanasi, none of us here have found anyone to go out with, and you have managed it in six weeks.'

I gave them a brief update on Moon, mentioning that I hadn't seen her in the past few weeks. I explained that I couldn't afford to take her out, and she was also occupied with her studies.

'Well, at least we can solve the cash problem, Raja,' Fatty said, handing me a thick envelope filled with ten- and fifty-rupee notes.

I was astonished by their generosity. When I regained my composure, I protested, 'No, I cannot accept this. Not at all. You guys did all the demanding work; all I did was have fun. It is not fair.'

Fatty replied, 'Come on, fresher, it is yours. Just accept it, or I might have to start ragging you now. Remember, the ragging period hasn't officially ended.'

Fatty gave me a mischievous wink, then turned to Das and Funny, who were sitting on the bed, and said, 'Now, let us get serious. We need money for some rum, coke, weed and beer. I have already asked Munna to prepare some special snacks. Ranjit, your dad works in the Air Force. Can we get some special rum from the army canteen here?'

Army folks had access to alcoholic drinks at prices less than half of what normal citizens paid!

Ranjit replied, 'Yes, I can go to my father's friend's house in the cantonment area and ask him to arrange a couple of bottles.'

'Then, let's go now. We could be back in a couple of hours,' Ramulu exclaimed, waving his motorcycle keys in the air.

'Well, Ramulu, why don't Ranjit and I get the rum? Let me at least take care of that for the party—please! I know all about the freshers not spending, but I am sure this is the least I can do for you guys.'

Fatty chimed, 'Machchan, are you sure you want to go for the rum, or do you have something or someone else in mind? Ha ha?'

Ramulu handed me the motorcycle keys, and soon Ranjit and I were riding through the congested Varanasi streets. We reached Ghosh uncle's house, where Ranjit took him aside to ask for the rum discreetly, so his wife wouldn't find out and berate us. Meanwhile, Moon and I exchanged pleasantries while sitting on the veranda.

'Hey Raj, *Graffiti* was fantastic! Thanks for sending me a copy. I shared it with my friends, and everyone wanted one. Your articles came out very well; evidently, you do have some skills after all,' she said, her words followed by a pearly laugh. She was the only person who ever called me 'Raj', which sounded quite endearing.

'Thanks, but Krish had just as much to do with the articles as I did. I will bring a few more copies next time—it is no problem. Interesting that you liked the mag. During our discussions about the content, we debated on what kind of articles readers would like. I quoted from Sherlock Holmes to bring the matter into a group consensus, rather than focusing on what a particular individual would prefer.'

'Sorry, you are as usual obtuse with me. What do you mean?'

'Nothing much. We were discussing what would appeal to a certain individual as a test case, and for that person, the mag seemed stilted and full of poor-quality humour, almost slapstick. That was a let-down, our first experiment being such a failure. But I remarked to the *Graffiti* gang that while the individual man is an insoluble puzzle, in the aggregate, he becomes a mathematical certainty. For example, you can never foretell what one person will do, but you can say precisely what an average number will be up to.

'Individuals vary, but percentages remain constant. By the way, what I said isn't my monologue but something Doyle wrote a century ago, and it remains a constant truth. While the first individual didn't find the mag any good, the next dozen or so pre-readers found the mag awesome, restoring faith in humanity and ourselves. All's well that ends well, and now we have enough money to start paying our mess bills and perhaps treat you to dinner one of these days.'

'Sure, let us plan dinner. I have exams until next weekend, but we can arrange something after that. By the way, I saw Ranjit sneak off to the den with my father into his den, carefully staying out of my mom's earshot. I don't need to be Sherlock Holmes to deduce that he is after liquor, and you guys are planning a party today.'

Thinking that was indeed a brilliant deduction, I said, 'Awesome! You are correct, my dear lady. This isn't elementary at all.'

I mused for a moment before adding thoughtfully, 'Yes, I plan to enjoy the party. It's quite funny that in all my life, I have barely tasted alcohol, except for a couple of occasions when I had some beer at one of the seedy joints in Lanka.'

'Well, don't think you have missed much, like my mom would say. She tried to wean my pop off his rum drinking in the early days of their marriage, but all she could do was limit his intake. The armed forces' life revolves around the canteen, pub and clubs after work, so it's difficult to be a teetotaller. But it's funny how Ranjit managed to stay far away from anything harder than Thums Up.'

'Yes, that is indeed very remarkable. Perhaps he gets his strength of character from his father. Ranjit told me his father quit smoking when he learnt he was going to be a father. Apparently he was in the garden, smoking, when his uncle delivered the good news. He looked at the cigarette, then at his uncle, and declared it would be his last. He has not smoked since. Quite incredible!'

'Yes, I have heard that from Ranjit's mother. I wonder how people find such mental strength.'

We sat in companionable silence, each wondering about the circumstances that led men and women to make such far-reaching decisions.

Ranjit's shouting abruptly broke our train of thought. 'Raja, let's go!'

I turned to see him standing near the motorcycle, gesturing with his left hand. I figured he must have used the back entrance to avoid meeting Moon's mother, as we hadn't noticed him exiting through the main entrance. In his right hand, he held a seemingly heavy black bag—our visit had not been in vain.

We said our goodbyes, and for a change, the farewell with Moon didn't feel as sad as it normally did. We were back at Vish in less than 40 minutes, where the drinking session had begun, with several beer bottles scattered outside Fatty's room. I was looking forward to the evening party—the first real one of my life.

The lobby next to Fatty's room was filled with people, all sitting and chatting with each other, holding bottles in their hands. Das saw us approaching, gave me a short wave, and handed me a beer bottle. He turned to the group and introduced me, 'Guys, meet Raja, a fresher, but someone who has put in an enormous amount of effort to bring out *Graffiti*. I am unsure if we could have brought out this mag without him, and more importantly, you wouldn't have gotten rum to drink without our friend here, Ranjit, another fresher. I propose a toast to these two freshers who have done what it takes to keep the name of BIT flying high. Cheers, guys!'

A loud cheer erupted from the group, and several students rose to extend a handshake and introduce themselves to us. For a change, there was no typical fresher introduction, no strict dress code of full shirts and trousers—just a lot of fun.

After my first bottle of beer, which tasted more delicious than usual—probably because I was already on a high after *Graffiti's* success, then meeting Moon and finally Das's introduction—I was pleasantly tipsy. Fatty handed me a glass with a finger or two of dark, amber-coloured liquid and asked, 'Thums Up or water?'

I looked at him blankly and asked, 'Sorry, but what is this?'

'That's rum, my friend. I think you haven't had it yet, so let me mix it with some Thums Up; it will taste better for a first-timer.'

I took a sip gingerly, wondering how it would feel,

and found the taste quite good—a little bitter, which the soda did well to camouflage. It was cold, with generously added ice cubes, making it seem refreshing in the hot and humid evening. I looked around and saw Ranjit sitting with Das, deep in conversation about how he managed to get the bottles of rum, with Das asking how many bottles we could get from his uncle every month!

Meanwhile, Funny emerged from Fatty's room carrying a bottle of beer in his hand. He saw me sitting by myself and immediately came to sit beside me.

'Cheers,' he said, extending his bottle for a clink with mine.

'Cheers,' I repeated, raising my glass in a toast, and asked him, 'So, how are you feeling today? Your labour of love completed and deemed a success.'

'Worried about the next one. We have a lot to live up to, my friend.'

'Come on, Funny, we have a semester to think about it. We have time, and I'm sure more folks will contribute now that people are aware of *Graffiti*. Look at Ranjit—I am confident he will do what is needed; and Chaaku is very smart—he can perhaps take over the crosswords and some articles from us. Relax and enjoy the feeling of success. You and Das, especially, have worked hard for this.'

'You are right; we should let our hair down a bit. But remember, the first success is always the easiest—it's often seen as inevitable. It's the second one that determines just how good you are.'

His last statement made me ponder for a few moments, and I couldn't agree with Funny more. I turned towards him, extended my right hand for a handshake, and said,

'Boss, I just learnt something enlightening today—thanks. It is indeed a very pertinent point you have just made.'

We solemnly shook hands and went back to our musings. I was engrossed in thinking about how much time had passed and how many experiences I had gathered in the past 70 days. Funny, presumably, went back to thinking about how to make *Graffiti* even better the next time.

'A penny for your thoughts,' smirked Das, standing in his dirty jeans and a torn T-shirt. 'What are you thinking so hard? And Raja, where is your drink?'

It was then that I realized I had consumed the glass of rum without any thought or taste recognition. Ranjit went to fetch more rum and cola, while Das made himself comfortable to my right, his own glass of rum dangling casually from his spindly fingers.

'So, tell me, guys, what's happening? You were in a different world altogether.'

I started, 'Well, Das, it is strange to think I didn't know any of you a couple of months back, and in just this short time, I have found a bunch of folks I want to know and remain close to for the rest of my life.'

'Well, hostel life is like that, Raja,' Das replied. 'It is a tremendous learning experience for everyone. You know what happened when I was in the first year and being ragged by a guy in the fourth?'

'Well, I haven't heard your ragging stories. I would love to hear them sometime.'

Das nodded and continued, 'Don't know how we came to discuss life and death—must have been the mixing of liquors. I recollect we began with beer, quickly moved to whisky and then on to rum. What I do remember is the statement Amit made when we were sozzled: "I want to live as long as I can get my dick hard, not more. Don't see the need to live beyond that."'

I burst out laughing at the statement before the import of the words and Das's serious countenance, viewed through an alcohol-induced stupor, broke into my thought process. It suddenly dawned on me with the full force of reason, and I was back to being sober again. Well, what a time to go!

Das turned to Funny and said, 'Well, why are you looking so bloody glum, like an ordained priest at a nudist club?'

Funny replied, 'Das, do you realize I only have nine months left of this life? If all goes well, I should be leaving the campus, gainfully employed somewhere in the world by this time next year. It is a scary thought, and I don't know how to take it. I am so used to the way we are living here.'

Das chirped up, 'You are drinking beer, I see. That causes all sorts of incorrect thoughts. Here, sip my rum and cola; it will make you feel better. Ranjit,' he shouted once Funny took the glass from his hands, 'get one more rum and cola for Funny, please. He is drinking crap.'

Das turned to me and said, 'So, Raja, what's happening? Did you get to meet her?'

I gave a sheepish smile and said, 'Yes, Das, I did. We just had a couple of minutes, though.'

Ranjit joined us and handed Das and me a glass of rum and cola each. Then he sat down on the floor at the edge of the verandah, his spindly legs dangling awkwardly in his half-torn shorts.

Das commented, 'Strange that Ranjit doesn't drink. Army boy and all that.'

I shook my head in wonder and said, 'That's precisely what Moon and I were speaking about; not just Ranjit, but even his father gave up smoking, just like that, one fine morning. Amazing willpower; we know where Ranjit gets it from.'

Das rummaged through his jeans pocket, fished out a crumpled Gold Flake cigarette packet, and lit it up. Taking a deep puff in contentment, he said, 'Funny seems depressed; we need to cheer him up.'

Turning to Funny, he said, 'Well, Funny, do you realize we have nine months to enjoy! What are we doing? Do you think you, me, this young bloke here, and all of us, will lose touch the minute we step out of this campus? Well, my friend, we will be friends for all our lives. Cheer up.'

'You are right, Das. Honestly, the past three years have been the finest in my life, and I don't know what more can happen to top them. Just a sense of nostalgia; it feels like I entered this institute yesterday, took admission in Mining, and spent the first days shacked up with Mangotra before individual rooms could be found for all of us... awesome memories, yaar.'

Funny then leaned forward, turned to me, and said, 'Raja, do whatever you want during the next four years you will be here, but remember to enjoy this time. I know many of you feared getting ragged and were uncomfortable with staying in a hostel, in a different city, but this is the best time. Enjoy it; it will make you a better person at the end of four years.'

Prophetic words, indeed. Funny believed it would take

all four years to change us; however, the first 80 days were sufficient to make a new me.

I don't remember the time we ended the party; besides the numerous rum and colas, there was a lot of dancing and loud music blaring from someone's speakers. I lost count of time or the number of glasses of the amber liquid I consumed. It was perhaps around 2 a.m. when I dozed off right there in the lobby outside Fatty's room, and my last recollections were of Das, Funny, Fatty, Pods, Krish, Ranjit and me sitting adjacent to each other for a photograph. That photo survives to this day as a reminder of my first daaru party—a beautiful memory of some of the best learning experiences in my life and some of the finest and most selfless friendships ever forged.

19

Journey to the Centre of the Indian Earth

The institute and its denizens placed great emphasis on cultural, social and athletic growth, in addition to the more obvious academic aspects. The institute had three key student organizations—Cultural, Sports and Engineering. Each had a General Secretary elected by its voting members. My interests naturally gravitated towards the cultural side, with some encouragement from the *Graffiti* gang, all of whom were active members of the cultural association.

Das was the secretary for the literary wing, and the tallest man on the campus—a six-foot-seven bloke named Ankit Suchetu—was the Quiz Secretary. Pankaj Singh, a stout and swarthy person with a perpetual smile on his face and blessed with a sensational voice, was the Indian Music Secretary. Brian, the gifted lead guitarist with an encyclopaedic knowledge of rock music, was the General Secretary as well as the secretary of the Western Music Association. He occupied the room next to Fatty's and soon became a good friend of mine. I will never forget how he saved me from what could have been a very nasty situation with Reema and her cohorts.

Brian and Ankit encouraged me to be a part of the cultural wing, and I soon joined the first-year quiz team with Bhoopathy and a budding mechanical engineer called James Anthony. To draw freshers into quizzing and popularize this division, Ankit and his team organized a written quiz contest. Interested freshers were asked to answer a hundred questions spanning topics from Hindi movies to geography and hand the answer sheets back for verification. There was significant interest in the quiz, and dozens of freshers participated. Funny enough, I finished third in the contest. I suppose a lifetime of reading eclectic literature and being interested in esoteric subjects had some benefits!

Ankit commented that I had exceptional knowledge of trivia, cricket, football, literature and Indian movies, which made me a good fit to team up with Bhoopathy, who was strong in general knowledge, and James, who excelled in Hollywood movies, rock music and American sports. Thus, the freshers' quiz team had an all-rounder look, Ankit's opinion was justified when we began winning tournaments in inter- and intra-collegiate festivals over the next few months.

❋

It was a cloudy morning in early October when Ankit woke me from a deep slumber on a Sunday.

'Bloody hell, Ankit, what are you doing at 6 a.m. here?' I protested groggily as I opened the door and gestured for him to follow me inside the room.

Ankit sat on the chair and said, 'Sorry, Raja, but we

have an emergency. I promised to go to LSR for Whale, but I can't. I need to go home tonight. I was hoping you could go instead.'

My mind, never the sharpest before morning coffee and the associated ebullition of the large intestine, meandered along some unexpected lines before I could comprehend that Ankit had asked me a question. I sat bewildered when I realized Ankit was looking at me expectantly, waiting for an answer. I had no clue what he was asking. All I could recollect was about a whale.

'Sorry, but what do you mean? I understand nothing. What whale?' I asked.

'Oh, I thought you knew about Lady Shriram College in Delhi. They are hosting a cultural event called "Blue Whale", and our quiz team is supposed to participate. Also, I had promised to be the quizmaster for one of their events since my sister chairs the organizing committee. Now, I have to leave for Jampot—Jamshedpur to most—tonight, and I was hoping you could take my place. Represent me in our quiz team and conduct the audio-visual quiz. I have everything ready, the questions, music, videos, etc. I just need you to conduct it.'

'So, when do I have to leave? You mean I need to go to Delhi? For how many days?' I was still a little confused, and the lack of coffee wasn't helping my thought process at all.

Ankit knew me well enough by then, I guess, and suggested, 'Come, let us get some tea from DG Corner. Don't think the mess would be open at this hour.'

We quietly made our way to the teashop, scuttling under the awning as we braved the intermittent drizzle that had just begun. The rain only added to my already dreary and forlorn mood. Early mornings did not ever agree with my constitution, and the lack of coffee or something hot and fulfilling gnawed at my vitals. We sat in companionable silence until the glasses of tea were served. It was only after we took a refreshing sip of the golden brew that the silence finally broke.

'Look Raja, LSR is a wonderful place for a first-timer to experience a cultural event. I went there in my second year, and it was a great show. The girls organized it well, and I am sure they will do a wonderful job this time too. So, I suggest you go since the team representing us is good. NPT is going, and Dilip Mahanta and Das are off too, along with the third-year Hindi music band. You will have good company there.'

'Sorry Ankit,' I began, my mind thawing enough to start processing, 'but can you please explain? I am still confused about the cultural stuff you mentioned and LSR. Well, thanks to college life, I have heard of LSD now, but never of LSR,' I joked.

'Well, my friend, LSR is probably worse than LSD,' Ankit replied, smiling. 'It is rumoured that the prettiest girls in Delhi go to LSR for their education, and when they organize the cultural meet, half the student population in North India wait expectantly for an invite. The security is about as bad as it gets, but once you are on the campus, it is great fun. We won the Western music event and the quiz event when I was there last, but last year, we were unfortunately unable to send a team. So, this year, we absolutely have to go, or else they might not come to our festival.'

I nodded in comprehension and said, 'Well, I would love to go. How do we go about it?'

Ankit heaved a sigh of relief and said, 'That's good to hear. I was wondering who else I could ask. The second-and third-year guys cannot go next week as they have their assessments, so I was left with the freshers or fourth-year students. Plus, I was keen to give a chance to someone like you who has done a good deal at the institute in a brief period. It isn't easy to become so close to Das and the team, and contribute to the cultural wing to the extent you have done. Excellent job; I think this trip would be a wonderful experience for you.'

'Thanks,' I muttered weakly, sipping the brew and wondering why I should be thanked for something that gave me a lot of pleasure.

Over the next half an hour, Ankit explained what I needed to do, and soon it was time for me to leave with Das, NPT and a few others who made up the institute's team for the Blue Whale cultural festival. Das, NPT and I sat together in the auto's back seat, with Mahanta hanging on for dear life in the front. I sat between Das and NPT, and they lost no time teasing me about going to my first cultural festival, and that too amid the prettiest girls in Delhi.

My ears were red with embarrassment by the time we landed at Mughalsarai Station. Even after two odd months in a hostel, the seniors had enough in them to make me blush, primarily detailing the options open to a young, virile man in a room full of pretty young ladies. It was obvious I had a lot more to do before I could deem myself to have been transformed!

We arrived at the station as dusk began to fall, giving us a good three hours to procure the tickets and, as Das put it, 'let loose Mahanta on the ticket inspectors' to find us reserved berths. There were 11 of us in the merry gang, with NPT as the team leader and thus responsible for our conduct, performance in the event, and most critically, for ensuring we would not be marked absent for the classes we would be missing! While waiting at the station's portico, waiting for Mahanta and others to get our travel organization confirmed, I asked Das, 'Well, is it always like this? We buy the tickets at the last minute? And why is NPT the team leader? He is normally in a grassed-out state.'

Das smiled and said, 'NPT, well, it is easy. That is perhaps the only way to make him behave—giving him the necessary responsibility. We all love him to death, but we know he will let us down if he doesn't have that responsibility, so this will keep him out of mischief.

'And regarding logistics, we usually decide on events we would be attending earlier in the semesters, and at that time, LSR wasn't on the shortlist. While the girls are great, we normally prefer to attend the IIT fests and the BITS ones only, as we have a limited budget, and the professors don't take too kindly to us missing too many exams. In this case, we had to make an exception for Ankit's sake when we heard his sister was part of the managing committee for the festival. Can't let down a good friend now, can we?'

I nodded in understanding and wondered what would happen to us once we entered the hallowed portals of the institute—these guys found ways to do anything for each other. At that time, I wondered whether we freshers would be able to measure up to such high benchmarks.

An hour or so later, we saw a previously dapper Mahanta, now sweating copiously and looking much worse, his shirt tails hanging out of his crumpled cotton trousers, approach us with a sheaf of tickets in his hands.

He reached us and said, 'I got the tickets, but was unable to find more than three berths. We will have to take a chance inside the train. Luckily, Magadh is a super-fast train, and the next stop is at least two hours away at Allahabad. I should be able to find the TTE and coax him to find us some places to sleep.'

Brian said, 'Well, there are 11 of us, and we have three berths; I suppose we can at least sit and go, I think.'

The Magadh Express was on schedule, and we were all trooped inside the compartment. Due to a paucity of space, many of us stood by the entrance, waiting and hoping for Mahanta to perform his magic. Half an hour or so later, he returned with not-so-good news. He had managed to coax the TTE for three more berths, which was all that was left; that meant a few of us had to spend the night on the cold compartment floor.

After a light meal, NPT, Mahanta, Das, Steven D'Souza and I squatted as comfortably as possible next to the compartment entrance. We closed and locked both entrances to ensure anyone entering or exiting had to use the other exit, and made ourselves comfortable to spend the night. It was post-midnight, and the last light in the compartment had been turned off while we were still chatting.

I listened with interest to the experiences of the guys who had gone to such cultural events earlier, and it was wonderful to hear some of their fascinating stories. Suddenly, NPT dug into his handbag and pulled out a small hookah. He got up to fill the container with a little water from the faucet and gave it to Das, who, in the meantime, had dug out a little, brown-coloured granular substance from a small packet in his handbag. He proceeded to stuff it into the top portion of the hookah; soon, we had a small hookah firing up. After ensuring the light was well and truly lit, took a mouthful of the acrid smoke and passed it on to NPT, who was sitting next to him.

I turned to Steven, seated beside me, and asked him, 'Now, what is that? It works the same way as a pipe, with the water filtering the smoke. But what is the powder? It doesn't look like tobacco.'

'Well, that's grass.'

Grass—Handy Guide to IT Lingo

I looked at Steven, perplexed at what was going on. Steven smiled and passed the hookah to me, saying, 'Well, try it. Just remember it hits you hard, so take a small puff.'

Trepidation filled me as I took a small puff. The acrid-smelling smoke immediately sent me into a paroxysm of coughing and sneezing, tears streaming down my face. A few minutes later, when I felt reasonably normal, I asked, 'What the heck is that?'

Das asked, 'Are you okay?'

I nodded a yes, still not fully trusting myself to speak.

'Grass is the stuff cows eat; that's why they always look so content. Have you ever seen a hyper, aggressive or misbehaving cow? Those buggers don't even misbehave when some old milkman touches their udders and extracts

milk. Wonder why we don't get high on milk, though!'
That was NPT speaking, no prizes for guessing.

NPT always had enough talent to teach a Harvard
professor lateral thinking and, after a couple of drinks,
could potentially successfully argue a complicated case in
a crowded courtroom against Percy Mason, even when
assisted by the beautiful Della Street.

I don't remember much of what happened next, but
I gathered from Steven that I had gone to sleep almost
immediately after my second puff, and had to be carried
and placed on a bunk to sleep off the effects. I sat,
shame-faced, as Steven recounted this to me over a cup
of steaming coffee the next morning, as we neared Delhi
station. So much for my first taste of 'grass'.

Delhi station felt quite different from Howrah. It gave
the impression of being a much smaller station, and as
we exited towards Ajmeri Gate, it was less crowded, with
very few hawkers and just a handful of trains standing in
desultory splendour at a few platforms. Most signs were
in Hindi, and at several places, I noticed the English
rendition of the names had been painted over in black,
presumably by some misguided, fanatical, parochial group.

Soon, we were on the LSR bus with some of the
students from a Lucknow-based college, heading towards
South Delhi. The roads, I noticed, were considerably
broader than those in Calcutta, with wide pavements that
were largely free of hawkers. We crossed the Rashtrapati
Bhavan, and other modern monuments built as a signal
to the world of a newly independent, confident India, and
soon we were at the gates of the famed college.

We were stopped at the gate, and a couple of guards
demanded to see our college ID cards and checked our

names off against a list they had with them. Security was tight; after all, the prettiest girls in Delhi were reputed to study here, and a bunch of rowdy gatecrashers at a cultural festival wasn't exactly what a festival required.

After registering at the administrative complex and receiving guest tags, were shown to our lodgings for the next three days. It was a large, narrow room with a door on its shorter side, lined with a dozen cots against a longer wall and several large, cheerful windows letting warmth and light into the room. I took the bed farthest from the entrance and rested my back as I waited for the next steps. Our escort spoke a few words to NPT, who nodded and followed them out of the room.

'What's next?' I asked Das, who had taken the bed next to mine.

'NPT has gone to check the status; we should know the plans soon,' he replied. 'In the meantime, I wouldn't mind a bit of shut-eye. It has been a long night, and well, not everyone could get a good night's sleep,' he added, winking at me as he settled into the bed.

I must have dozed off despite the light, noise and commotion, and it was a good hour later when I felt myself shaken awake by Steven.

'Hey, sleepyhead, wake up! Ankit's sister wants to meet you. I suggest getting a quick shower and a shave before meeting her. Can't let our institute down with shabby looks, eh!'

After a quick shower and shave, I went down to the lobby, accompanied by Steven, where we saw some young girls talking animatedly to each other. On seeing us approach, one of them moved away from the group and asked, 'Are you guys from BIT?'

We chorused a 'Yes,' and I continued, 'Well, you must be Ankit's sister, Anamika.'

That was an easy guess; she stood about six inches taller than my five-foot-seven in her heels and had the same unmistakable sharp nose that Ankit had. Ankit was easily the tallest student in the institute, and if there were taller students than his sister at her college, they would have to be very tall indeed.

'Yes, I am, and I guess it was easy to figure out, right?' she said with a wink.

I smiled and said, 'Well, I am Raja, and this is Steven,' pointing to Steven, who stared open-mouthed at a stunning young lady to his immediate left.

I gave Steven a sharp nudge, and he turned to Anamika and hastily said, 'Nice meeting you, Anamika.'

'Well, good meeting both of you.' Anamika continued, 'Raja, I need some time from you today. Ankit mentioned you are an exceptionally good quizzer, and I was keen for you to spend some time with our quiz team here. I hope you had a comfortable journey and have had some rest, because I am keen to introduce you to them as soon as possible—now, if you are up for it. Also, I hope you have the questions ready for the audio-visual quiz, which is the first programme tomorrow.'

I said, 'Yes, I have the stuff for the quiz. I will need a projector and a cassette player. I trust that won't be a problem?'

Anamika nodded. 'Great, no issues. We can check everything at the quiz club if you are ready to go now.'

I turned to Steven. 'See you in a bit,' I said, before following the tall lady out of the lobby.

20

Freshers' Nite

A gala event called the 'Freshers' Nite' marked the end of the ragging period at college. On that day, for the last time as a fresher, we had to wear our severe attire. However, by the end of the night, most freshers would be clad in far less—less severe anyway! But we are getting a little ahead of ourselves.

Ragging is a hotly debated topic in India. At various times the press and the public have called it unnecessary, illegal, barbaric and pernicious to the well-being of naïve young individuals just stepping into college life. While this book in no way tries to justify ragging or condones any of the excesses or boorish behaviour that sometimes accompany it, the fact is that this period was squarely responsible for my transformation. Anyone who knew me before college would agree that this—dramatic, quick and disruptive transformation—was for a better Raja. It shaped me into who I am today—someone capable of founding start-ups, leading large firms and collaborating with people from diverse cultures with broad success.

While there have been documented instances of freshers being subjected to serious injuries and even odd cases of abetment to suicide, I personally never came across any incident that caused physical harm to a person. Despite the quantum of ragging many of us were subjected to, we rarely even felt that we were ever in physical danger. On the contrary, ragging made me think laterally and quickly, as I had to answer questions raised by minds twisted by years in an eclectic institution. It made me confident to speak and express myself well, formed a handful of friendships that have stood the test of time and even led to a disruptive institution called marriage.

> *Once upon a time in IT,*
> *Far away from any bustling city,*
> *I came to study engineering,*
> *After hearing tales so intriguing,*
> *About the education in the IT.*
>
> *Four years flew by in a blink,*
> *Indians, Palestinians, without even a chink,*
> *All living together in total harmony,*
> *As thieves after a successful felony,*
>
> *It is with a heavy hand that I write,*
> *The end of the ragging sojourn in sight,*
> *And all the seniors seen in new light,*
> *Are friendly to us with all their might.*
>
> *A new dawn beckons us to proceed,*
> *On the paths with our seniors at lead,*
> *Ahead with the energies of body and mind,*
> *All offers for change of institute we rescind.*
>
> *Happy, content and homely we at IT feel,*
> *With the seniors often joining us for a meal,*

And with all the problems they help us deal,
And with all the problems they help us deal.

Freshers' Nite marked the moment we came out of our cocoon to claim our place as equals with students from other years in one of the finest colleges in the country—and, as most would insist, in the world. This event featured a gala evening where freshers were expected to showcase their talents through cultural performances, ranging from plays and drama to music and dance. Our batch was as talented as any, and a couple of my classmates took charge of organizing the festivities.

I was conspicuous by my absence from any of the preparatory activities, but as Pondy, who was responsible for getting everything together, humorously told anyone who cared to hear, 'Raja is too busy with *Graffiti* and answering fan mail from all the girls he swept off their feet at LSR, so we need to let him have some rest.'

That Friday morning, the 81st day since starting college, dawned sunny and crisp. The monsoon clouds had retreated since it was October, leaving the grounds covered with green grass, overgrown in places, and the buildings freshly washed. I was woken up early that day by heavy knocking on my door, as if someone was attempting to assess the lateral strength of the woodwork.

'Hey guys, what happened? What is on fire?' I groggily asked as I opened the door, surprised to see Ranjit and Pondy, who loved their early morning sleep as much as I did, looking remarkably fresh and dapper.

'Nothing is on fire but get moving quick. Let's get you some coffee,' Ranjit answered, fully aware that I would refuse to do anything without my morning cup of Joe.

I brushed my teeth while the two waited in my room, and soon announced I was ready for the coffee. Aware that it was the last day of the ragging period, I thought that possibly the seniors had called me for one final session to make me a more presentable human being.

'Okay guys, what's up?' I demanded once I had sipped the steaming coffee the mess boy had thoughtfully placed before me. 'You guys would not have woken up at 8 a.m. unless something was happening.'

Ever the consummate sales guy, Pondy took over from Ranjit, and I immediately realized these were still waters and they ran deep.

'Well, Raja, you know that today is Freshers' Nite. The event kicks off at seven in the evening, and we need your help with something.'

I nodded, waiting for him to continue, as I sipped the hot liquid, its warmth and taste waking me up.

'As you are aware,' Pondy continued after a sip of his coffee, 'Brian and the fourth-year guys have helped us organize the evening. He was very keen, and we all, at the Organizing Committee, agree with his observation, that you would be the best person to deliver the opening address.'

I choked on my coffee, sputtering and coughing. When I could finally speak, I exclaimed, 'You guys are crazy. You know very well I cannot do this.'

Rubbing my thigh vigorously after sprinkling water where the hot coffee had spilt, I continued, 'I have never spoken in front of more than five people, and you guys want me to address five thousand. You are out of your minds. Ask someone good at such stuff, not a blinking idiot who never knows when the stammering bug will hit him—and remains the only person who flunked in elocution in class nine.'

Pondy, seated across from me, nodded sagely and said, 'That is precisely why Brian suggested your name.'

Ranjit, who had been quietly sipping his tea, took over. 'Raja, this isn't something that we have decided over a drink. We all considered it carefully and concluded that the most popular freshman is best suited to deliver the opening address. You speak very well and passionately, and you have a command of the language; most importantly, everyone knows you. As Brian pointed out, this would be the best possible indicator of overcoming your speech-related problems that were painfully obvious when you first came here.'

Ranjit put his arms around my shoulders, giving them a friendly, affectionate squeeze, and said, 'Raja, don't be nervous. We know you will be sensational. Just be natural.'

I tried to object. 'No, Ranjit, no. First, I lack the confidence to walk up to the podium and address a thousand people. Second, it is just not fair. You guys, Bhuvan and Bala have worked hard to organize this event, and someone from your team needs to take the bow, not someone like me who has done nothing to assist. Third, I am hardly the best public speaker; we need to find someone like Bhuvan, who regularly won debates at school. We need to get our best speaker for this opportunity.'

Pondy chimed in, 'No, Raja. Bhuvan is also very keen that you address the people. Honestly, we cannot think of someone better than you to do the honours. To increase your confidence, let us spend the rest of the morning preparing your speech; we are here to help you in any way you think we can.'

Ranjit added, 'And, by the way, we have selected PK to deliver the vote of thanks, while the masters of ceremonies are Manish and Pondy here.'

I shook my head in disbelief, 'Crazy guys! PK is just learning English, and Manish and Pondy are as different as chalk and cheese. Manish rarely speaks, and Pondy here has no clue when to start or stop speaking.'

'That is the idea, Raja,' Ranjit said. 'Let us be disruptive. PK will never have a complex about his English after today. Manish will have to step out of his shell and speak more, and Pondy will need to show restraint. Add you to the mix, and we have a disruptive proposition here.'

I shook my head, still unconvinced, and said, 'No, guys. I can't do it. I neither have the talent nor the guts. Why, at school, I regularly got the lowest marks in class for elocution. I must have been the only person to have failed at elocution in my school's hundred-year history.'

'You are doing it, my friend. That is final. I have even informed Moon, and she is coming to the function today as my guest.' Ranjit gave Pondy a wink, and they both roared with laughter, confident they had me now.

I held my head in resignation and misery, scared for the first time in over 10 weeks.

We spent the next hour sketching out key points for the address. Pondy had helpfully prepared a précis, which Brian had reviewed already, helping us develop the content quickly. Soon, I was addressing Ranjit and Pondy in my room, looking more confident than I felt. Funny though, the speech in the evening turned out to be quite different from the one I had so diligently practised all morning.

✳

The clear blue skies soon gave way to dusk with a suddenness I had hardly seen anywhere. One moment, the sun seemed to be shining low, bright and orange at the horizon, the next moment it disappeared, leaving the evening resplendent with a full moon shining bright amongst the countless twinkling stars in the cloudless sky. I was at King's Pavilion, sitting on the railing, my heart pounding in nervousness.

King's Pavilion, nicknamed an unassuming 'KP' by the students, was a square-shaped two-storey building painted in the same dull yellow colour as the rest of the institute. The entrance on the ground floor, which faced the larger of the two football grounds, led to a spacious hall flanked on either side by two large rooms. A steep staircase led to the first floor, which had four rooms. A narrow staircase led to the roof, which had a small room in one corner and a long podium that served as a makeshift stage.

The area was large enough to easily accommodate four hundred seated guests and, on an occasion like this, it could hold perhaps twice that number, with many standing and craning their necks to witness the performances. The organizing committee had thoughtfully arranged several chairs for the professors and honoured guests, who typically spent an hour or two before leaving the students to commence the festivities. That evening was to be no different.

I sat on one of the chairs nervously looking and re-looking at the speech I had jotted down in my irregular hand, even though I knew the two-page note by heart. Bhuvan came to me and gave me a friendly slap on my shoulder.

'Hey, Raja, don't look so nervous. You will do fine.'

'Bhuvan,' I replied, 'you should be doing this address, not me. I lack the skills, and you chaps know it. I will happily take three more months of ragging than face a crowd to address them.'

'Don't be ridiculous, Raja. You underestimate your abilities. The trick to any good address is to relax and let passion take over—don't worry too much about the script. Your command of the language is excellent, and you have clever ideas; use them. If you stick to a script, the passion disappears, and so does the spontaneity that makes an address memorable. Just remember the key points you need to bring out and relax. You will do great.'

With another friendly slap on my back, Bhuvan walked off to discuss some other nuance with the organizing committee, leaving me to ruminate over his monologue. It did make sense, I concluded.

Soon, the students began arriving, followed by the professors, and it was time for me to commence the proceedings. Amidst the melee, I did not see Moon arrive, but when I walked up to the stage, I saw she was seated on the second row, beside Dr Basu from the Electronics department.

I walked towards the podium with more confidence than I felt, tapped the microphone to check it was working, and looked at the crowd for the first time from my new vantage point. Suddenly, no words came out, the speech forgotten as my mind went blank. All my fears of failure came rushing, and I looked at the crowd, then at the microphone, and then at Moon, sitting demurely, waiting patiently for me to begin, in a daze. I was dumb in shock for several agonizing seconds till I noticed Moon pouting a kiss at me.

Crowds are queer things. The atmosphere felt magnetic that night, and Moon's presence and her pout heightened the charge. I came under the influence of something quite indescribable. I had practised the speech for several hours, and had a neatly written note in front of me with the salient points, but as I looked upon the sea of upturned expectant faces, I suddenly ceased to remain a stammering dolt. I became an actor. I had an audience before me and I wanted to move them. Something clicked, and I began to speak, not from the rehearsed script but on my own—the hours of practice and the key points jotted down by the seasoned Brian all forgotten—as Pink Floyd would claim, in a momentary lapse of reason.

Initially, I even failed to offer the traditional greetings to the professors and the honoured guests, and instead began:

'Friends, part of this institute and friends because of this institute, it is an honour and a pleasure to stand before you today, representing this amazing class at this august institution. This is an important occasion, and we, the incredibly talented class of freshmen, feel privileged to be here and take our place as first-year students.

'As a class, we hope to live up to the reputation, pedigree and history of this college. We hope to prove ourselves worthy of this institution and promise to be diligent students and citizens, and endeavour to remain honest to ourselves, this institution and our country.'

I took a deep breath and continued.

'All of us came into this institution as naïve, innocent students with dreams in our eyes and a song in our hearts. Over the past 12 weeks, those dreams have become closer to reality, and the songs in our hearts have become more melodious; all of us, without a doubt, have intensely enjoyed these past 12 weeks. It has been a period of intense learning and some great friendships have been forged; we have received selfless assistance from all interactions, and we want to thank the professors and the seniors for making us feel at home.

'While some seniors use some quirky ways to achieve this and mistakenly call it ragging, they do so with the fair intention of making us more comfortable in our new and unfamiliar environment.'

I paused as claps and laughter rippled through the crowd before continuing.

'I must admit, when I entered this college, I could only associate the colour blue with VIBGYOR and the sky. Now, I have learned a sex—sorry, sen—sational new idiomatic expression related to what I once thought was just a colour, and it has a much less depressing usage in idiomatic contexts.'

Once again, I had to wait for the applause and laughter, this time louder and more prolonged than the earlier one, to die down before I could continue.

'The learning over these past 12 weeks has been sensational, and I am not just referring to our newfound appreciation for some colours.'

There were a few desultory claps when the message sunk in, and I continued.

'Now we know a "murga" does not necessarily refer to a "hen", the "air" has numerical connotations, and "UFOs" stands for "unidentifiable fried objects". Well, I am sure we can spend the rest of the evening discussing the different acronyms we have learnt over the past weeks.'

There was a lot of laughter and some clapping, and I waited for the noise to abate.

'Capra wrote that physicists do not need mysticism, mystics do not need physics, but humanity needs both. Dare I say our seniors and professors have demonstrated humanity when they could have focused on their work instead of trying to make us freshers more attuned to life here. After these 80 days, I can confidently claim that we freshers needed the ragging to help transform us.

'I still remember the Saturday morning I entered the desolate Rajputana Hostel for the first time. I felt like Alice, who peeked into her sister's book and wondered about the value of a book without pictures or conversations. Well, the past few weeks seemed to have transformed the desolate landscape into a vibrant wonderland, and this Alice—pardon the gender pun—is still here with an entire assortment of well-meaning Mad Hatters.

'I also remember the day I first arrived at this institution, when my uncle and I debated whether it was the right place for a teenager to grow up. Now, I KNOW it is the best place for anyone who wants to live and not grow up. After all, Peter Pan was born here and still lives here, waiting to grow up sometime. Or rather, never.'

There was a smattering of applause, even from the professors, as the students at the back hooted their approval. I paused, all pretence of the script and any thoughts of a logical recital of the key points forgotten in the enthusiasm and adrenaline of the moment. I saw Moon smiling widely, and she raised her hand in a V sign when she noticed I was looking at her. I took a deep breath and continued.

'School rarely prepares us for college life—this is something we have constantly heard from our seniors and elders. However, we could only realize how little it actually prepares us after coming here. Those first days—alone in a room, staring at the ceiling, willing for sleep to envelop us in its warm cocoon; hesitantly making new friends; wandering the corridors trying to locate the right room for our next class; coming to terms with the freedom that one can actually NOT go to class if so desired, and, well, no one even asks for a letter from the parents when one misses a class—was all a unique experience.

'While we had been warned that school life and college life in a hostel are very different, I don't think anyone was prepared for the sheer scale of it. I think it is a credit to us, and with no small assistance from our seniors and professors, that we have adapted well and have begun to enjoy the moments.

'So, thank you, our dear seniors, for showing us, in uncertain measure, how to efficiently rag the unsuspecting kids who will take admission next year. Nothing could have prepared us for this one piece of education!'

There were huge guffaws amongst the students, and I could hear Steven's screechy voice declare loudly, 'Well, Raja, we can always extend the ragging period to teach you guys something we might have missed.'

I smiled at his comment and thought a repartee

should be in order. 'Well, Steven, it would be great if we could demonstrate to you and others how well we have learnt the art. Well, my class, do you think a day where we demonstrate ragging techniques to the seniors should be in order?'

There was a huge roar of approval from my batchmates, with several shouts of 'Hear, hear!' echoing through the space. I waited for the noise to subside before continuing,

'Friends, we hope you will enjoy today's show; I know you would appreciate the efforts we have put in to demonstrate some of the talent this class possesses, and we would also love the constructive feedback that is so critical for us to improve. Some of the shows and skits may even be sarcastic and derogatory; we have taken some liberties, and I would like to apologize in advance if we occasionally go beyond the straight and the narrow. I can assure you that we don't mean any disrespect to anyone.

'I passionately believe that "all is fair in love, war and engineering". And with that, I would like to introduce you to the MCs of the evening, the M, and the P of our batch, who will keep you company for the rest of the evening.

'My friends, thank you for everything—most of all, for teaching us how to live fearlessly and be adaptable. As Tolstoy said, "everyone thinks of changing the world; no one thinks of changing himself". I think all of us have understood the true import of these words in these past few weeks. Thank you for that.'

I stepped off the stage to a standing ovation, and Ranjit and Bhuvan, who were waiting at the foot of the stage, hugged me, carrying me to the corner where a large group of students had gathered.

There was much backslapping and a general sense of euphoria, when Brian walked up to us and said in his dry humour, 'Well, someone claimed he couldn't speak.'

It suddenly struck me then—I had not stammered; not only that, but I had also not felt that I was going to! How had this happened? How did a pathetic, stammering, diffident Raja, who regularly flunked in elocution at school thanks to his inability to speak in front of 40 students, suddenly have the confidence to go on stage in front of a few hundred people and talk without stammering for a dozen minutes? Wonders never cease!

PK was so obviously sincere in his efforts to deliver the vote of thanks that everyone instantly warmed up to the rustic but kind-hearted batchmate of ours. Kalpana was sensational in her rendition of a Geeta Dutt classic, and Santosh and the team put on an exceptional short play. The evening was rendered resplendent by a super performance by the first-year rock band—they managed to play complex and popular numbers like 'Smoke on the Water' in the little time they had had to practise. It was obvious to all listening that the proud rock culture of BIT was in excellent hands.

All in all, the two-hour programme was deemed a success by all those concerned, and the organizing committee consisting of Bhuvan, Ranjit, Pondy and Bala were given a round of applause by the entire institute for a job very well done.

That was one of the few occasions I saw Ranjit blush.

I didn't get the occasion to exchange more than a

few words with Moon as she was closeted with Dr Basu, but she—in a quick gesture unnoticed by anyone in the crowd—gave my hand an affectionate squeeze, a peck on my cheek, and said, 'Well done.'

The first kiss is always special, and the first one in the middle of a crowded room? Even more so.

I don't recall washing my face for the next couple of days.

21

From Freshers to Not-So-Fresh

Very few of us slept on Freshers' Night. The sheer euphoria was intoxicating, and the abundance of liquor did little to enhance the already heightened sense of well-being. I felt somewhat disoriented; the enormity of what I had done hadn't yet sunk in. The fact that I had addressed a large crowd without stammering even once was scarcely believable. Even the brief, sweet meeting with Moon after the event paled in comparison to the potentially life-changing 15 minutes on stage. I had spoken in front of 500 people!

10 October was unnaturally chilly, though sunny and bright, with not a speck of cloud in the sky. I lay in bed, lazily contemplating the past 80 days. I was wondering if it would be worth getting up for coffee, when a loud knock interrupted my musings. I managed to rouse myself and opened the door to find Fatty, Funny, Krish and Das. Funny gave me a big hug, and the rest followed him in.

'Well, my friend,' Funny began, 'it looks like you have actually arrived, in more ways than one. I was speaking to Adesh last evening; by the way, Shailesh was asking about you and sent his best regards. I mentioned that you are among the most popular freshers in this batch, which surprised your old school chum significantly. Apparently you had a major stammering problem during school and, according to Shailesh, you were very shy and introverted, only speaking when spoken to. Seeing your transformation is incredible—it's truly amazing.'

Das nodded thoughtfully. 'You know, Raja,' he added, 'we've seen kids change dramatically in the first few weeks of hostel life, but not like you. If what Adesh and Funny say is even partly true, your transformation is incredibly positive; this experience will leave you much better suited to life in general. Congratulations, my friend—and on last evening's speech, too. It was fantastic. I didn't get a chance to say that last night.'

Fatty grinned, gave me a high-five, and exclaimed, 'Thod-phod boy!'

Thod-phod—Handy Guide to IT Lingo

We all went out for tea, discussing what makes people change. While some change for the better, others lose control and misuse opportunities. Then there are those who resist change, clinging to their little cocoons.

As we walked to the tea shop, I reasoned with Funny and Das that it was the company that had helped me change so dramatically for the better. I felt lucky to have come into contact with the *Graffiti* gang and knew I owed Shailesh and his brother Adesh my thanks for introducing me to them. These guys had made me strong. After all, a hard-boiled egg is hard to beat!

'You're right,' I said. 'I feel a lot more confident now.

Being accepted into this university and this eclectic group of highly intelligent guys has boosted my confidence. That's probably why I've been able to adapt to a different lifestyle and come out of my shell. Honestly, you guys—the *Graffiti* gang—are the reason for my change!'

Fatty then mentioned that Ankit was looking for me and suggested I return with them to Vishvesvaraya Hostel. I nodded in agreement, and we continued our leisurely walk towards the hostel, each lost in thoughts. During the five-minute walk, I reflected on the significant change that had come over me in the past 12 weeks and wondered if there was a lesson there.

As we entered Vishvesvaraya, a thought struck me— change is the only constant. The sooner one appreciates and embraces it, the better it is for them. At the same time, one needs the good fortune to be surrounded by the right people for the right change. I was still mulling over this when my thoughts were abruptly interrupted by Fatty's loud voice reverberating through the hostel, assaulting my ears.

'Ankit!' The walls seemed to tremble with the sound waves, creating a perfect storm of discordant notes.

'Ankit!' Fatty's voice ballooned again.

I wondered if anyone would respond to stop the incessant noise. Finally, Ankit emerged from the mess area and waved his hands, possibly entreating Fatty to cease calling his name and restore the morning's tranquillity.

'God, you haven't changed in four years here now, have you?' Ankit said to Fatty. 'Your voice is still as loud as it was the first day I heard it in Morvi.'

'Funny you mention change,' Fatty replied, pointing at me. 'We were just discussing it with the kiddo here.'

Still recovering from the assault on my eardrums, I shook my head and said, 'Hey Ankit, what's up? I heard you were looking for me. I don't have your experience of coping with Fatty's voice, so I'm still a little groggy. Nothing a coffee in your mess can't cure, though.' I gave him a broad smile as I said the last line.

Ankit smiled back and suggested, 'Yes, let's go to the mess. I have something to show you.'

We walked leisurely to the mess while Das updated Ankit on our discussions at DG Corner, and Funny and I chatted about the GKWs that had sprung up in abundance after the rains.

Once in the mess, Ankit asked us to wait while he went to his room to fetch something. We ordered coffee while we waited. Ankit returned with a large brown envelope in his hands.

'Hey, Raja,' he began, 'you seem to have made quite an impression on my sister—not to mention her friends.'

I nodded noncommittally and replied, 'Well, all I did was conduct the quiz and participate in a couple of events. Mahanta and I even won the antakshari, and Das won the rag-mag competition, as usual. Nothing too exciting.'

With a sly smile, Ankit opened the envelope and pulled out a glossy photograph. 'Strange, these pictures say otherwise.'

We all crowded around the photograph, and my face flushed with embarrassment. It was a picture of me holding up a sequined red dress towards the camera, surrounded by six of Delhi's prettiest girls, all wearing outfits that left little to the imagination. I hadn't mentioned to the gang that, during the LSR fest, I had been invited to the girls' fancy dress competition and somehow ended up in the dressing room. The girls were busily trying to adjust their outfits when I, jokingly, held up the dress to make room for me to sit down and asked one of the girls, Sheba, if she thought I'd look good in it. I ended up in the photograph since the girls had decided to take a picture.

I explained, 'I was in the dressing room for just 10 minutes before they asked me to leave so they could have more privacy. But, you know, what happens in front of a camera stays forever.' I'm just glad YouTube had not been invented back then!

Suddenly, Das gave me a hard slap on my back, making me wince in pain, and I let out a loud 'Ouch!'

He looked positively livid and didn't hold back in expressing his frustration. 'You son-of-a-gun! You never mentioned this to any of us. Fuck, man! You had an exciting time with the girls, and here we were, trying to win some trophies for the Institute,' he exclaimed.

Defending myself, I said, 'Hey, Das, nothing much, yaar. Remember the girl who conducted the antakshari... Rashmi? After the event, we got talking—she was keen to understand how a South Indian like me knew all those old Hindi songs. Then she realized she had to rush into the dressing room for her fancy dress event and asked me to follow her to continue our discussion. That's all, nothing else happened.'

Another slap on my back and Das retorted, 'Nothing else happened? Eh? *Chuppa rustom.*'

Chuppa rustom–Handy Guide to IT Lingo

Ankit then proceeded to take more photographs out of the envelope, and we looked at group photos of the quiz contest, the rag-mag competition, the antakshari and others.

I asked Ankit, 'Hey, do you have more copies of these? I wouldn't mind having some.'

With a wink, Ankit replied, 'All except the *special* one.'

In mock surrender, I said, 'Fine, all of them then. And I need to ensure the one special one is hidden somewhere.'

As we continued chatting about less dangerous topics, we remembered that the Durga Puja vacations were only a few days away.

Das inquired, 'So, what are your plans, Raja? I recall you mentioning that you were considering going home for the vacation. Is it still on?'

I replied, 'Don't know, Das. If I go, I will have to go to both Bokaro and Calcutta. I wonder if it's worth the trip for just ten days. What about you? Patna is just a hop, skip and jump away.'

'Yes, I am off for a few days; Funny is coming with me. There's no way he can make the three-day trip to Madras for such a short break.'

I nodded in agreement. The Kashi Vishwanath Express was the only train running between Varanasi and Madras, and it took more than 48 hours.

'That's good. How about Fatty, Krish or any of the guys who can't make it back home? Want to visit a small town and a large city in a week? It would be fantastic if you guys could spend time with my folks in Bokaro and Calcutta,' I suggested.

Fatty was happy to come with me, but Krish mentioned he needed to check if he could travel. His department was considering organizing special classes to make up for the time lost during sine die. We decided to wait a few days before purchasing the train tickets, even though we were warned that getting reserved seats would be difficult due to the holiday rush in the woefully underfunded Indian railway system.

Ankit mentioned that Ramulu and Pods would be joining him in Jamshedpur for a week, and perhaps we could all meet up in Bokaro or Jamshedpur, just over 120 kilometres apart but a good five-hour-drive thanks to the lousy pothole-ridden roads.

'That sounds like a great plan, Ankit,' I responded. 'It would give us something to do during the holidays. Nothing ever happens at Bokaro. Of course, you can enjoy some of my mom's delightful vegetarian cooking at home!'

Suddenly, Krish, who usually remained quiet and measured, piped up, 'To hell with the classes! I haven't had home-cooked vegetarian grub for months now.' Turning to me, he added, 'Raja, count me in—and please ask your mother to make rasam daily.'

'That's easy,' I replied. 'She loves rasam and makes it daily. I never liked it, but funny enough, my mouth is watering at the sound of it.'

Funny how one's taste could change so dramatically. I used to be a fastidious eater, carefully picking out vegetables and sauces, but now, anything home-cooked seemed heavenly.

'Sick of UFOs already, eh?' Das teased. 'You have another four years to go!'

UFO—Handy Guide to IT Lingo

'Yes, Das,' I replied. 'And to think I hated rasam and roughly 90 per cent of the things Mom cooked. But right now, I would gladly eat anything she makes.'

'It happens, machchan,' Fatty chimed in. 'Look at me. One would think I eat a lot and eat everything I can find. But I used to be very finicky too. Now, when I go home, all I do is eat and eat everything home-cooked.'

After a while, I started walking back to my hostel. At DG Corner, I found Nilesh with his arm around Shashank's shoulder, a picture of perfect friendship. It was strange to see this, considering my most vivid memory of the pair was from Shashank's first day when Nilesh had made him measure the entire lobby with a five-paise coin. Smiling at the thought, I called out, 'Hey, Nilesh! Looks like you are best friends with Shashank now. Great to see you guys.'

Nilesh gave me a friendly wave, high-fiving me when I was close enough. 'Well, Shashank is from my school, and there was no way I could have let him go through four years of university weighing approximately 120 per cent more than his ideal weight. Look at him now,' he continued. 'Doesn't he look reasonable?'

I smiled at Shashank and commented, 'Well, he does seem to have lost considerable weight.'

Shashank, who had taken full advantage of the post-ragging period's lax attire, was back in his hideous Bermuda shorts, this one with two colours—red on the right leg and blue on the left. I considered the colours and wondered what would happen if they mixed; would someone get maroon-ed? Pun intended.

'Yes, I feel slimmer,' Shashank said.

'Off to Calcutta for the pujas, Raja?' Nilesh asked.

'Yup,' I said. 'How about you guys? Off to Delhi?'

Both nodded in agreement, and we spent a few minutes catching up before Shashank and I headed back to our hostel. As we walked, we discussed the freshers' night and the funny way the seniors had behaved.

'All in all, it was a great experience,' Shashank said, referring to the ragging period. 'Even though there were several occasions when I felt like dropping the nearest flowerpot on some senior's head.'

'I know what you mean,' I responded. 'Some of the ragging, particularly by the second-year Electronics and third-year Civil students, was obnoxious.'

'I think my worst experience was with second Chem.'

'Oh, so you had an encounter with those guys. They made poor Achintya run half a kilometre, praying for his life.'

'He he, I remember that. But in my case, it was a lot more mundane. They turned me into Superman and then made me perform some stupid Bollywood dance routines.'

We said our goodbyes at the hostel entrance, Shashank going up the stairs near the entrance, while I walked towards the far side for mine. As I climbed up the stairs, my mind lingered on the past few weeks. I wasn't the only one who had changed dramatically. Some of us had even become slimmer versions of ourselves!

22

Calcutta Part III

A week later, we arrived in Calcutta, pulling into Howrah Station on the Coalfield Express from Dhanbad. The train rolled on to Platform 11 just after 10 in the morning. Overall, the journey had been comfortable, as my father had bought us reserved seats in the air-conditioned coach. During the five-hour trip, we relished superb kachori and samosa at Asansol, sweet son-papdi at Durgapur, and the exceptional tea served by various vendors in small earthen pots called bhand in Bengali.

Fatty and I chatted throughout the journey, while Krish dozed off in the window seat, snoring gently and waking up intermittently to munch on the goodies.

'This bhand concept is great,' Fatty remarked from his aisle seat. 'I don't know why folks in Madras cannot adopt this concept. It is sometimes sickening to drink from a dirty glass.'

'Yes; this is also eco-friendly and supports small enterprises,' I responded.

Fatty nodded in agreement and said, 'Machchan, I had a great time at your place. Your mom's a wonderful person, and your pop is cool. He offered me whisky from his stock! Far-out!'

I smiled at the memory of Fatty torn between accepting the whisky and trying to be polite by refusing it. Eventually, the devil in him won, and my father and Fatty spent the entire evening drinking Chivas and entertaining us with their irreverent humour.

'Yup, my old man is cool. Can you imagine? A South Indian Brahmin boy like me, never asked to study by his old man?' I said with a chuckle.

We woke Krish from his slumber as the train reached the platform and made our way to the station's grand entrance, lugging our bags. As Fatty and Krish marvelled at the gigantic ceilings and the sheer size of the station, I explained that it was India's biggest railway station. I also mentioned Sealdah, another station in Calcutta primarily catering to trains bound for the east and northeast of India, smaller in size but reputed to be the busiest due to the local trains.

Outside, we joined a long taxi queue facing the Hooghly River. Krish and Fatty were captivated by the view—the iconic Howrah Bridge rising majestically to their left, while the second Hooghly Bridge—a few weeks away from inauguration—was visible to their right. The foggy morning lent an enchanting atmosphere, with the sun trying to break through the mist, casting weak rays of light.

Behind us, bus conductors called out their destinations for passengers in staccato rhythm.

Krish turned to me and said, 'Raja, this is incredible. I've never seen such activity in my life. Bangalore is big, and Madras perhaps bigger, but this is beyond imagination. It's an uncommon blend of beauty and chaos. The river and the bridge, the station—they're all uncommonly beautiful, but the squalor and filth make the place hideous.'

I nodded in agreement. 'Yes, that's probably a good approximation of Calcutta—the splendid and the squalor coexisting in perfect equanimity.'

After a 20-minute wait, we finally boarded a taxi. As we climbed in, the sun broke through the fog, bathing us in golden light. Krish and Fatty sat in the back seat while I sat beside the driver and told him, 'Hazra Road *jabo*, Ritchie Road *crossing er kache*,' instructing him to take us to Hazra Road near the Ritchie Road crossing.

To my surprise, I didn't stammer while giving the directions—not even on the letter 'R'. All my life, I had struggled with stammering, especially when asked to name myself or my address. It was a pleasant surprise to realize that a lifetime of regret and reluctance to converse with strangers due to my stammer could finally be put to rest.

As the taxi crossed the Hooghly River on the stately Howrah Bridge, Krish and Fatty looked on with admiration at the engineering marvel. Krish remarked, 'Proud that we will soon be engineers—after all, it took an engineer to visualize and build this bridge.'

'Three cheers for us engineers—hip, hip, hurray!' Fatty bellowed, momentarily startling the taxi driver and causing him to lose control of the wheel. The driver seemed horrified at the realization that someone other than his wife could have a voice that loud and shrill. He muttered in Bengali, '*Amar bou er thekeo beshi* (Even louder than my wife),' and we both laughed at the remark, which I translated into English for Krish and Fatty.

We inched our way through Brabourne Road and moved silently through the distinguished Old Courthouse Road, with the grandeur of East India Hotel on one side and Lal Dighi and GPO (General Post Office) on the other; soon we were gliding down Hospital Road and Red Road.

Fatty expressed his fondness for trams, which he missed in Madras. 'No trams in Madras anymore,' he lamented.

We entered Harrington Street (now Ho Chi Minh Sarani), then took a right on Russell Street, before proceeding to Lower Circular and finally reaching Ballygunge Circular Road. As we passed my school, I pointed out the majestic edifice to Krish and Fatty. 'That's my school,' I said proudly.

'We should come take a look, Raja,' Krish commented. 'It looks fantastic.'

'Yes, we can do that tomorrow. SLOBA, our old boy's association, runs a clinic every Sunday; we can even meet some teachers and alumni,' I suggested.

'That sounds good,' replied Krish, and Fatty nodded in agreement. He seemed a little embarrassed by the driver's comment about his voice being louder than his wife's. For the past 20 minutes, he had been unusually quiet, brooding or muttering softly. But I knew Fatty well enough to realize that he would soon revert to his old self. He never took anything seriously, and his sheer zest for life was infectious.

As we reached home and rang the doorbell, my aunt opened the door and shrieked gleefully—a sound that could comfortably compete with Fatty's decibel levels— then hugged me. I introduced my friends to her, and she excused herself to get us some coffee.

She returned with three steaming cups, sat opposite me and stared intently at my face. I raised a questioning eyebrow at her scrutiny and she commented, 'Raja, you have changed. You are a very different person now. You are no longer the little boy who left home three months back.'

I smiled at the memory of my shy, stuttering self, mumbling goodbye to everyone as my uncle and I got into the taxi. Time had flown, leaving me wondering about the transformation that had taken place.

Curious about my aunt's observation, Fatty and Krish looked at me. While they both knew me well, they probably never realized how different I used to be.

I turned to my aunt and said, 'Well, *Mami*, I weigh the same—around 50 kgs! Don't think I've put on any weight, and I'm too old to grow taller now.' I chuckled lightly at my weak joke and asked her, 'So what's changed then? I even shaved just so that you'd let me in.'

During my Class XI examinations, I had not shaved for over five weeks. My aunt had ordered me to visit the local barber before setting foot inside the house on the last exam day. As usual, I forgot her directive and landed home with my straggly facial hair. She took one look at my face and insisted I get a shave before entering the house.

'You don't necessarily have to put on weight to be different,' she replied.

'Well, talk about yourself, Mami,' I retorted, laughing.

My aunt smiled, and for a moment, we both reminisced how, about five years ago, she married my uncle and joined the family as a thin, sensitive young woman, fearful of the myriad experiences that come with leaving behind her parents' home to come live with her new husband and his family.

'Well, it took me five years to put on 20 kgs and to shed some of my timid nature. It's taken you 10 weeks,' she said.

Krish chimed in, 'You are right, Mami. We said the same thing to Raja a few days ago.'

My aunt leaned back against the chair, gave me another appraising look, and said, 'Look at his eyes—they're different. The way he walked into the house, the way he's speaking…everything has changed. Raja would have never dared to comment on my changes three months ago. My brother warned me about letting Raja go to Banaras; he suggested Raja should stay in Calcutta and study at the ISI. I didn't realize how right he was.'

At this, Fatty spoke up, his temporary embarrassment in the taxi clearly a thing of the past. 'Well, isn't it good that Raja has changed? He is so much more confident now.'

Mami nodded thoughtfully and said, 'Absolutely, I think it is great. But I want to ensure that his warm nature remains intact. Other than that, it's great. I am so happy to see him confident, speaking clearly and making friends in Banaras. I always thought he didn't have enough friends in Calcutta and depended more on his cousins than his schoolmates.'

Krish commented, 'Well, he is one of the most popular first-year boys at uni now.'

My aunt turned to me, her eyes brimming with pride and warmth. 'I always knew Raja was special. Give me a minute,' she said, stepping out of the room to discreetly wipe away her tears of joy. She returned with a small piece of cloth clutched tightly in her hand and stood before me, performing a small prayer, waving her hands in a circular motion to ward off the evil eye.

As she sat down again, the low hum of the television filled the room—a particularly erotic Bollywood number was playing. As I watched idly, I couldn't help but reflect that not all the changes in me had been positive. It seemed an inappropriate occasion for such thoughts, but I realized I had developed a certain mischievous streak. I was no longer scared or embarrassed about admiring women in various stages of undress, unlike that first day with Nutty and the gang in Vivekananda!

Sunday dawned sunny and bright, a typical October morning in Calcutta—crisp, beautiful and infused with the scent of fresh flowers. The city seemed to be on its best behaviour just after the monsoons. The fresh air and the rains had washed away the accumulated heat and grime of the humid summer months. There was an undeniable air of joy with the festive season in full swing, as most schools had declared a vacation for children to enjoy the celebrations. Durga Puja was also a time for Bengalis to mingle; it was when relatives and friends came to visit from far and wide—a prime occasion for matchmaking among bachelors and spinsters.

The previous evening had been spent in easy conversation with my grandfather and uncle when they returned from their respective offices. Fatty and Krish took immediately to my taciturn but warm-hearted grandfather and my ever-smiling uncle. My aunt prepared some delicious

South Indian food, and Fatty declared her cooking to be as good as my mother's, which made Mami's day!

Early on Sunday, after a breakfast of coffee and hot idlis, Fatty, Krish and I set off towards my school. It was only a couple of kilometres away, making for a pleasant walk. We passed Maddox Square, where a large puja pandal had been erected, the idol of the goddess and her family hidden behind a large piece of cloth. I gave Fatty and Krish a quick rundown on the significance of Durga Puja and mentioned that the drapes covering the idols would be removed the next morning—on *Sashti*, the sixth day.

On our way, we crossed a group of young women dressed in beautiful Bengali silk sarees. Fatty looked at them, then back at me, and said, 'And you told us Bong females are not hot.'

I smiled at him before glancing back at the group, who had noticed us staring. One of them looked at me and flashed a fleeting smile. I returned the smile, losing myself in her grey eyes. They were mesmerizing—like watching the sunrise on Puri beach, with the warm water lapping at your ankles and a sense of contentment filling your heart. Suddenly, the girl burst into a laugh and darted across the road to join her friends, who had by then crossed the narrow lane.

We soon arrived at St Lawrence. The school had two large gates—the main entrance, flanked by two grand columns with a wrought-iron gate and a uniformed guard keeping unwanted visitors away, and another on Ritchie Road, which led directly into the school grounds. The latter was closed with a sliding iron gate, and only opened during school hours for buses ferrying children.

We walked around the imposing building, Krish and Fatty gazing at it in speechless awe, until we reached the main entrance.

'Well, Calcuttans sure know how to build grand structures, machchan,' the awestruck Fatty said. 'This is massive.'

'My school had 12 classrooms in one row and a tiny lawn where we ate lunch. There was no proper playground—not that the teachers ever wanted us to play, in case we didn't clear the IIT entrance exams,' Krish added dryly.

'This school has three football grounds, one basketball court, a volleyball court, and even a small zoo on the campus. Two of the football grounds are fit to host any international tournament, and we have hosted a few. The third one is slightly smaller but perfect for hockey. Yes, we are lucky to have such expansive ground, and to ensure we all got our playtime, our lunch break was an hour long each day,' I explained.

'Massive,' Fatty repeated, shaking his head in wonder.

At the entrance, a uniformed guard accosted us, standing firmly in our path. '*Ki chai?* (What do you want?)'

'I am a former student,' I responded in Bengali, 'and I am here to meet the SLOBA guys.'

His weathered face broke into a smile as he welcomed me, quizzing me about my companions. I told him that they were my classmates from college.

We climbed a set of stairs leading to the school foyer, which looked like a gothic castle; it had four rooms on either side, all leading to the football grounds. We entered the room on our far left, which had a board proclaiming it as the office of SLOBA, and found half a dozen men sitting on straight-backed chairs, engaged in an animated discussion. One of them looked up and asked what we were looking for.

'I am a former student; I passed my *Uchha Madhyamik* (Higher Secondary) this year and just came to visit the school,' I replied. 'These are two of my college friends who were keen to see it.'

At this, all the men stood up to shake hands with me, asking how I was doing and what I was up to. They introduced themselves in turn, sharing their names and the year they had passed out. I realized that one of them, Soumitra, had been my uncle's classmate; he chuckled when he heard that his old friend had been tasked with depositing me in Banaras.

One of the men went outside to order tea for everyone, and soon we were sitting on the uncomfortable straight-backed chairs, discussing schools, universities, and whether school prepared someone for life in a prestigious engineering institution.

Sitting with my back to the wall, adjacent to the open door, I looked up to see Kartikeyan Grover entering the room, followed by two of his usual cohorts, Pritish and Sachin. I went quiet and a lifetime of embarrassment caused by these three students made me squirm with discomfort. Kartikeyan didn't notice me at first, heading straight to shake hands with Soumitra. Pritish noticed me and exclaimed 'Raja!' just as Kartikeyan finished shaking Soumitra's hands and was about to greet the gentleman sitting next to him.

At Pritish's exclamation, Kartikeyan turned, his face flushing red. He muttered a weak 'Hi' to me and asked how I was doing.

'What are you doing here?' Sachin asked, shaking my hand. 'I heard you study at an IIT.'

'Yes, I am at BIT,' I replied. 'How about you guys?'

'Well, none of us got into engineering, so we decided to sit for the exam again next year. We are studying for a science degree now while preparing for next year's IIT entrance test.'

'All the best,' I replied, not knowing what else to say.

I was amazed to hear that these three, among the smartest kids in my school, had failed to crack the entrance exam. For a moment, I almost felt sorry for them, but it soon vanished when I remembered my last encounter with the trio. It had been immediately after the school final examinations and, as usual, they had used the occasion to poke fun at me.

'Oh, by the way, it would be great if you could spend time with us to help us with our preparation,' Sachin continued, snapping me out of my brief reverie.

I murmured 'Of course', and looked at Kartikeyan properly for the first time. I had never seen him embarrassed, bereft of a wisecrack, and considering me with anything other than supreme contempt. *Life has a funny way of dealing in circles*, I thought.

I suddenly remembered Fatty and Krish, who were sitting quietly in the corner. I introduced them to my schoolmates, and Sachin said, 'Great, we have three IITians in this room. Can we step outside for a few minutes and bounce some ideas off you for the exams?'

I nodded, and we all trooped out to the empty football ground. We squatted on the fresh, verdant grass, which had never looked greener to me; the sun had never felt warmer on my back, and I had never felt happier in that moment, flanked by Fatty and Krish, watching Kartikeyan and Pritesh squirm while Sachin asked all the questions, which Krish answered with his usual passion and detail.

I thought about Moon then, wondering what she was doing, and felt a sudden anticipation for the moment I could be back in Varanasi to tell her all about this incident. Suddenly, I realized I was unexpectedly looking forward to boarding the Himgiri Express and making the journey back to Varanasi, eager to spend the next few years at the eclectic institution.

Life had indeed come full circle. I felt like Gregor Samsa, who woke one morning from uneasy dreams to find he had transformed into a gigantic insect while still in his bed.

He took one night. I took 80 days. In Varanasi.

In Gratitude

This book is dedicated to several people and places—all those who enabled me to seize the inflexion points in my life. In no particular order, they include:

My parents, who found the time and effort to bring me into this world and lavished love and care as only parents can.

My mom for, well, everything really, but especially for helping me copy study notes from my classmates in Class 9, which enabled me to avoid flunking my exam that year.

My dad, who never asked me to study for exams but consistently encouraged me to read for knowledge and imagination.

My cousins, Srikant and Jayshree, who believed in me more than I did myself.

My uncles, Sankar and Kumar, who supported my escape into dreamland at Priya Cinema and encouraged my love for table tennis, respectively.

My uncle, Kannan, who, as my Mathematics teacher, imbibed in me a ruthless focus to get things done.

Assorted uncles, aunts and cousins too numerous to name. Every single one of them is a key message from Someone Above.

My maternal grandmother, the loveliest woman who ever lived. Due apologies to my sweetheart—now, my stunning wife.

My maternal grandfather, who locked the front door from the inside to extinguish my cricketing dreams and instead pushed me to study for the IIT entrance exams.

My teachers at school and college, who consistently made me feel I could achieve nothing in life. And as usual, they were proved right.

My friends, who have been true blessings.

Shankar–Jaikishan, Doyle and Wodehouse, whose influence on me was profound and who gave me a virtual identity at a time when the Internet was merely a reference to a tennis shot hitting the net cord.

My sweetheart, who deigned to become my better half and ensured this ugly duckling didn't become an even uglier duck—and later, for correcting the numerous errors in this manuscript.

My daughter, for sheer *joie de vivre*.

Finally, to the late Surajit Das, my buddy and the man with the finest sense of humour ever, who left us too soon.

Handy Guide to IT Lingo

Chapter 1

Aaya	Arrived / has arrived.
Abe	Pronounced 'Abey'—typically used to holler at someone. In P.G. Wodehouse's Psmith parlance, it roughly equates to 'Ho'y'.
Dhakkan	Literally means a lid; usually refers to individuals without one.
Fresher	First-year students, typically referred to as a 'fresher' till the end of the ragging period.
Itian	The elite of the Varanasi society.
Naya	New.
Padha	Read/to read.
Pondy	Invigorating literature, often read alone at nights to 'educate' oneself on reproductive systems; not intended for medical students.

Chapter 4

Chappal	Slippers.
Chhotu	Errand boy; heir apparent to the Maharaj.
Chirkut	A person who is unpredictable but usually a dhakkan.

GKW	Ghas Katne Wali—a source of entertainment for frustrated, budding ornithologists.
Machchan	Literally means brother-in-law; often used to denote a friendly relationship.
Maharaj	The chief cook in the mess.
Makku	Madras, Andhra, Karnataka and Kerala Union—sometimes used to denote someone from the non-northern part of India.
Murga	As freshers, during the ragging period, it refers to an unseemly position of squatting on one's haunches while holding their ears. For the seniors or at other times, it refers to a particularly delicious meal.
Patao	To flirt successfully.

Chapter 5

Chai	Literally just a cup of hot tea, but, in practice, the source of our existence, especially during exams.
Chick	The young of a hen; generally used to refer to pretty young things.
Yaar	Close friend, mate.

Chapter 6

Arbit	Has several connotations; usually means 'generally'.
Chaat	The normal activity of a chaatu.
Chaatu	A person who bores others.

Goli	Addictive tablets generally consumed as an antidote to classes.
GPL	G pe laath; translates to a major force applied to the posterior section of the human body. In physics: instantaneous transfer of momentum, generally delivered by the foot to the posterior section.

Chapter 7

Café	The place where students while away time and wish they were in instead of the classroom.
Classroom	Where students feel the sleepiest; a centre for snores.

Chapter 8

Ajhel	Something very rotten, like leftover food with no refrigeration in the Indian summer months.
Female	The antonym of a male; used to refer to pretty (and not-so-pretty) middle-aged individuals.
Gali	Narrow lanes; as a proper noun, it refers to the narrow, winding lane housing the main Shiva temple of Varanasi.
Godowlia/ Gods	The largest shopping centre in Varanasi.
Lingo	Language used in everyday life.
Mishrambu	Sweet alcoholic drink, usually consumed during Holi.

Chapter 9

Chutti	Official declaration that classes will not be held.
Fag	Smoking medium—could be cigarettes, cigars, pipes or, given the usual economic constraints, more often than not, bidis.
Graffiti	Resident opinion of the Itian in the form of a humour tabloid.
Grass	Uplifting when consumed; a type of tobacco.
Hajaar	Literally means 'thousand' but generally refers to a large number one cannot be bothered to count. For example, hajaar dhakkans.
Junta	Assembled people, a mob; often denotes a widespread opinion.
Karra	Literally means 'tight'; often refers to slim, athletic females.
Lafda	Major problem requiring immediate attention.
Lavda	The visible component of the male reproductive organ.
Mochu	Local fast-food centre; a sort of Pop Tate's.
Phatta (or Fatta)	A joke, usually a pun.
Shutta	A kind of fag, usually cigarettes or hand-rolled cigarettes with a modicum of grass.
UFO	Unidentifiable fried objects; often aloo (potato) fry.
Wardy	The warden of a hostel.

Chapter 10

Cul Wing	The centre of activity in the gymkhana.
DG Corner	The chai shop opposite DG Hostel.
G-Secy	The general secretary of the cultural wing. There were two other G-secys—one for sports and the other for miscellaneous affairs—but they were generally ignored and unrecognized.
WC	Women's College—the location for current and future Romeos to congregate every evening.

Chapter 11

Aloo-fry	Cubes of potato deep-fried and garnished with Indian spices; a source of sustenance during the first year.
BSDK	A gaali, not referring to incestuous acts; instead, it considers birthing from the excretory passage a distinct possibility
KLPD	Major disappointment.
Lanka	The suburbs of BIT.
Munna	The number-one Maharaj in BIT, residing in Vishvesvaraya Hostel.

Chapter 12

Freak-out	Major enjoyment.
Fundu	Very good, like seven As in a report card.
KLPRR	An even bigger disappointment. The difference between KLPD and KLPRR can

be illustrated by the story of a totally mother-in-law-pecked man who was informed that his mother-in-law was drowning. He exclaimed that it was a misfortune. The next second, he was informed that she had just been saved. He felt that it was a catastrophe. In ITian terms, the first would be a KLPD and the second a KLPRR. RR stands for 'road roller'. And the other words refer to a male organ that sometimes brings pleasure to the female and often to the male. Check Lavda under L.

Chapter 13

Far-out   Something extremely good, like discovering your favourite band is playing a surprise concert in your town.

Funda   The raison d'être of anything and everything, usually denoting 'fundamentals'.

Gaali   Swear words used in normal conversations, often referencing incestuous relationships or puerile genitalia jokes.

Chapter 14

Khotte   Essentially refers to a duplicate currency coin; usually used for someone who is unreliable.

Chapter 16

Dhobi	A washerman, without whom the campus would be a stinking mess. Also key to understanding Six Sigma processes—not a single item of clothing was lost or misplaced in the four years.

Chapter 17

Daaru	Alcoholic drinks.

Chapter 18

Fest	Inter-college youth cultural festivals.

Chapter 19

KP	King's Pavilion; the hive of gymkhana activity. 'King's' because it had junk that a palace would not have and 'Pavilion' because the pavilion that was to be constructed never got built.

Chapter 20

Chuppa rustom	Hidden talents or hidden information.
Dip/Dep	The department, regrettably, of choice.
Thod-phod	Major achievement.